PINNED DOWN

A bullet ricocheted off the iron rim of a wagon wheel as Garrett ran to his rifle. He levered a round into the chamber, then turned and yelled at Annie, "Get back! Farther into the arroyo!"

He had no time to watch if the woman had done as he'd ordered because the Indians had shaken out into a line and were riding fast toward the mouth of the canyon.

Above him on the crest of the hill, Ready's Henry hammered a shot, then another. One of the warriors threw up his hands and toppled backward off his pony. But the rest kept on coming.

Garrett drew a bead on an Indian with red and black streaks of paint across his nose and cheeks. He held his breath and fired. The man jerked as the bullet hit; then he bent over the withers of the horse before slowly sliding to the ground.

Ready was shooting steadily and with deadly accuracy. Another Indian went down, then another. Garrett fired, fired again, and missed both times. . . .

Ralph Compton

The Tenderfoot
Trail

A Ralph Compton Novel

by Joseph A. West

A SIGNET BOOK

SIGNET
Published by New American Library, a division of
Penguin Group (USA) Inc., 375 Hudson Street,
New York, New York 10014, USA
Penguin Group (Canada), 90 Eglinton Avenue East, Suite 700, Toronto,
Ontario M4P 2Y3, Canada (a division of Pearson Penguin Canada Inc.)
Penguin Books Ltd., 80 Strand, London WC2R 0RL, England
Penguin Ireland, 25 St. Stephen's Green, Dublin 2,
Ireland (a division of Penguin Books Ltd.)
Penguin Group (Australia), 250 Camberwell Road, Camberwell, Victoria 3124,
Australia (a division of Pearson Australia Group Pty. Ltd.)
Penguin Books India Pvt. Ltd., 11 Community Centre, Panchsheel Park,
New Delhi - 110 017, India
Penguin Group (NZ), cnr Airborne and Rosedale Roads, Albany,
Auckland 1310, New Zealand (a division of Pearson New Zealand Ltd.)
Penguin Books (South Africa) (Pty.) Ltd., 24 Sturdee Avenue,
Rosebank, Johannesburg 2196, South Africa

Penguin Books Ltd., Registered Offices:
80 Strand, London WC2R 0RL, England

First published by Signet, an imprint of New American Library,
a division of Penguin Group (USA) Inc.

First Printing, July 2006
10 9 8 7 6 5 4 3 2 1

THE IMMORTAL COWBOY

This is respectfully dedicated to the "American Cowboy." His was the saga sparked by the turmoil that followed the Civil War, and the passing of more than a century has by no means diminished the flame.

True, the old days and the old ways are but treasured memories, and the old trails have grown dim with the ravages of time, but the spirit of the cowboy lives on.

In my travels—to Texas, Oklahoma, Kansas, Nebraska, Colorado, Wyoming, New Mexico, and Arizona—I always find something that reminds me of the Old West. While I am walking these plains and mountains for the first time, there is this feeling that a part of me is eternal, that I have known these old trails before. I believe it is the undying spirit of the frontier calling, allowing me, through the mind's eye, to step back into time. What is the appeal of the Old West of the American frontier?

It has been epitomized by some as the dark and bloody period in American history. Its heroes—Crockett, Bowie, Hickok, Earp—have been reviled and criticized. Yet the Old West lives on, larger than life.

It has become a symbol of freedom, when there was always another mountain to climb and another river to cross; when a dispute between two men was settled not with expensive lawyers, but with fists, knives, or guns. Barbaric? Maybe. But some things never change. When the cowboy rode into the pages of American history, he left behind a legacy that lives within the hearts of us all.

—*Ralph Compton*

Chapter 1

The barber snipped away the last errant curl that hung over the collar of Luke Garrett's shirt, switched to smaller scissors, then carefully trimmed the young rancher's sweeping dragoon mustache. That done, the man stepped back to admire his handiwork, nodded to himself and reached for a bottle of pomade on the counter. He vigorously rubbed the lavender-scented oil into Garrett's unruly auburn mane, then combed the hair straight back from his forehead.

"A little wax on the mustache, maybe?" the barber asked, his hands clasped together at the front of his chest as he gave a solicitous little bow.

Garrett shook his head. "Let it be. I reckon I smell like a sheepherder's socks already."

This entire operation had been watched, to his evident satisfaction, by Simon Carter, chief of the Fort Benton Honorable Vigilante Committee.

"Stand up, boy," Carter told Garrett. "Let's take a look at ye."

The young man swung out of the chair and rose

to his feet. Garrett was twenty-five years old that summer and stood a couple of inches above six feet. He was thin in the waist and hips, but wide across the shoulders, where it mattered most. Hard muscle bulged under the sleeves of his washed-out denim shirt and his hands were big and scarred from twenty years of working cattle. Garrett wore fringed shotgun chaps and wide canvas suspenders over his shirt, and his ten-dollar boots were hand-made but much scuffed and down-at-heel. His eyes were hazel, but showed more ice green than brown when anger was on him, as it was on him now.

"Satisfied, Carter?" Garrett asked, his voice sharp-edged as a slow-burning fury rode him.

Carter tipped his chair against the shop wall, looked the younger man up and down, then beamed. "You look crackerjack, boy! I swear, it's going to be a real honor to hang you."

Garrett rubbed his shaved cheeks and briefly glanced at himself in the mirror, where his eyes caught and held Carter's. "Seems like a lot of trouble to go to for a hanging," he said.

The vigilante nodded his agreement. "There are some might say that, but Simon Carter will send no man to hell without a shave, a haircut and a full belly. You'll get beefsteak and eggs this afternoon, boy, an' a mess o' buttermilk biscuits if'n such is to your liking."

Carter looked his prisoner up and down again, eased his chair away from the wall, and his beaming smile grew wider. "Crackerjack!" he said.

The vigilante nodded his satisfaction and asked the barber: "Don't he look crackerjack, Sam?"

"Crackerjack," Sam said without noticeable enthusiasm. "An' that's why he's gonna cost you a dollar, Carter."

"Tender your bill to the committee," Carter said. "In triplicate, as usual."

The man called Sam swore under his breath. "And as usual I won't see a red cent."

"It's your civic duty to curry the condemned, Sam." Carter smiled. "There are some might see it that way."

"Civic duty my ass," Sam snapped. "A pat on the back don't cure saddle galls or an empty wallet either."

Garrett reached into the pocket of his shirt, found a dollar and spun it to the barber. "Take that. It's the only one they missed."

Sam caught the coin expertly and brandished it in Carter's direction. "See that? A real gentleman, he is."

The vigilante was no longer smiling. "You held out on me, boy," he said. "That dollar should have gone toward your keep."

"So what are you going to do about it, Carter?" Garrett asked. "Hang me?"

Carter rose to his feet, a long, lank string bean of a man in a shabby black suit and cracked patent leather shoes. His dirty, collarless shirt showed what he'd eaten for his last ten meals and a battered silk top hat was tilted on his bald head. By profession, Carter was the town's undertaker and it showed. He looked and walk-hopped like a seedy, molting crow.

"Now you get buffler steak for your last meal,

boy," he said, his face flushed. "And maybe you won't get any of them biscuits I was talkin' about neither."

For a few moments Carter's black eyes locked with Garrett's. But gradually the man relaxed and his smile returned. "Nah, beefsteak it is. Damn it all, I like you, boy. I'm going to hang you, but I like you."

Garrett did not reply as he measured the distance between him and the vigilante, figuring his chances. He tensed, knowing that if he was going to make a play, it had to be now.

But Carter read something reckless in the younger man's eyes and the shotgun in his hands came up fast, the muzzles pointing right at Garrett's belly. "Don't even think about trying it, boy," he said, his voice soft, without threat. "I'd cut you in half with this here Greener afore you took a single step."

"Buckshot always means a buryin', that's for sure," the barber observed. "An' nobody knows that more'n you, Carter. In your time you've gunned your share."

The vigilante nodded and smiled, as though Sam had fairly stated the case.

Garrett glanced at the shotgun, rock steady in Carter's hands. Dirty and unkempt the man might be, but the weapon was clean, a film of oil glistening the length of the barrels. The man's fingers were white-knuckled on the triggers and Garrett knew that if he even developed a sudden eye twitch Carter would cut loose.

Forcing himself to relax, the young rancher unclenched his fists and managed a slight smile. "When I got right down to it, I plumb lost my confidence." He nodded toward the Greener. "Came on me all of a sudden."

"Wise decision," Carter said, without humor. "Now get your hat. Time you was heading back to the jail afore you get any more of them bright ideas and step into a passel of trouble."

After Garrett collected his battered Stetson from the hook on the wall, the barber whisked a brush across his shoulders. "I'd say you're welcome to come back, son. But on account of how by sundown you won't be around no more, I'll just"—Sam stuck out his hand—"say so long and good luck."

Garrett shook the barber's proffered hand and stepped outside, Carter alert and ready behind him.

The young man settled his hat on his head and briefly looked around, his nose lifted to air so thick a man might feel he could cut out chunks of it with a knife.

It was still an hour from noon, yet the sun was already blazing hot in a sky the color of washed-out denim, ripening the stench of manure from thousands of mules, horses and oxen and from piles of stinking buffalo hides. In winter the streets of Fort Benton became seas of vile-smelling mud, impassable even for freight wagons, but now, that hot summer of 1876, dust was the problem. Despite the recent rain, the ground had dried quickly, and choking yellow clouds hung in the air, kicked up by wagon wheels and draft animals. The dust sifted into every nook and cranny of the town, lying thick and indiscriminate like powdered mustard on furniture from parlor pianos to saloon faro wheels. It found its way inside the wool shirts of men and the silk dresses of women, mingling with sweat, trickling slow and gritty down muscular backs and between soft breasts.

A mile-long levee protected the town's scattered shacks, stables and warehouses from the annual flood of the Missouri and down by the loading docks were tied the elegant steamboats that had plied the river this far but could travel no farther.

Gold miners headed for Bannack, Virginia City or Last Chance Gulf had to complete their journeys overland.

The town was the very center of a vast transportation hub. All the major trails in Montana, including those leading into Canada, intersected at Benton, and that was the reason why the town prospered in freight and shipping operations.

The headquarters of the rich merchant princes who helped Benton thrive were clustered around Front Street, outfits like Garrison and Wyatt, Carroll and Steel, E. G. Maclay and Company and the Diamond R Transportation Company. Between them these firms employed three thousand men, four thousand horses and twenty thousand oxen and mules to haul goods in and out of the town.

The loud and profane men who jostled their wagons past Garrett on the street were for the most part professional bullwhackers and mule skinners, although Benton also had its share of wolfers, miners, gamblers, whores and whiskey traders.

Here and there, usually seen lounging outside

the town's dozen roaring saloons, were men of a different stamp. Lean, blue-eyed men wearing belted Colts, they looked at nothing directly but saw everything. Such men were few in Benton, but their presence was always noted, their movements closely observed.

Luke Garrett felt the muzzles of Carter's Greener dig into his back. "Get moving, boy," he said. "You've seen enough. And walk real relaxed and easy." The vigilante's voice dropped to a conversational tone and the younger man could hear his smile. "Two things you should learn about me, son—I got faith in shotguns and I don't never trust a dead wolf until he's been skun."

Without turning, Garrett nodded. "I've learned something about you already, Carter."

"An' what's that?"

"You don't ever need to worry about biting off more than you can chew. Your mouth is a whole lot bigger than you think."

Behind him, Garrett heard the vigilante cackle. "Dang it all, Luke, but I like you. Whooee, but you've got sand, boy."

The two men walked past the gallows built near the jail, a simple platform of pine boards six feet high surmounted by a T-shaped gibbet with iron hooks screwed into the underside of each end of the crossbar. Red, white and blue bunting had already been draped over the front of the platform in anticipation of Garrett's hanging.

Carter saw the younger man's head turn to look and he said, "Haven't had a double hanging in near a twelvemonth. Always draws a big crowd. But don't you worry none. A nice-looking young feller like you will bring plenty out to watch."

"Thanks," Garrett said. "That cheers me considerably."

"Bad thing about a hanging is you never quite know how it's going to go," Carter said as they reached the jail. "I've seen two-gun hard cases who claimed to be all horns and rattles go weak at the knees an' cry like babies when the time came for them to take their dose of rope medicine." He shook his head. "No, sir, a hanging is one dang thing you just can't practice for."

He motioned to Garrett with the shotgun. "Now you step over there to the side of the door and don't move a muscle."

The vigilante pushed the muzzle of the Greener into Garrett's belly and removed a large iron key from his pocket. He turned the key in the lock and the bolt clanked back. Without moving the shotgun muzzle an inch from its spot just above the buckle of Garrett's chaps, he swung the door wide and nodded toward the opening. "Now get inside—and don't be trying no fancy moves."

Garrett stepped into the jail and the door slammed behind him. Carter's face appeared at the small barred window cut in the heavy oak. "I'll bring your supper around four. That'll give you a quiet hour to eat afore we hang you."

The young rancher turned. "Thanks, Carter. You're all heart."

Garrett's sarcasm was lost on the man. "Me, I always try to be a bit nicer to prisoners than is called for," he said. "But I don't take no guff either."

Before Garrett could answer, the vigilante swung on his heel and walked away, his choppy, crow-hopping steps kicking up little puffs of dust around his patent leather shoes.

Garrett watched the man go, then sat on the edge of the bunk. The narrow bed with its filthy straw mattress represented the extent of the jail's furnishings. The jail itself was a single room about twenty feet long by half as much wide, built low and sturdy of heavy pine logs. To discourage escape attempts, the floor was concrete. The roof was a shallow, inverted V of pine beams and rough wood shingles topped by a layer of sod. A tiny window barred with iron was cut high in the wall opposite the bunk, through which angled a ray of sunlight where flickering dust motes danced.

Rising to his feet, Garrett crossed the cell, walking from gloom into light and back to gloom again. He reached up and tried the bars on the window. But they refused to budge, the iron set in cement by a man who knew his business.

Discouraged, Garrett stepped back to the bunk and flopped down on his back. Carter had left him with his makings and he reached into his shirt pocket, found tobacco and papers and built a smoke. He thumbed one of his remaining matches into flame, lit the cigarette, and through a curling cloud of blue smoke stared moodily at the shadowed roof, trying to grapple with the reason why his life had changed so completely and rapidly—and for the worse.

In less than twenty-four hours he'd gone from being a prosperous, good-looking young rancher with a herd to sell to a condemned criminal who'd soon be dancing at the end of a hemp rope.

And now, as he studied hard on it, he remembered that the coffee thirst of an Arbuckle-drinking old man had been the start of it all. . . .

Chapter 2

In the early summer, when the corn lilies were in full bloom, Luke Garrett and his hired hand, bearded, sturdy old Zebulon Ready, moved the young rancher's small herd off their pasture in the Judith Basin country and hazed them north toward Fort Benton, at the southern end of the Whoop-Up Trail.

For six days Garrett and Ready drove the fifty shorthorn Durhams and small remuda of six ponies across good grass that in places grew belly-high to a steer. By the time they made camp a couple of miles outside of town, the cattle were fat and sleek, a fact that did not go unnoticed by Ready.

"Luke, I'd say this herd is worth ten dollars a head in anybody's money," he said. "I reckon we can push those redcoat Mounties at Fort Whoop-Up to go fifteen, maybe more."

"Maybe so," Garrett agreed. He reached for the coffeepot and filled his cup, his eyes restlessly scanning the darkness around him where the herd was bedded down. They were quiet right now, but anything could set them to running. Garrett saw lightning flash to the west and heard the distant grumble of thunder.

"How little will Deke Waters take for the bull?" the old man asked. "Could be we'll have enough money to buy the Angus and have enough left over to put in that artesian well you're always talking about."

Garrett smiled. "Trouble is, there's no little to it, Zeb. Deke wants five hundred and he won't back off on the price a cent."

"Mean ol' cuss, that Deke Waters," Ready said, his bearded lips moving around the stem of his pipe.

"He's just a toothless old dog that chews real careful," Garrett said.

"Five hundred is a heap of money, Luke."

Garrett nodded. "I reckon it is, but then, that Red Angus of Deke's is a heap of bull."

The bull was the reason Garrett had rounded up his herd early and pushed it north. He'd been told by a passing rancher down from Fort Benton that the Royal Canadian Mounted Police in Alberta were right then paying ten dollars a head in silver for Indian agency beef.

Prodding him too was the parting remark Deke Waters had made. "I'll hold the Angus for you, Luke, but not for too long," the old rancher had told him. "I'm short of ready cash my ownself and my old lady is agitating for a shade porch around the house. So you see how it is with me."

When a man calls your bluff, it's time to look at your hole card again, and this Garrett knew. In his case, the card was his fifty young shorthorns and the five hundred dollars in Mountie silver they'd bring at Fort Whoop-Up.

His mind made up, he and Ready had gathered the herd the next day.

Ready, a long and lanky seventy-year-old with far-seeing blue eyes, stretched out a buckskinned arm and grabbed the coffeepot. He filled Garrett's cup and said, "Drink up, Luke. After this, we have a handful of coffee for breakfast and then it's all gone."

The young rancher set the cup between his legs and began to build a smoke. "I'll ride into Benton tomorrow and buy some," he said. "And we need salt pork and flour."

Ready nodded. "And a sack of sugar and maybe some raisins. And when it comes to the coffee, buy only Arbuckle, Luke. Accept no substitute."

Garrett smiled. "I'll bear that in mind."

Ready was lean and long muscled, all the tallow burned out of him by a lifetime of hard trails. He'd been a Texas Ranger, Indian fighter and later, as a top hand, had helped Oliver Loving and Charlie Goodnight blaze their cattle trail from central Texas to Fort Sumner in the New Mexico Territory.

That association had ended a few years later when Goodnight's new foreman, a sour man called Wilson, told him, "Ready, I'm a man of few words. If I say come, you come." Zeb nodded and answered, "Wilson, I'm a man of few words my ownself. If I shake my head, I ain't comin'."

Ready figured it was high time to pull his freight and for a while he'd prospered in the restaurant business before giving it up to work for Garrett. It was a decision neither man had found cause to regret.

Zeb was a talkative, friendly man and he had a relaxed, even-tempered way about him. In the past, a few hard cases, mistaking his casual manner for weakness, had thought him an easy mark. Five of them lay buried in Boot Hills from Texas to Montana, men who learned too late that Ready could also do a sight of talking with his gun.

He was good with the Colt, better with the Henry, and there was no backup in him. As he'd told Garrett many times, "Luke, when your talking is all done, and you go to the gun, coolness and a steady nerve will always beat a fast draw. Take your time and you'll only need to pull the trigger once."

Garrett had never been in a gunfight, but he'd listened and learned and stored away what Ready had told him. He didn't know it then, but the old man's advice would very soon save his life—and land him in more trouble than any young rancher could be reasonably expected to handle.

Now Garrett looked across the fire at Ready as the man talked again. "Thunder to the west, Luke. I reckon I'll saddle up and do some singing to the herd."

"I'll do it," the younger man answered. "You can spell me in a couple of hours."

As Garrett rose to his feet, Ready asked, "Luke, you heard anything about this here trail to Fort Whoop-Up?"

Garrett shook his head. "Not much, except it's

two hundred miles of difficult country where everything that grows has spines and everything that walks has fangs. Add outlaws of every stamp, whiskey traders and downright hostile Crows, Blackfoot and Sioux, and the Whoop-Up Trail shapes up to be no place for a pilgrim." The younger man smiled. "Or us either, come to that."

Ready stretched, his face untroubled. "That doesn't do much to inspire confidence in a man. Outlaws don't scare me none, but the Blackfoot are a handful. The Sioux will back off once in a while and go on their way, but the Blackfoot keep a-comin' right at you."

"I reckon. Just sleep with your rifle close."

"Hell, I always do," Ready said. "In Indian country a man can never tell which way the pickle will squirt, and that's a natural fact."

Garrett left the fire and saddled a mouse-colored mustang from the remuda. The little bangtail barely went eight hundred pounds and had the disposition of a curly wolf, but it was good with cattle and sure-footed in the dark.

Lightning glared in the distance, silver light flashing inside the building clouds, and thunder muttered threats as Garrett made a circuit of the herd. Most of the shorthorns were still bedded down, though a few were on their feet, grazing around the wild oaks that grew at the edge of the meadow.

But there was a tension in the air the young man didn't like. It crackled around him fragile as crystal, as though the slightest noise could shatter the night into a million pieces.

And it seemed that the crowding darkness had eyes that watched . . . and ears that listened.

"Damn it all, Luke," Garrett whispered to himself, shaking his head. "You're acting like an old maid, hearing footsteps behind you and a rustle in every bush."

Nevertheless, he loosened the .44-.40 Winchester in the scabbard under his left knee and, in an effort to soothe his nerves and settle the cattle, began to sing in a low, tuneless baritone that more than once had made a cook stop the chuck wagon to look for a dry axle.

Oh, slow up, doggies, quit roving around.
You have wandered and trampled all over the
*   ground.*
Oh, graze along, doggies, and feed kinda slow,
And don't always be on the go.
Move slow, little doggies, move slow—

A gunshot hammered apart the fragile fabric of the night.

Immediately the cattle were up and running. Garrett swore, shucked his rifle and levered a round into the chamber. From somewhere behind the herd, he heard a man whoop, and another gun banged, a fleeting orange flare in the darkness.

Lightning blazed among the clouds and in the sudden light Garrett caught a brief, flickering glimpse of a rider galloping hell-for-leather near the wild oaks.

The thunder was now right overhead. Every few moments the sky flashed from horizon to horizon, constantly switching the surrounding country from darkness to a shimmering white glare where the trees, grass and stampeding cattle stood out in stark detail.

Garrett angled toward the oaks, trying to cut off the running rustler.

Ahead of him in the gloom he heard the pounding of hooves. As the lightning blazed again he and the rustler saw each other at the same instant. The brightness flickered into darkness just as the man's gun flared in the night, then flared once more.

Garrett reined up the mustang and waited, rifle to his shoulder. Thunder roared and rain spattered into his face. Then lightning burned across the sky and he saw the man who'd shot at him. He had slowed his horse to a walk and was riding under the branches of the oaks, his head turning.

In that single, blinding instant, as the branded sky sizzled, Garrett fired. He heard a shriek and as the darkness again fell around him, he got off two more quick shots in the general direction of the now unseen rider.

The raid on the cattle ended as abruptly as it had begun.

The bellows of Garrett's rifle bounded away, fading into the distance like the beats of a distant drum, and the hiss of falling rain now filled the echoing silence.

Suddenly Zeb Ready was at Garrett's side, his Henry slanted across his chest. The old man looked up at Garrett and said, "I was about to bed down when I heard the shots. What happened, Luke?"

"Rustlers. I think I discouraged them, but they've scattered the herd to hell and gone."

"You get any of them?"

Garrett glanced down at Ready, the man's buckskin shirt already glistening black at the shoulders from the rain. "I took a shot at one of them over by the wild oaks. Don't know if I hit him, but I sure thought I heard him holler."

Ready's deeply lined face was grim. "Let's go take a look."

With an effortless ease that belied his years, the old man vaulted onto the rump of the mustang and Garrett kicked the little horse into motion. After a few minutes of searching, they found a man's body lying facedown in a clump of squawbush, the petals of its tiny yellow flowers scattered across his blood-stained shirt.

Ready swung off the mustang and kneeled beside the downed rustler. He rolled the man onto his back, then looked up at Garrett. "You cut his suspenders, all right, Luke. This one's about as dead as he's ever gonna be."

Garrett stepped out of the saddle and looked down at the dead man. The rustler's blue eyes were wide open, staring into nothingness, and his thin, hard mouth was stretched across his teeth in a final grimace of pain. He looked to be somewhere in his middle twenties and was dressed in the nondescript range clothes of a puncher.

As though Ready had read his thoughts, the old man said, "Judging by his spurs and boots, I'd say he was out of Texas, maybe the Panhandle country.

He'd been a bull nurse in his day, though he hadn't punched cows in quite some time."

"How so, Zeb?" Garrett asked, his voice slightly unsteady. He'd never killed a man before, and there was a sickness in him—and an impossible yearning to go back in time and restore things to the way they were before he'd pulled the trigger.

If Ready heard the tremor in the younger man's voice, he didn't let it show. "Luke, when you take the measure of a man, take the full measure. That engraved Colt on his hip isn't a puncher's twelve-dollar gun. And see here." He grabbed the man's right hand and showed it to Garrett, palm up. "He hasn't done an honest day's work with this mitt in quite a while. Fingernails are clean too."

"Outlaw?" Garrett asked.

The old man nodded. "Could be. Or a hired gun of some kind." He let the hand drop. "Now it don't matter a hill of beans what he was. His day is done."

Ready rose to his feet, his knees snapping. "We'll bury him come morning, then round up the herd."

Garrett shook his head. "No, I'll take him into Fort Benton come first light. There were others with him tonight and maybe the law will know his name and who he was running with."

"Luke, the only law in Benton is vigilante law," Ready protested. "Them boys could start into asking more questions than you got answers, especially if he was one of their own."

"He was a rustler, Zeb, and one of their own or no, vigilantes don't take kindly to his type." The young man smiled. "And besides, you need your coffee."

The night shaded into dawn under a watery gray sky, the dragon hiss of the teeming rain the only sound as Garrett saddled the mustang. Earlier, after they'd sat hunched and miserable around a smoking fire and drunk the last of their coffee, Ready had helped him drape the dead man face-down over his horse.

Then the old man had left to round up what he could of the herd, telling Garrett he'd be back no later than sundown. "Don't worry none, Luke," he said. "I'll find them critters. They won't have run far."

Garrett was about to swing into the saddle when he saw six riders approaching his camp, led by a tall, thin man in a canvas slicker, a battered silk top hat on his bald head.

Had the rustlers returned?

Deciding to take no chances, Garrett slid his Winchester from the boot and waited, his wary eyes intently watching the riders as they drew closer.

When the six men were still a ways off, Garrett saw a young towhead on a buckskin point to him and yell, "That's him, Carter! That's the dirty bushwhacker who killed Johnny Gibbs!"

Garrett stepped away from the mustang, the Winchester ready in his hands, as the riders trotted to within ten yards of him, then stopped.

"Put that rifle away, boy," the man called Carter said. "You're in enough trouble already."

The men with Carter seemed tough and capable,

all of them bearded and armed to the teeth. A couple carried scatterguns across their saddle horns, a way of making sure they would get the last word should any gun argument arise.

Carter jutted his chin toward the dead man and said, "Len, go see if that's Gibbs."

The towhead threw Garrett a look of hatred and swung out of the saddle. He walked to the dead man, grabbed a handful of hair and jerked up the head, looking intently at the gray face. "That's Johnny all right," he said. "Like I didn't know that already." Len turned, looking up at Carter, who sat his horse, his face grim. "He's been shot in the back."

"Could see that from here my ownself," Carter said. His eyes slanted to Garrett. "Got some explaining to do, haven't you, boy?"

"The explaining is easy," Garrett said. "This man tried to rustle my cattle last night and I shot him."

"In the back," the towhead yelled, jabbing an accusing finger at the young rancher.

"In the dark," Garrett said. "I just aimed in his general direction."

"Carter, good ol' Johnny never stole anything in his life," the towhead said, his eyes on the tall man in the top hat. "He was true-blue and no rustler."

A slight smile touched Garrett's lips. "Seems to me outlaws and martyrs are greatly improved by death. Did you call him good ol' true-blue Johnny when he was alive?"

The towhead opened his mouth to speak, but Carter waved him into silence and nodded to Garrett. "What's your name, son?"

"Luke Garrett. I plan on driving my herd to Fort Whoop-Up. I hear tell the Mounties are buying Indian beef."

"Maybe you will at that," Carter said. "But in the meantime we got a difficult situation here. Len says you bushwhacked him and Gibbs last night for no other reason than they were riding too close to your herd."

"Len said that?"

Carter nodded.

"Then he's a damn liar."

The towhead's face flushed and he swore as his hand dropped for his gun. But Garrett's rifle swung on him and his cold voice cut across the quiet of the rain-slanted morning like a knife. "Shuck that black-eyed Susan and I'll blow you right out of the saddle."

Len hesitated, seeing something in Garrett's green eyes that he didn't like.

Carter stepped into the tense silence. "Do as he says, Len, or he'll kill you for sure." Then to Garrett: "You're coming with us, boy. You can do your explaining to the Fort Benton vigilante committee."

Garrett waved the muzzle of the rifle toward the dead man. "I was bringing him in anyhow. Hardly the action of a guilty man, is it?"

"You was getting rid of the body, is what you were doing," the towhead said. "You take us all for fools?"

Garrett shook his head. "Only you, Len. Only you."

*   *   *

"Johnny Gibbs rode shotgun for the Diamond R freight line, and they set store by him," Simon Carter told Garrett as the two men sat drinking coffee in J. C. Hepburn's Saloon and Pool Room, where the younger man's trial was due to take place in less than an hour.

The vigilante blew across his cup, scattering the rising steam. "Johnny was a big spender, so the saloon keepers liked him." Carter shook his head slowly. "There are eight men on the committee who will hear your case. I'm one of them and four of the remaining seven own saloons, and two more work for the Diamond R."

"You telling me I'm facing a stacked deck?"

"Yup, I'm telling you that. And I'm also saying we only have your word against Len Swinton's that you shot Johnny Gibbs while he was trying to steal your cattle."

"That's exactly what happened," Garrett said, anger tugging at him. "My herd is scattered to hell and gone and my hired hand is out right now trying to round 'em up. You said yourself Gibbs was a big spender. Maybe he was running out of money and saw the herd as a way to fatten his bankroll."

Carter nodded, doubt plain in his eyes. "Could be. And maybe that's how the vigilante committee will see it."

"But you don't think so."

Carter shook his head. "Hell, boy, I'll say it plain. I like you. I like you just fine, but I got the feeling I'm going to end up hanging you."

                    *   *   *

Garrett's trial was a foregone conclusion and the verdict seemed to surprise no one.

The committee voted seven to none, with one abstention, that on the evening of July 13, 1876, Luke Garrett, drover, had murdered John F. Gibbs, wagon guard, after accusing the said Gibbs and the deceased's friend Len Swinton of trespassing near a cattle herd with mischief in mind.

Sentence: death by hanging, said sentence to be carried out by vigilante Simon Carter and certain others one hour before sundown on the day following.

Freshly shaved and barbered, Garrett was later confined to his cell—where he was assured a last meal of steak, eggs and biscuits—to be purchased out of petty cash by the Fort Benton Honorable Vigilante Committee. Then he would keep his appointment with the noose.

Chapter 3

Garrett rose and ground out his cigarette butt under the heel of his boot. Restlessly he stepped to the bars of his cell and tried them again, but they were as immovable as before.

He crossed the concrete floor and sat on his bunk and rolled another smoke from his dwindling supply of tobacco. He studied the slim sack, calculating if he had enough to last until the hanging. That much was doubtful, so he decided to roll them thin and hope the makings held out.

Garrett knew he'd been railroaded—and the trumped-up murder charge by the vigilantes would do nothing to make his dying easier.

It seemed that Johnny Gibbs had been a well-liked man around Fort Benton, would-be rustler or not, guilty or not. The four hundred men who worked for the Diamond R freight company wanted to see his killer hanged—a fact of life that had not gone unnoticed by the alert vigilantes.

Garrett looked up at the changing light streaming through the small window into his cell. He had no watch and wondered how close it was to sundown. A couple of hours maybe, no more than that.

When a man is facing death, his perceptions sharpen. Garrett watched the dust motes swim in the light slanting into his cell and heard the creak of wagons on the street outside, the yells of "Hee" and "Haw" from the bullwhackers as they guided their teams of fifteen oxen through drifting clouds of yellow dust. From somewhere close by a saloon piano played "The Hills of Mexico" and a woman laughed, a harsh, strident shriek empty of humor, then fell silent.

Garrett realized that in a few hours he'd be gone, but the noise would continue, the world going on its way without him, as though he had never been. It was a depressing thought that the young man forced from his mind. He rose and stretched, but froze in that posture, his arms above his head, as he heard a voice at the tiny cell window.

"Pssst . . ."

Garrett slowly turned his head and looked up at the window. He could see only a pair of bright, intelligent black eyes and a single thick eyebrow.

"Come closer," a man's voice ordered.

Garrett stepped to the window and the man thrust several fingers through the iron bars and waggled them at the young rancher. "Sorry I can't get my hand through," the man said. "The bars are too close together."

Garrett reached up and took the proffered fingers. "Name's Charlie Cobb," the man said. "Pleased to meet you, Luke."

"Likewise," Garrett said, puzzled. "What are you doing here?"

The young rancher caught a glimpse of white teeth and a pencil mustache as Cobb smiled. "Going to bust you out of this here hoosegow. You're too good a man to end up doing the Texas cakewalk at the end of a rope." The teeth flashed white again. "Got that puddin' foot mustang of yours all saddled and ready to go over by the front of the livery stable. A Winchester is in the scabbard and I hung a gun belt and holstered Colt on the horn."

"Cobb," Garrett said, "I appreciate the help, but this place is built rock solid. How are you going to bust me out of here?"

"Gunpowder," Cobb answered. "Got me a keg of the stuff—small keg certainly, but big enough, I'd say. It's right up against this wall."

"When are you planning—"

"Oh, judging by the fuse, about ten seconds from now. This whole damned jail is about to blow a thousand feet into the air. See ya."

Cobb's face vanished—and in a panic Garrett ran to the cot, yanked off the thin straw mattress and covered his head.

A split second later, with an ear-shattering roar, the Fort Benton jail blew sky-high.

Logs, dust and debris clattered and crashed around Garrett, shattered shingles and one heavy beam thumped onto the mattress over his head. His ears ringing, he warily removed the mattress and glanced around him.

The entire wall opposite his cot was gone, and so was the roof. A few flames fluttered like scarlet moths on the ends of the remaining logs and a thick cloud of brown smoke rose into the air.

Garrett staggered to his feet and hurled himself toward the opening. He heard a man yell and a gun bang; then he was running. The livery stable lay across a hundred yards of open ground, mostly soft sand with patches of prickly pear growing here and there.

A bullet split the air near Garrett's right ear as he reached the stable and saw the saddled mustang in the doorway.

The man called Cobb stood in the gloom of the interior and yelled, "Get on the hoss and ride. Head north and you'll come up on the Teton River. Hole up there."

"What about my herd?" Garrett asked.

"I'll bring it to you," Cobb said. "Now get the hell out of here. Don't try any shooting. You'll have plenty of time to look tough when you're out of sight."

"Thanks, Cobb," Garrett said. He set spurs to the mustang, rounded the livery stable and swung north at a gallop as guns roared behind him.

The mustang was game and stretched out, the bit in its teeth.

Garrett glanced to his rear and saw armed men clustered in the street. A few were running toward the stable for their horses. He saw Simon Carter look after him, then throw his top hat to the ground in frustration, his face flushed with anger.

A bullet burned across Garrett's left shoulder, drawing blood, and a moment later he felt the mustang stagger, then regain its balance, running as hard as before.

Ahead of Garrett a steep-sided dry wash angled away from the Missouri. He headed the mustang into the wash, its hooves pounding on sand and scattered rock. Garrett followed the wash for several hundred yards, then clambered up a section of bank that had been broken down by the passage of a buffalo herd. He cleared the wash and swung the horse due north, riding between a pair of shallow hills, their slopes covered in Indian grass made bright by streaks of evening primrose and Rocky Mountain iris.

The young rancher turned in the saddle and studied his back trail. A dust cloud rose in the distance and that could only mean that the Fort Benton vigilantes were still coming after him.

Garrett glanced at the sky. Heavy violet clouds were rolling in from the west as the sun dropped lower and the late-afternoon light was slowly dying around him.

If he could stay clear of the vigilante posse until dark, he might have a chance of living through the night.

Drawing rein on the mustang, Garrett scanned the land ahead of him, gently rolling hills cut through by arroyos where dark blue shadows were already gathering. An errant gust of wind spattered a few drops of rain against his face as he stepped out of the saddle and walked the mustang toward a break in the hills. Behind him the rain had not yet settled the dust on his back trail and it looked like the posse was starting to crowd close.

But the mustang had been running hard and badly needed a few minutes' rest.

Garrett buckled on the gun belt Cobb had left for him—and only then saw the blood dripping from the skirt of the saddle and the slender scarlet fingers that ran down the horse's left flank. After a few moments' search he found the wound. A bullet had plowed under the bottom of the saddle and had ranged across the pony's back, cutting deep. He could see that the bullet had not exited and had to be buried in the animal's back.

Garrett swore under his breath as he patted the horse's cheek. "It's a sorry cowboy who'll ride a sore-backed hoss," he said, trying to make the animal understand. "But right now, little feller, I have no choice in the matter."

The mustang tossed its head, the bit jangling, and seemed as eager as ever for the trail. It was a small animal, with a mean disposition most of the time, but it was tough and hard to kill.

Shaking his head over what he had to do, Garrett swung into the saddle and sat back in the leather as gently as he was able. He glanced once again at the dust cloud behind him, then set spurs to the mustang's flanks.

The little horse bounded forward and Garrett swung toward an arroyo between the nearest hills and entered its shadowed floor at a gallop.

He rode through the narrow gulch, then over the crest of a low saddle-backed hill, coming upon a wide meadow streaked by wildflowers and a scattering of tall white spruce.

Garrett found a stream near the pines, a shallow brook bubbling over a pebbled bed, and he let the mustang drink, then drank himself.

The rain was falling heavier now, settling the dust behind him. Where was the posse?

He had ridden fast and far, but Garrett had no idea how determined the vigilantes were. Rain or no rain, darkness or not, they might keep on coming. The mustang was still losing blood and suddenly seemed tuckered out, its ugly hammerhead hanging, the reins trailing.

Garrett had no slicker and he was getting thoroughly soaked. He brushed rain from his mustache and with a pang of regret for the horse stepped into the saddle again.

No matter what, he had to keep moving. He must be close to the Teton where Charlie Cobb had told him to hole up. Could he trust the man? Cobb had saved him from the hangman, so it was unlikely he'd planned to lure him into a trap.

Garrett shrugged. Faint heart never filled a flush, so he would trust Cobb, at least for now. Studying on it, as he did as he urged the horse forward, he knew he had no other choice in the matter.

He rode up on the river an hour later, just as the day was beginning to shade into night and the raking rain relentlessly cascaded from a ragged sky.

Garrett was pretty sure the vigilantes would have turned back by this time. No matter how badly they wanted to hang him, riding through a rainstorm chasing shadows was nobody's idea of fun. He was willing to bet that Carter had headed the posse back to Fort Benton and the saloon. They could always catch him another day when the weather was more obliging.

Still, he decided to take no chances.

He led the mustang into the thin shelter of the cottonwoods along the riverbank and slid the Winchester from the scabbard before unsaddling the horse. What Garrett saw shocked him. The bullet had done much more damage than he'd thought. It had burned along the horse's back, then hit a bone and gone deep into the mustang's chest, leaving a raw, nasty entry wound.

The little horse wheezed with every breath and showed no interest in the grass at its feet. There was blood on the animal's lips and teeth and it seemed too weak to lift its head.

Garrett walked to the river and filled his hat with water. He returned to the horse and poured water on the wound, then used his fingers to wash away most of the crusted blood. Normally the mustang would not have stood for this kind of treatment and would have kicked out at the man, but it seemed to be beyond caring, its eyes showing white arcs of pain, its breathing becoming even more labored.

The vigilantes might be close, but after Garrett examined the wound again he made a decision. The mustang had done well, but now it was in pain. It was a tough, enduring little cow pony with plenty of sand, and that was the reason it was dying so slowly, much too slowly.

Garrett led the horse away from the cottonwoods and drew his Colt. A single shot shattered the quiet of the night and the mustang's suffering was over. The young rancher stood, the smoking gun in his hand, and stared down at the animal's body, now looking even smaller in death.

"Thank you, little feller," he whispered aloud. "Thank you for everything."

Then he holstered his gun and sought the lean shelter of the trees, a sad kind of hurt in him. In all his life he had never seen a critter, tame or wild, feel sorry for itself, and the mustang had been no exception.

Tonight the little pony had taught him something about living and dying. It could be he'd lost his herd and maybe there was a necktie party on his trail, but life isn't about holding a good hand, it's about playing a poor one well.

Garrett had been dealt some bad cards, but he decided right there and then to make the most of them. Come first light, he'd backtrack toward Benton and find Zeb Ready and the herd. Then he'd trail the shorthorns to Fort Whoop-Up like he'd planned.

Afoot, in a country where every man's hand was turned against him, it wouldn't be easy, but it had to be done. The little mustang had shown him the way.

In the teeming rain, Luke Garrett sat soaked and miserable at the base of a cottonwood, wishful for hot coffee but wanting only tomorrow.

Chapter 4

Luke Garrett slept as the night fell around him, rain pattering through the leaves of the cottonwoods and the distant voice of the thunder the only sound. In the early hours of the morning, in deep darkness, coyotes were drawn to the place by the smell of blood. On wary feet, the little animals nosed closer to the dead mustang but then caught a human scent from somewhere among the trees and backed off into the gloom, their eyes glittering.

Garrett slept on, undisturbed.

Just before dawn, the rain stopped, the clouds parted and a weary moon vanished over the far horizon.

The light brightened and was starting to banish the night shadows as a lone horseman approached the river. The man dismounted, slid his rifle from the scabbard and stepped purposefully toward the trees.

A kick on the sole of his boot instantly brought Garrett to full wakefulness. He saw the dark silhouette of the man towering over him and his hand dropped for his holstered Colt.

"Don't shoot! It's Cobb!" the man said. He stepped closer, and as his body emerged from the gloom it took on shape and form. Garrett saw a grinning face under a dripping hat, a glistening yellow slicker falling to the figure's ankles.

"Maybe a little too quick to go to the draw there, Luke," Cobb scolded, his smile taking the sting out of it.

"I'm a hunted man," Garrett said. "And a hunted man trusts nobody."

"A hunted man without a hoss," Cobb said. "Saw your mustang over there."

"He was shot as we left Benton. Carried me all the way here, and then I had to put him out of his misery. That little pony was as game as they come." Garrett rose to his feet. "Why did you save my life, Cobb? I'm a stranger to you."

The man shrugged. "I figured if I did you a favor, you'd do me one in return."

"You only have to name it."

Cobb's smile was suddenly sly. "Oh, don't worry about that. I will."

Charlie Cobb was as tall as Garrett, but slimmer in the shoulders. He had lively brown eyes that missed nothing, and his mouth under a black pencil-line mustache was thin and hard, arcs showing at the corners of his lips when he smiled. The man took off his hat and slapped it free of rainwater against his legs, revealing slicked-down hair, parted in the middle, carefully arranged curls lying on his temples.

Garrett decided Charlie Cobb looked like a cathouse pimp. Then, suddenly ashamed of the treachery of his thoughts, he smiled and said, "I never did thank you properly for saving my life. If it wasn't for you I'd be lying in Boot Hill by this time."

"That's a natural fact," Cobb said. "And nobody sheds tears at a Boot Hill buryin'."

"You said you'd ask a favor of me," Garrett said. "What is it?"

"Later. I've got coffee in my saddlebags and some grub, on account of how I know a man who ain't exactly on speaking terms with the law travels light. Let's see if we can rustle up some dry wood." Cobb grinned. "Oops, Luke, sorry about that word—rustle, I mean. It can't be settin' too well with you about now, can it?"

Garrett laughed, rose to his feet and went about the task of gathering firewood around the roots of the dripping cottonwoods.

After a meal of broiled salt pork sandwiched between thick slices of fresh sourdough bread, Luke Garrett sighed, poured himself another cup of coffee and began to build a smoke.

"Here." Cobb grinned, throwing the younger man a sack of tobacco. "You can roll 'em a mite thicker with that."

Garrett nodded his thanks, rebuilt the smoke, then dragged luxuriously on the cigarette.

"First one of the day is always the best," Cobb said. He studied Garrett for a few moments, then asked, "Feeling better now you ate?"

"Fair to middlin'," the young rancher answered.

"I'm still worrying considerable about Zeb Ready and the herd."

Cobb waved a negligent hand. "Then worry no more," he said. "I spoke to your hired hand early this morning before I headed this way." Cobb shook his head. "He ain't exactly a trusting man, had a Henry on me the whole time."

Hope spiked in Garrett. "Where is Zeb? And how many cattle has he?"

"He's headed this way, should be here in a couple of hours or so, maybe less. You'll be able to count 'em your ownself."

"Zeb's a good man, but he's driving fifty head. Could slow him up some."

"He doesn't have fifty head, or at least he didn't when I spoke to him."

"How many?" Garrett asked, anxiety spiking at him.

"Less than thirty. Ready told me the herd is scattered all over hell and half of the territory. It seems once those cows took the notion to run, they kept on going. Your man says it will take weeks to round 'em all up, if ever." Cobb hesitated a few moments, then said, "He also told me about the Red Angus bull."

"When he takes it into his head, Zeb is a talking man," Garrett said, without bitterness.

His dream of owning the bull and improving his stock had vanished like a fairy gift in the morning light. Deke Waters was not a patient man and he wouldn't wait much longer. Garrett knew he had no time to put another herd together, even if he had the cows, which he did not. He was down to less than thirty head, and if he lost more on the trail he'd fall way short of the five hundred dollars he needed to buy the bull.

Cobb was talking again. "Just as well I'm here," he said, "because I can do you another favor."

Garrett shook his head. "I'm beholden to you, but you've done me favors enough."

"This favor isn't one-sided, Luke. Fact is, it's the reason I saved you from Simon Carter's noose. I heard you were headed for Fort Whoop-Up and I decided you were the only man I could trust to take something precious of mine along with you."

"Cattle?" Garrett asked.

Cobb smiled. "No, not cattle." The man's eyes glowed. "Something of greater value. I'm talking virgins, Luke. Five sweet virgin brides."

Chapter 5

For a few moments, Luke Garrett sat too stunned to speak. He opened his mouth, his jaw working, but could not form a sentence. Finally he managed a single strangled word: "Brides?"

"Mail-order brides, to be exact. Catalog brides as some call them, each of them pledged to wed a lonely and pining gold miner at the fort. Romance is in the air, my boy, *l'amour du jour*, as they say."

"But . . . but why me?"

Cobb shrugged. "There was no one else at Benton I could trust. Luke, these little gals are the genuine article, not soiled goods, each one intact, if you know what I mean. And they need to get to Whoop-Up and their prospective husbands still in one piece."

"You busted me out of the *juzgado* for that? Why not take them yourself?"

Cobb nodded and smiled. "A good question, that. Yes, in fact it's an excellent question. The trouble is I can't show my face at Fort Whoop-Up. A few months back I had a little misunderstanding with the Mounties at the fort, a minor disagreement over the legality of selling whiskey to the Indians. The upshot was that I was forced to make a dash for the border on a fast horse. Those redcoats are long on justice and short on mercy, so it was either make a run for it or end up as a cottonwood blossom, my boots a-swaying gently in the breeze."

"Cobb, I still don't understand," Garrett said, a puzzled frown gathering between his eyes. "I asked you before. Now I'll ask you again—why me?"

"That's easy," Cobb said. "I was close by when you drove your herd into the meadow near town. Right then and there, as soon as I clapped eyes on you, a fine, upstanding young rancher, I knew you were gold dust. You were the very man I needed to safely escort my lovely virgins along the Whoop-Up Trail with your herd. You were safe, Luke, safe. And that's what made the difference."

Garrett tossed his cigarette butt into the smoky fire. "If you'd asked me then, I would have said no."

"Maybe," Cobb said, "but then I would have told you my proposition."

"And that is?"

Cobb looked uncomfortable. He shifted position and found under his rump a rock, which he looked at for a couple of moments, then threw away. "Luke, each of the eager, and let me say rich, grooms-to-be has agreed to pay two thousand dollars in gold upon the safe delivery of his bride to Fort Whoop-Up. That's ten thousand total, and your cut will be five percent." The man smiled. "I don't know if you've studied your ciphers, Luke, but that's five hundred dollars. Now how much is that bull you want so badly?"

"Five hundred dollars," Garrett answered.

Cobb eased back, his smile stretching into a smug grin. "Well then, there you have it. Is that a great proposition or not, huh? You tell me."

The rain had stopped and the sun had begun its climb into a pale blue sky. Jays had begun to quarrel among the branches of the cottonwoods and a fish jumped at morning flies in the river, making a sudden plop.

Garrett looked into Cobb's eyes, the man's shiftiness apparent by the way his gaze slanted quickly away and found something of great and immediate interest in his coffee cup.

"You've been up that trail, Cobb," Garrett said. "It's two hundred miles of the roughest country on earth, and there are outlaws up from the Nations and hostile Indians every foot of the way. It's no place for women."

"I think you and your hired man—what's his name?"

"Zebulon Ready."

"Ah yes, Zeb Ready. I think you and he will have nothing to fear from desperadoes and Indians. I saw how that old man handled his Henry, like it was a part of him. You did all right your ownself when you shot Johnny Gibbs off his horse in the dark."

Cobb lifted the coffeepot from the coals and gestured with it to Garrett. The young rancher extended his cup and the man filled it. "And think of the five hundred dollars, Luke. Hell, no, don't think of the money, think of that Red Angus bull. Keep it in your mind."

Cobb settled the pot back on the fire. "And perhaps you might think, just a teeny bit, mind you, that the man asking a favor of you saved your life."

"I'm not likely to forget that, Cobb," Garrett said, a testiness edging his voice. He thought things through for a few moments, then said, "Let's wait until Zeb gets here and I see what's left of my herd. I'll give you your answer then."

"Seems fair enough," Cobb said. "Though if there's even thirty of those shorthorns left I'll be very surprised."

As it turned out there were twenty-seven shorthorns in the small herd Zeb drove up from the south just before noon.

"Sorry, Luke," he said as he stood with Garrett and Cobb under the cottonwoods. "That's rough country to the south of Fort Benton, and I swear some of those cows must have run clear to the Highwood Mountains."

"It's not your fault, Zeb," Garrett said, disappointment tugging at him. "Nobody but cattle know why they stampede, and they ain't talking."

"What do we do now, Luke?" Ready asked as Garrett handed him a cup of coffee. "I know you'd set store on buying that Angus bull."

"Charlie Cobb here has made me a proposition," Garrett said. "And right about now I'm inclined to take it."

Zeb threw Cobb a hard look. "Spoke to him this morning. Told me what had happened with the vigilantes and how he'd busted you out of jail afore you was hung. Don't mean I trust him any. What's he sellin', Luke?"

"Virgins," Garrett answered.

Ready choked on his coffee, his face stricken. "What the hell is they?"

"Mail-order brides, Zeb." Cobb smiled. "Five chaste and lovelorn ladies bound for their panting grooms-to-be at Fort Whoop-Up."

Turning puzzled eyes to Garrett, Ready said, "I don't want to hear any more from him. You tell me, Luke."

"Cobb's just about told all there is to tell," Garrett said. "We take the brides with us to the fort, then collect two thousand dollars from each of the miners."

"Luke gets five hundred for his trouble," Cobb said, finishing it for him. "Enough to buy the bull and with what he gets for the herd, he'll have money to spare."

"Maybe enough for an artesian well, Zeb," Garrett said.

Ready stood quiet for a few moments, thinking. Finally he said, "Luke, there are two critters that are never welcome on the trail, a woman and a wet dog. But you're the boss, and I'll do as you say, even though I don't like it none."

Cobb beamed and clapped his hands. "Then it's settled. You boys head due east until you meet up with the trail and wait for me there. You can't miss the Whoop-Up. Just look for the wagon ruts."

"What about the vigilantes?" Garrett asked.

"They've lost interest in you by this time," Cobb

answered. "You spoiled a good hanging, Luke, but even so, Simon Carter and the rest don't like to be away from Fort Benton for too long. The town can go to hell fast when there's no law around."

Cobb nodded toward the dying fire. "You can keep the coffeepot and what's left of the grub. I'll have plenty more supplies in the bridal wagon." He smiled at Garrett. "Well, *buena suerte, mi amigo.* I'll meet you on the Whoop-Up the day after tomorrow."

After Cobb was gone, Ready kneeled by the fire and poured himself more coffee. Then he looked up at Garrett and asked, "Luke, you trust that feller?"

The younger man grinned. "Yup, I'll trust him until we collect the money from the miners. After that, only about as far as I can throw a ninety-pound anvil."

The sun was dropping low in the sky as Garrett and Ready drove their small herd into a wide coulee off the Whoop-Up Trail. Recent rains had fed the grass growing along the bottom of the arroyo and the cattle and horses found plenty of graze between stands of prickly pear and a scattering of cholla.

As Ready made camp, Garrett mounted the rangy buckskin he'd saddled that morning from the remuda and headed east at a trot, swinging to the south only when the muddy Marias River blocked his way and the distant purple peaks of the Bear Paw Mountains came into sight.

Riding through gently rolling country, the young

rancher was only a couple of miles from the Missouri River when he looped to the west and rejoined the trail.

He headed back toward the arroyo, scattering a small herd of pronghorns that had come close to the trail to graze, and rode up on the camp just as darkness was falling around him and the coyotes had begun to talk.

He had seen no sign of vigilantes, or any other humans, a fact that greatly eased his mind.

Zeb Ready had coffee on the boil as Garrett unsaddled the buckskin and stepped up to the fire, put together by the old man using scraps of driftwood that had been washed into the arroyo during some recent flood.

"See anything?" Zeb asked, handing Garrett a steaming cup.

"Not a thing, except for some antelope."

"Glad they're around. We may need to hunt for meat if Cobb doesn't get here on time. Salt pork's almost gone, and so is the coffee."

But Charlie Cobb showed up the next morning.

He rode along the trail ahead of a four-wheeled, canvas-covered beer wagon, drawn by three yoke of oxen. A red-faced bullwhacker in dirty buckskins walked beside the team, his rawhide whip cracking.

Garrett and Ready had been watching Cobb and the wagon since they'd spotted the dust cloud churned up by the wheels in the distance. They rode out of the coulee to meet them. Cobb threw up an arm and the bullwhacker halted the plodding oxen.

"Well met!" Cobb exclaimed. His eyes slid to the

coulee. "And you found a hiding place. Excellent choice, right in the middle of grizzly country. Did you lose any cattle?"

"Nary a one," Ready snapped, his growing dislike for Cobb obvious.

If Cobb noticed he didn't let it show. The man waved a hand toward the bullwhacker, who was standing by the wagon lighting his pipe, his deeply lined face sullen.

"That fragrant creature goes by the name Jacob McGee," he said. "In lieu of wages I've told him he can sell the wagon and oxen after my brides are delivered at the fort." Cobb winked at Garrett. "Of course, if you want to keep the money for yourself, Luke, well"—he looked pointedly at the Colt on the young man's waist—"I think you know what to do."

Garrett let that pass and his eyes traveled over the wagon. "Where are the women?"

"Inside, and no doubt anxious to meet you. Though I must warn you, they are shy, timid creatures."

But a strident female voice from the wagon immediately put the lie to Cobb's statement. "Hey, Charlie, get your low-down, thieving rump over here!"

Cobb had the good grace to flush red as he glanced from Garrett to Ready. "That's Annie Spencer. She's like a mother hen to the rest of her little brood."

"Hey, Charlie! Don't make me come the hell out there after you!"

"Be right back," Cobb said quickly, his eyes worried. "I'm on my way, Annie!" he yelled. He waved a hasty hand and rode to the wagon.

"Virgin brides, huh?" Ready said and spat.

"Could be them timid virgins are just a might tetchy this morning," Garrett offered.

Ready did not reply, but the exasperated sidelong glance he threw at the younger man was answer enough.

Chapter 6

A tall, angular woman in a black dress climbed down from the wagon. She held a glass with three fingers of bourbon in her hand, and wore a sour expression on her face.

Cobb turned and waved to Garrett. "Luke, come and meet the charming Miss Annie Spencer."

The young rancher ignored Ready's muttering and rode toward the wagon. He swung out of the saddle and touched his hat to the woman. "Right pleased to meet you, ma'am."

For her part, Annie ignored the pleasantry, looking Garrett up and down from his battered hat to the toes of his scuffed, down-at-heel boots. She made a face and turned to Cobb. "Don't stack up to much, does he?"

Cobb grinned. "I guess that's what Johnny Gibbs thought."

"Johnny is a *mucho* hombre," Annie said, her brown eyes alight, remembering.

"Maybe so," Cobb said, "but Johnny ain't with us no more. Garrett here killed him."

"Then Johnny got it in the back," Annie snapped, a frown gathering on her lined face.

"As a matter of fact he did," Garrett said defensively. "He was trying to rustle my cattle. I was shooting in the dark at a man on a galloping horse. I'd no idea where the bullet would hit."

"That's your story, cowboy." Annie took a deep pull on her bourbon, her eyes like ice over the rim of the glass. "And I guess you'll stick to it."

Annie Spencer was tall and thin with wide, bony shoulders. Her body was all sharp corners and had width but no depth, like the Queen of Spades on a playing card. Garrett guessed she was in her late twenties, but her eyes were old and knowing, a woman who had been used and abused by men and had now run out of any trace of affection or compassion for males, or for anyone else.

Her eyes still on Garrett, she nodded toward Cobb. "Did he tell you why he can't make the trip to Fort Whoop-Up?"

Garrett saw a sudden tangle of masked emotions in Cobb's eyes, one of the more obvious a shifty uneasiness. "Annie, I told him," he said quickly.

"What did he tell you, cowboy?" the woman asked Garrett, her smile thin and cynical.

"He said the Mounties are after him. Something about him selling whiskey to the Indians."

Annie nodded. "That much is true. Ol' Charlie is a whiskey trader from way back and the Mounties would love to hang him, but there are few of them and they're spread mighty thin. You're not afraid of the Mounties catching you, are you, Charlie? Tell the cowboy the real reason." She waited a few moments, but Cobb said nothing, looking down at his feet. The toe of his right boot dug into the dirt.

"Cat got your tongue, Charlie?" Annie asked. "Then I'll tell it." Her frosty eyes slanted to Garrett. "I got to hand it to Charlie. He isn't scared of much. But one man scares him—I mean, scares him real bad. Isn't that right, Charlie?"

"Who is he?" Garrett asked. "An outlaw?"

"You could say that. His name is Weasel and he's been out for the past three months."

"Don't know the man," Garrett said.

"You might get to know him real well on this trip, cowboy. Weasel is a Crow war chief, and he's been raiding all over the Whoop-Up Trail. Caught four miners north of the Milk River a few weeks ago and lifted their scalps, and the latest we heard he'd murdered a settler family over to Pondera Coulee. Weasel's got maybe, twenty, thirty young bucks with him, and they're painted for war."

Annie motioned to Cobb with her glass. "Weasel blames Charlie and another whiskey peddler by the name of John Healy for destroying his people with their rotgut." She smiled. "He wants your hair real bad, Charlie, don't he?"

Anger flared on Cobb's face. "Hell, Annie, you should lay off the bourbon in the morning. All you've done is talk Luke out of taking the job."

"Cobb, I told you I'd take the job," Garrett said. "I won't go back on my word."

Annie shrugged. "Weasel has nothing against you, cowboy. Maybe he'll let us be."

Reassured by Garrett's assertion that he would

stand by his promise, Cobb twisted his lips in a malicious smile. "Annie, why don't you tell Luke about Thetas Kane while you're at it?"

For the first time, Garrett saw real emotion in the woman's eyes, a knot of fear and something akin to panic. "I don't want to talk about Thetas Kane," she said, her thin body shuddering. "Thetas Kane is dead."

"So they say." Cobb's smile was malicious as he twisted the knife. "So they say. But then, who knows?"

"Who is Thetas Kane?" Garrett asked, feeling a quick pang of sympathy for the woman.

Annie shook her head. "Cowboy, that's something you don't want to know."

A few moments of uncomfortable silence stretched between the three of them; then Garrett cleared his throat. "Well, it's time we were moving out." He turned to the woman. "Miss Annie, could you please tell the rest of the . . . um . . . virgin brides to get ready for the trail?"

Annie threw her head back and laughed, a harsh, strident cackle. "Hear that, girls?" she yelled. "We're virgin brides."

From behind the canvas four female voices joined in the laughter, and Garrett felt his cheeks flame.

Before Garrett headed out with the wagon and the herd, Cobb showed him the supplies stacked in the storage box: .44-.40 ammunition, bacon, flour, coffee, sugar and a plentiful amount of canned meat, beans and peaches.

"Starting two weeks from this date, I'll begin riding out to this spot every day," Cobb said. "Bring the miners' money here and I'll give you the five hundred."

Garrett grinned. "You're a trusting man, Cobb. I could keep on riding."

"If I thought you were the kind to do that, you'd be hung by now," Cobb said. He reached into his coat and produced a sheaf of papers. "There's one more thing you can do for me when you reach the fort. Tack up these posters everywhere gold miners gather—probably the saloons. It's a list of lovely young ladies who are eagerly looking for husbands."

Garrett glanced at one of the posters and the large print across the top that read:

CHARLES J. COBB ESQ.
MARRIAGE BROKER
Send orders by mail c/o Fort Benton,
Montana Territory

Garrett nodded and shoved the posters in his saddlebags. Then, as he tightened the cinch on his buckskin, he said, "One more thing. Who is this man Thetas Kane you and Annie were talking about?"

Cobb's smile was thin and faded fast. "Don't you worry none about Kane. Like Annie said, he's dead."

Garrett opened his mouth to speak again, but Ready rode up beside them and cut him off. "Time to head 'em out, Luke."

The young rancher nodded. He turned to Cobb. "Be watching for me."

"Adios, Luke. Ride careful."

As he trotted away, Garrett glanced back and saw Cobb looking after him. Even at a distance the young rancher saw that the man's knuckles were white on the stock of the rifle he seemed to carry everywhere and his black eyes were shadowed.

Garrett moved out trail-drive fashion, the wagon ahead of the herd, he and Ready riding swing.

The Whoop-Up Trail was well marked, the ground scarred by the passage of wagon wheels and the hooves of countless oxen. Less than a hundred miles ahead lay the Sweet Grass Hills. Ten miles to the east was the cone-shaped peak of Mount Brown rising almost seven thousand feet above the flat. Once the hills and the mountain came into view, they'd be almost halfway to the fort.

When Garrett mentioned the peak to Ready, the old-timer nodded. "Heard about that mountain. It was discovered back in 1827 by a feller named David Douglas during his crossing of the Athabasca Pass. He named it for a friend of his who was an expert on plants and the like. It's a right pretty mountain, especially in the winter when there's snow on the top, but it sure has a homely name."

Garrett smiled. "Pity he didn't know you, Zeb. He could have called it Ready Mountain. Now that's a crackerjack name."

"Damn right." Ready smiled, pleased.

They were pushing the herd through open country with rolling hills on each side of the trail. Here and there grew massive clumps of prickly pear and cholla, home to the pack rat, which used the cactus for protection as well as for food and water. A pack rat's abandoned nest, a spiny fortress of dry sticks and cactus parts, was an excellent fire starter, and as he rode, Garrett scanned each clump, hoping to spot one.

His shorthorn Durhams didn't move as fast as rangier, long-legged longhorns, and the oxcart was slowing them even further. But all going well and if the weather held, Garrett was sure they could reach Fort Whoop-Up in seven days, maybe a little less. It couldn't come fast enough for him. The responsibility of taking care of five women was already beginning to weigh on him, and Zeb became downright surly every time the virgin brides were mentioned.

At around two in the afternoon, they stopped to give the horses a break and boil up some coffee, and Garrett met all of his charges for the first time. The women tumbled out of the wagon, giggling at him and Ready, and Annie made the introductions, the names and faces flying past Garrett so fast he made no attempt to memorize them—all but one.

Jenny Canfield was small and shapely, a thick mass of yellow hair piled on top of her head with pink ribbons, stray ringlets falling across the forehead of her heart-shaped face. Her eyes were dark, her nose pert, her mouth full and inviting, and in the single instant when their gazes first met, Luke Garrett fell hopelessly in love.

Jenny was younger than the rest—he guessed no more than eighteen or nineteen—and she had none of the others' hardness around the mouth and eyes. When the other women looked at Garrett, their gaze was bold and measuring, experienced and knowing of the ways of men, and when they walked their hips swayed an invitation.

By contrast, Jenny seemed reserved, almost shy. When she realized Garrett was staring at her in open admiration, her face stained bright pink and the lashes of her downcast eyes lay on her cheekbones like lacy black fans.

Two people noticed right away that Luke Garrett was smitten. One was Annie Spencer and the other was Zeb Ready.

Annie was amused, her smile cynical, contemptuous of the follies of men. But Ready's expression was guarded as he kept his thoughts to himself.

Another man's thoughts were much more obvious. Garrett saw Jacob McGee's eyes on Jenny, hot with lust. Aware that Garrett was watching him, the bullwhacker threw him a look of disgust, spat and walked away, a huge, dirty, shambling figure with hands that hung by his side like massive, curled claws.

Jenny flashed Garrett a demure smile as she stepped away from the wagon, carrying a notepad of some kind and a handful of colored pencils. The young man stood and watched her go, his heartbeat suddenly loud in his ears.

A small stream ran close to the trail at this point, curving away from the wagon where Ready already had coffee boiling on a small fire. The bend of the stream was hidden from view by a stand of cottonwoods and a solitary willow, and among the roots of the trees grew thick clusters of vermilion butterfly weed, bees droning from flower to flower.

As he watched Jenny vanish from sight among the trees, Garrett heard Ready yell, "Luke, coffee's on the bile." Then, using the old trail cook's call, he added, "Grab 'er now or I'll spit in the pot."

Garrett tore his attention away from the grove of cottonwoods and stepped to the fire. Ready handed him a cup, his eyes holding a question.

"Never seen a gal that pretty in all my born days," the young rancher said. It was lame and he knew it, but he realized that Ready had wanted to hear him say something.

One of the girls giggled, leaned over and whispered into Annie's ear. The woman nodded, grimaced and said to Garrett, "Haven't been around much, have you, cowboy?" Then, casually tossing the statement away as though it was too worthless to even mention: "Jenny's not that pretty and she's not for you."

Garrett opened his mouth to protest—but a scream from among the trees stopped him before he could utter a word.

Chapter 7

Luke Garrett sprang to his feet, the coffee cup dropping from his hand. Ready was also standing, and Annie was looking toward the cottonwoods, her eyes wide and fearful.

Garrett sprinted toward the stream and crashed through the lower branches of the trees. Beyond the cottonwoods lay a small meadow, strewn with wildflowers, and as Garrett entered the clearing he saw Jenny Canfield.

The terrified girl was a few yards away and Jacob McGee was standing in front of her, his eyes hot and glowing. The front of Jenny's dress was torn, the claw marks of McGee's fingernails angry red welts on her naked white shoulder.

As Garrett hurried toward her, McGee turned on him, his face a twisted mask of fury. "She's mine. After I'm finished with her, you can have what's left."

Anger flared in Garrett. He stepped away from the girl and crowded closer to the bullwhacker. He brushed aside McGee's clumsily thrown punch, then crossed a hard right to the man's jaw. McGee's head snapped to his left and he stumbled backward a few steps. Garrett had grown to manhood amid the rough-and-tumble of cow camps, where he'd learned to fight with fist, knee and skull. He went after McGee, giving the man no chance to get set.

He slammed a solid left into McGee's belly and as the man doubled up he took a single step back and slammed an uppercut into the bullwhacker's face. Blood splashed from McGee's pulped nose and the man staggered, his eyes uncertain and suddenly fearful.

The bullwhacker, thick and powerful in the shoulders and arms, outweighed Garrett by fifty pounds. But the young rancher, a searing anger riding him, was without fear, and relentless. He took a right to the chin from McGee, shook it off, and backhanded the man across the mouth with his own left. The bullwhacker let out a bubbling scream as his lips mashed against his teeth. Garrett followed up with another right, a short, powerful punch that was beautifully timed and hit the correct angle of the man's hairy jaw.

McGee's eyes rolled in his head and he dropped to his knees, then sprawled facedown in the grass.

Quickly Garrett stepped to Jenny's side, only vaguely aware that Ready and the other four women were standing in the meadow watching him. "Are you all right?" he asked the girl.

Jenny sobbed deep in her chest and fell into his arms. Garrett, feeling awkward, stroked her hair and made soothing sounds, as he would have done for an injured puppy.

"He tried to . . . He told me he'd . . ." Jenny couldn't find the words and her voice faltered to a stop.

"I know, I know," Garrett whispered. "It's all over now."

But it wasn't, not then.

"Luke!" Zeb Ready's voice held an urgent warning.

Garrett turned and saw McGee climbing to his feet. The man swayed for a couple of moments, then spat blood and broken teeth. "Next time you see me, Garrett, I'll be wearing a gun," he snarled.

The young rancher's hot anger bubbled to the surface. "Damn you, there's no time like the present," he yelled. He let go of Jenny, stepped away from her and turned to Ready. "Zeb, give him your Colt."

The old man hesitated and Garrett hollered, "Now, Zeb!"

Ready shrugged, drew his gun and offered it butt first to McGee. The man looked at the walnut handle of the proffered Colt like it was a rattlesnake. His tongue touched his split top lip and he said to Garrett, "If I take that, you'll kill me. I'm no gunfighter."

"You wanted a gun, McGee. Take the damn Colt!"

The bullwhacker stood right where he was, his hands hanging by his sides. "You go to hell," he said. McGee looked around the circle of hostile, angry faces. "I need a horse," he said. "From now on you can drive your own damned oxen."

"We don't have a horse to spare," Garrett said, his voice cold. "You can walk back to Benton."

"Be there by sundown, maybe," Ready said, smiling as he holstered his gun.

McGee threw a last look of implacable hatred at Garrett and stomped out of the clearing, wiping blood from his mouth with the back of his hand.

Ready watched him go, then said, "Luke, you ever run into that man again, step careful. When you see a coward with a gun, it's time to get scared or scarce, because the bullet he puts into you won't be in the front."

The other girls except for Annie Spencer were clustered around Jenny, comforting her as only other women could. But she looked over at Garrett and her lips formed the words "Thank you."

Garrett smiled and touched his hat, then grinned as he heard Ready say, "Luke, a word of advice— a man don't have thoughts about a woman until he's thirty-five. Afore then, all he's got is feelings."

The young rancher shook his head. "You're wrong there, Zeb. Right now I've got them both."

Ready shook his head. "Then God help us," he said.

After Ready left to throw the dregs from the coffeepot on the fire, Annie took his place. "Cowboy, I want to thank you for what you did for Jenny," she said. "Jacob McGee is an animal. I don't know why Charlie hired him."

Garrett grinned. "I'm getting thanks from all directions," he said. "It can give a man a swelled head."

Annie's smile was slight and fleeting. "Then don't let it go to your head, cowboy. I got the feeling you'll have to save Jenny a heap more times before this here journey is over."

As he watched the woman walk away, her straight, wide back stiff, Garrett thought about what she had just said. Did Annie know something about the Whoop-Up Trail she wasn't telling him?

And could it be something to do with a dead man named Thetas Kane, whose very name had seemed to scare her?

Garrett had questions without answers, and that made him uneasy. He didn't trust Charlie Cobb, and now it dawned on him that he shouldn't trust Annie Spencer either.

Deep in thought, Garrett watched a kestrel that had been hovering high over the slope of a nearby hill fold its wings and dive—and the small, violent death that followed was lost in the vast, uncaring wilderness that surrounded him.

That night after supper, Garrett saw Jenny standing beside the wagon and he left the fire to talk to her.

He brushed aside more of the girl's thanks and said, "Saw you carrying a notebook. Were you writing to your folks?"

Jenny laughed and shook her head. "No, Luke, I don't have any folks. They were took by the cholera when I was still a child. What you saw was a sketching pad." She looked up at Garrett from under her long lashes. "Would you like to see it?"

"You bet I would," Garrett said. "I've never met an artist before."

"Don't call me an artist until you've seen my drawings," Jenny said.

When the girl returned with her sketch pad, Garrett leafed through the pages and was stunned by what he saw.

There were landscapes of Fort Benton and of steamboats lined up at the levee, along with sketches of the gamblers and fancy women who worked them. She had drawn Charlie Cobb, capturing the man's shiftiness and slick good looks, and Annie Spencer, who looked stern and all sharp corners. But what impressed Garrett most were the drawings of the wildflowers Jenny had seen along the way, so precisely rendered and delicately colored they seemed to be blooming right on the page.

"These are really wonderful," he said after he'd carefully studied the last drawing. "I think you could become a famous artist."

"You really believe so?" Jenny asked, hope showing in her dark eyes.

"Sure I believe so. People would pay money for your pictures. One time in Denver I saw pictures for sale in a store window that were made by artists, and they weren't nearly half as good as yours."

Jenny drew her shawl closer around her shoulders as the whispering wind caressed her skin with an evening chill. "That's what I want to be, Luke, a professional artist. But an artist needs money to live until the pictures start selling."

"Is that why you plan on marrying a miner? Get hitched to a man who's struck it rich and can support you while you draw and paint?"

Garrett said this without rancor, but for some reason he could not understand, it gave Jenny pause. Finally she said, in a voice that faded with each word, "Yes, something like that."

The girl laid the tips of her fingers on the back of Garrett's big, work-scarred hand. "Luke, I want to be an artist more than anything else in the world, and I'll do anything it takes to realize my dream. Just two or three more trips and I can quit Charlie Cobb and—"

"Jenny, that's enough!"

Annie Spencer's voice slashed across the quiet of the night like a saw-bladed knife. "It's time you went to bed, girl," the woman said. "We'll be moving on at first light."

Garrett saw a flash of alarm in the girl's eyes. "Yes, yes, of course, Annie." She turned to Garrett. "Good night, Luke. And once again, thank you for saving me from that awful Jacob McGee."

After Jenny climbed into the wagon, where an oil lamp glowed, shading the canvas with pale gold, Annie motioned to Garrett. "Step this way, cowboy. I've got something to say."

Garrett followed the woman until they were out of earshot of the wagon, then she stopped and turned to face him. "Mr. Garrett," she said, "in the future, when you wish to speak with one of the young ladies in my charge, please tell me first so that I can properly chaperone her."

Garrett opened his mouth to speak, but Annie

held up a silencing palm. "Mr. Garrett, all these young ladies are already pledged to their prospective husbands. I do hope that is a thing you will keep in mind as we continue our journey."

Before Garrett could say anything in return, Annie turned on her heel and walked quickly away, her back stiff. The young rancher looked after her, his mind churning.

What had Jenny meant by two or three more trips? And why had Annie so angrily cut her off?

His sense of unease growing, Garrett had the feeling that Charlie Cobb and Annie Spencer had their own agenda. Did they plan to step over his dead body to achieve their goal, whatever it was?

From now on, Garrett decided, he'd ride with his gun loose in the holster and his eyes on his back trail.

He sensed danger all around him—and it was not a feeling that brought comfort to a man.

And what of Jenny? He had no doubt that he was madly in love with the girl. He had no explanation for how he felt. It was something that just happened. But in a few more weeks would she turn her back on him and marry another man, a man she had never even met?

That possibility troubled him more than any other.

Chapter 8

They made only ten miles the next day, traveling across level ground but slowed by the oxen. After clearing the lower reaches of the Teton, Garrett followed the trail to the northwest, pushing his cattle toward the great loop of the Marias River. He figured that at their present rate it would take seven or eight days to reach the Sweet Grass Hills, a prospect that brought him no joy.

"It's that damned cat wagon that's slowing us, Luke," Ready grumbled after they'd circled the herd and made camp that evening. "I say we mount the women on the spare horses and get shet of them oxen."

Garrett checked that Annie Spencer and the rest of the brides were talking around the wagon, out of earshot, before he said, "There's something eating you, Zeb. You've been as tetchy as a teased snake all day. Out with it. Say it plain."

The old man nodded. "I'll say it plain, Luke. I been seeing dust on our back trail since early this morning."

Alarm flared in Garrett. "You sure about that?"

"Sure, I'm sure. My eyes are no good up close anymore, but I'm a far-seeing man."

"Vigilantes?"

Ready shook his head. "A passel of riders would kick up a heap more dust. No, I reckon this was one man and he was keeping his distance."

"Jacob McGee maybe? Could be he's found himself a horse."

Ready added a few sticks to the fire. "Not his style. McGee won't come right at you, Luke. Too yellow for that. He's a dark-alley killer."

A frown gathered on Garrett's forehead. "Then who?"

"Beats me." Ready shrugged. "But it's somebody who knows what he wants and is willing to bide his time to get it."

The old man's eyes moved to the women talking by the wagon, his dislike for them obvious. He'd given them all nicknames, except for Jenny, and that only out of deference to Garrett. No matter the names they were born with, as far as Ready was concerned, Annie was Razorback Molly, and the others were Covered Wagon Liz, Rantin' Nell and Five Ace Flora. Every time Garrett mentioned them as "the virgin brides," the old-timer laughed.

"Seen something else today, just afore we bedded down the herd," Ready said in a conversational tone.

Garrett smiled. "Zeb, you're just a barrel of good news. What did you see this time?"

"Injuns," Ready said. "They've been out among the hills watching us for quite a spell."

Garrett turned his head, listening to the darkness. "You reckon they plan to attack us?"

"Maybe, but they'll talk first, I think."

Annie Spencer stepped up to the fire, her hands on her hips. "What's for supper, gents?" she asked.

"Bacon and beans," Garrett said.

"But that's what we had yesterday."

"An' that's what you'll have tomorrow, Molly ol' gal, an' the day after that," Ready said.

Annie gave Ready a hard look and turned to Garrett. "What did the old coot just call me?"

"A slip of the tongue was all," Garrett said, sliding a warning glance to the grinning Ready. "He meant 'Annie.'"

"I don't take no funnin'," Annie said, "especially from some broken-down old puncher who doesn't have sense enough to—"

The woman's eyes suddenly moved beyond the dancing scarlet shadows of the campfire and her fingers flew to her mouth as she gave a startled yelp of alarm.

Garrett followed Annie's gaze and he picked up his Winchester as he rose slowly to his feet, aware that Ready was doing the same.

Four Indians sat their ponies just beyond the circle of the firelight, tall, hard-boned men dressed in beaded hunting shirts, rifles slanted across their chests.

"Bloods," Ready whispered. "They're close kin to the Blackfoot and just as ornery."

Out of the corner of his eye, Garrett saw the women move closer, a shudder of fear rippling through them. Jenny came closest of all, standing near Garrett as though grateful for a strong masculine presence.

The young rancher waved a hand toward the fire. "We have coffee. And bacon if the Bloods are hungry."

The Indians sat very still, watching the camp. Finally one swung off his horse and stepped into the firelight. The others followed.

"You ride far?" the Indian asked. He was taller than the others and at some time in the past most of his left ear had been shot away.

"To the land of the Great Mother," Garrett said. "We ride for Fort Whoop-Up, and the redcoat police will very soon meet us along the way."

Garrett waited to see how the Indian would react, but if the man was intimidated by the threat of Mounties, he didn't let it show. His black eyes, glittering in the firelight, moved to Ready and then to the women, where they lingered for a few moments before they turned back on Garrett.

"Why do you travel with so many women? Are they your wives?"

The young rancher shook his head, smiling. "No, not my wives. But they will soon become the brides of other men, miners at the fort. They are"—he didn't know if the Blood would recognize the word "virgins" and settled for—"maidens."

The Indian's face was like stone, revealing none of his thoughts. "Coffee is good, and so is bacon," he said.

The Bloods did not seem hungry, but an Indian would fill his belly every chance he got, knowing that his next meal was a very uncertain thing and might be a long time coming.

As Garrett fried strips of bacon, Ready had his Henry across his knees, his finger on the trigger, the muzzle pointed at the tall Indian's belly. The old man made it seem casual enough that offense could not be taken, but the Bloods were aware of the rifle and the coolly alert eyes of the man who held it.

After the Indians had eaten and drunk coffee, the tall warrior wiped his mouth with the back of his hand and said to Garrett, "We will ask nothing more of you, except for the wooden crate that carried the Arbuckle."

Puzzled, Garrett answered, "We have no crate, only the sack that held the coffee."

The Indian nodded, his eyes distant, looking into the darkness, perhaps recalling a memory in the night. After a while he said, "Our women make use of the crate."

Now Ready spoke up. "I have the peppermint candy stick that was in the sack," he said. He reached into his saddlebags, his rifle still on the Indian, and produced the piece of red-and-white-striped candy that was packaged inside every sack of Arbuckle coffee. "For the children of the Bloods," he said, offering the stick to the Indian.

The man took the candy and nodded, acknowledging that Ready had performed a small act of kindness. "Better for them this sweet thing than the crate."

With effortless grace, the warrior rose to his feet.

His eyes scanned the shadowed camp and again lingered for a long time on the women.

"We will go now," he said finally.

Garrett watched the Indians fade into the night like gray ghosts, then said to Ready, "Why do the Bloods set such store by a coffee crate? Firewood, maybe?"

The old man shook his head. "Arbuckle's crate is just the right size to hold a dead child for burying, and Indian women have been burying a heap of them in recent years. They'll latch on to a coffee crate every chance they get and carry it with them until the need arises, as it does all too often."

Jenny had been listening to Ready and her damp eyes glistened. "That's sad. It's so very sad."

Ready nodded, his face bleak. "Hunger and disease take their toll on Indian kids, to say nothing of the ones who get gunned or sabered in the fights with the cavalry." The old man shrugged. "The Indians are living through some hard times, and that's why we're moving out—right now."

"Zeb, you think they'll be back?" Garrett asked. "They seemed friendly enough."

"I know they'll be back. Among the Bloods friendship with the white man has its limits. We've got women, cattle and horses, and only two guns to defend them. Luke, if you were an Indian what would you do?"

Realization dawned on Garrett and he needed no further urging. He turned to the women and yelled, "Get the wagon packed and I'll help hitch the oxen. We're leaving this place."

Annie Spencer hesitated for a moment before

she caught Garrett's urgency. She turned to the women, who were standing still, staring at the young man in disbelief, and snapped, "You heard the cowboy. Load up the wagon."

"But why now?" a small brunette with startled brown eyes asked.

"Because, Lynette, if you don't leave, your hair will soon be hanging in an Indian tepee," Annie said. She stepped closer to the girl, her cheekbones stained with red. "Now do you think that's reason enough?"

By the scared expression on the brunette's face, Garrett saw that it was. The women began to hastily throw the belongings they'd strewn around the camp into the wagon while Annie and Jenny left to fetch the oxen.

They pulled out less than ten minutes later, the wagon now in the center of Garrett's small herd and remuda. He and Ready rode flank, rifles across their saddle horns.

As they moved through the crowding tunnel of the darkness, the only sound was the plodding hooves of the cattle and the creak of the wagon. At Annie's insistence, she and the other women walked to lighten the load for the oxen and hopefully increase their slow pace. The brunette was sobbing with fear, a tiny lost sound in the stillness.

Out among the hills the coyotes were talking to the moon that was now rising high in the midnight blue sky, touching the ragged edges of a few passing clouds with silver. There was no breeze, as though the night was holding its breath, waiting for what was to happen.

After an hour, Garrett rode closer to Ready, exchanged a few quick words, then dropped back behind the herd. He swung his horse around and cantered in the direction they'd just come, his eyes straining into the gloom ahead, looking for any sign of the Bloods.

The lifting moon was lighting up the ribbon of the trail as Garrett slowed his buckskin to a walk and swung toward the low hills to the east. He rode up a gradual sandy rise, the horse picking its way through clumps of cactus, sagebrush and a few stunted spruce before reaching the crest.

Garrett sat his mount and squinted into the darkness. Nothing moved, and when the buckskin tossed its head, the chime of its bit was loud in the silence.

The moon had hidden its face behind a cloud, and when its light again spread over the surrounding land, Garrett saw a gleam of white at the base of the next hill. He leaned forward in the saddle, trying to make out what the object was, but in the darkness his eyes could not put form to it. An outcropping of rock, maybe? It was possible, though surface rock formations were more common farther to the east and a lot closer to the Missouri River.

It was in Garrett's mind to dismiss the thing, whatever it was, and ride on. Yet, as the moonlight glowed on it again, revealing a stark white mound almost hidden among the tall grama grass, he was intrigued.

Kicking the buckskin forward, the young rancher rode down the slope and into the shallow arroyo between the hills. He stepped out of the saddle when he was still fifty yards from the white object and walked toward it on cat feet, his rifle held hammer back and ready across his chest.

The moon disappeared behind a cloud and Garrett waited until light again touched the bottom of the arroyo before he walked on.

Only when he was just a few steps away did he recognize the white object for what it was—the naked body of a man spread-eagled and staked to the ground.

That man was Jacob McGee.

The bullwhacker's death had been agonizing and long drawn out. His jaws were stretched wide apart, his last terrible scream now echoing through eternity, and his eyes, when Garrett looked down at his face, still clung to his horror at the manner and the pain of his dying.

A green sickness curling in him, Garrett saw where the man had been cut and burned, slowly and with great care, done with the purpose of inflicting the maximum amount of pain while holding back the mercy of death. But, after a few hours, his torturers had tired of his screams and, like boys who torment a kitten then kill it when they become bored, they'd finally disemboweled Jacob McGee and allowed him to shriek his way into the pit of darkness.

Garrett gulped down his revulsion and wiped suddenly damp palms on his chaps. He looked around him, his haunted eyes staring into the night, but saw only moonlit hills and a sky ablaze with stars.

Was this the work of the Bloods?

Thinking it through, Garrett doubted it. The Indians who'd come into his camp had been a hunting party, and though they might casually murder a white man they happened to meet on the trail, it was unlikely they'd take the time to torture him.

Glancing at the body again, Garrett decided this had been done by men who knew how to hate.

And, if what Annie Spencer had told him was true, no one hated the white man more than the Crow war chief who called himself Weasel.

The night was warm, but Garrett shivered.

If Weasel and his young warriors were out there among the hills and coulees surrounding the trail, they had already seen the wagon, the five women and his herd.

And they'd counted his guns.

When he glanced down at the body again, Garrett looked into Jacob McGee's staring eyes—and saw a warning from hell.

Chapter 9

When he rejoined the wagon and herd, Garrett told Ready about McGee, but he decided to keep it from the women. The sudden night dash along the trail had scared them badly enough and nothing would be served by scaring them further. They traveled through the darkness, stopping every four hours to graze the herd and to let the women rest.

But there was no rest for Garrett. He switched his saddle to a blaze-faced black and scouted the moonlit hills and shadowed coulees on each side of the trail. He saw nothing.

At noon Garrett led the wagon into a narrow arroyo where there was some shade and sufficient grass for the animals. The recent rains were now a distant memory and the day was hot. Jenny and the other women were soon covered by a layer of dust that worked its way inside their clothes and tangled in their hair.

Around him, Garrett saw that only the cactus were prospering as the land surrendered to the summer drought. Finding water for the herd would soon become an urgent problem.

After hazing the shorthorns and the remuda into the canyon, he and Ready blocked the mouth with the wagon and laid their rifles against the wheels, ready for action should the need arise.

Annie Spencer, a glass of bourbon in her hand, stepped beside the water barrel and rapped its oak side with her knuckles. "Sounds like it's getting low, cowboy," she said, turning to Garrett. Then, by way of explanation: "Me and the rest of the girls need to bathe."

The young rancher shook his head. "As you just said, we're running low on water. We can't spare any for bathing."

Annie sipped her bourbon, her eyes on Garrett. The dust on her face had settled into every wrinkle, so that she looked years older than she was.

"You could head east for the Marias," she said. "Plenty of water there."

"Maybe so," Garrett allowed, "but it would take us a couple of days out of our way, there and back. Zeb says if we keep heading north, we'll catch the bend of the Marias about fifty miles south of the Sweet Grass Hills. Then we can trail along the west bank of Willow Creek all the way to the Canadian border. You women will have plenty of chances to bathe then. Zeb says the creek water is a little thick and you may have to chew it some before you swallow it, but it's good water."

"That's then, this is now," Annie said, her anger flaring. "We're all of us hot, gritty and tired"—she gave Garrett a sidelong look—"including Jenny.

We need to wash off at least the top layer of this dust."

Garrett glanced up, where the sun was a molten ball of white, scorching the cloudless sky into a pale, washed-out blue. Beyond the arroyo, out on the flat, heat waves shimmered and the long grama grass seemed to twist and curl as though in a wind.

He thought things through. There was probably enough water in the barrel to get them to the big bend of the Marias. But even if worse came to worst and the barrel ran dry, they could always head east to the river as Annie had suggested.

His mind made up as sweat trickled down his chest and back, Garrett nodded and said, "You can fill one bucket and share it among you. And even then we'll be wasting too much water."

"Wouldn't be a waste if you used some your ownself, cowboy," Annie said.

Garrett filled a water bucket for Annie and as she called the other women to her, Ready spat and said, "Nothing's better than a cool drink of water, but too much of it can give you a bellyache, and right now seeing a bucketful go to waste is hurting my belly considerable."

Garrett shrugged and smiled. "Women like to bathe, I guess."

Ready's eyes moved from Annie to Garrett. "You sure it was Weasel and his Crows that killed McGee?"

"I don't know for sure, Zeb. But I'm willing to bet it wasn't the Bloods."

"Bloods will torture a man," Ready said, "but they don't take to it the same as the Crows. There are some who say the Crows learned how to torture from the Apaches who learned it from the Spanish." He wiped sweat from his brow with the sleeve of his buckskin shirt. "Maybe that's so."

"Whoever did it, they had a powerful hate in them," Garrett said. "I'd say McGee screamed every foot of his way to hell."

Ready's gaze shifted to the hills on either side of them. "I don't like being penned up like this," he said. "It's way too close. Crow or Bloods, if them Indians come over the rises they can pin us down and pick us off at their leisure."

Ready grabbed his Henry and nodded to the hill behind Garrett. "I'm going up there to take a look-see." He smiled. "Luke, if I come back down a-runnin' an' a-hollerin', you'll know we're in a heap of trouble."

Garrett watched Ready climb the hill and when the old man had taken up position near a sprawl of prickly pear, he walked to where Jenny was standing in a patch of thin shade near the grazing shorthorns.

The girl had unbuttoned the top of her dress, and her head was back, her eyes closed as she dabbed a wet cloth against her throat, water trickling between the generous swell of her white breasts.

Garrett's breath caught in his chest as he stopped and watched Jenny for a few moments; then, feeling oddly guilty, he coughed to make his presence known.

"Luke, I didn't know you were there," the girl said, smiling. She opened up the cloth and rubbed the back of her slender neck, dampening the small curls that hung there. "It's so hot."

Garrett nodded. "That's why I miss the mountains already. They're a sight cooler than down here on the flat."

"Is that where your ranch is, in the mountains?"

"They're close by, the Rockies, the Judiths and the Big Snowy. Zeb and me, we ride some steep trails, time to time. Can't do that with a center-fire rig, you know. That's how come when we're up in the high rim country, we always double-cinch our saddles." Suddenly Garrett was embarrassed. "Sorry, Jenny. That's just dumb cowboy talk. I should be talking pretties to a gal like you."

"Luke, do you know any pretties?"

Garrett shook his head and grinned. "Now when I study on it, nary a one."

Jenny smiled. "Then telling me about your ranch is pretty enough. Can you describe it to me?"

"Not much to describe. A log cabin shaded by wild oaks. Tall cottonwoods by a stream that flows fast and cool when she doesn't run dry. A barn, a pole corral for the horses and a smokehouse. But it's the country I love, wild and magnificent country that maybe I don't have the words to describe. Jenny, the mountains are so high they touch the sky and the cool, clean air smells of pine and sage and the silence of morning lies on the land like a blessing." Garrett grinned. "I reckon it's about as close to heaven as I'm ever likely to get."

Jenny stepped closer to Garrett, the fingertips of her small hand on his chest. "I'd love to see it,

Luke. Visit your ranch and see the mountains touch the sky and listen to the silent mornings."

"I don't want you to visit, Jenny. I want you to live there, as my wife. They say cowboys have too much tumbleweed in their blood to settle down, but not me. I want you by my side, always."

A sadness shaded the girl's eyes as she shook her head. "Luke, you don't know anything about me, what I am, what I've been. I could never make you a wife."

"I love you, Jenny," Garrett said. "Nothing else but that matters."

"Maybe once, a few years ago, it would have worked . . . but not now."

"Why not? Is it because you want to marry a man you've never even met?"

"That's not the reason," Jenny said quickly, her eyes misting. "I have a past, Luke. Maybe too much past for you to overlook, maybe too much past for you to ever let go."

"Try me, Jenny. Let me make that decision."

The girl nodded. "I will. Sometime. But not now and not here."

Garrett opened his mouth to speak again, but Zeb Ready's shout from the hill stopped him.

"Luke, Injuns coming! An' man-oh-man, there's a whole passel of 'em!"

A bullet ricocheted off the iron rim of a wagon wheel as Garrett ran to his rifle. He levered a round into the chamber, then turned and yelled at Annie, "Get back! Farther into the arroyo!"

He had no time to watch if the woman had done

as he'd ordered because the Indians had shaken out into a line and were riding fast toward the mouth of the canyon.

Above him on the crest of the hill, Ready's Henry hammered a shot, then another. One of the warriors threw up his hands and toppled backward off his pony. But the rest kept coming.

Garrett drew a bead on an Indian with red and black streaks of paint across his nose and cheeks. He held his breath and fired. The man jerked as the bullet hit; then he bent over the withers of his horse before slowly sliding to the ground.

Ready was shooting steadily and with deadly accuracy. Another Indian went down, then another. Garrett fired, fired again, and missed both times. But the charge had been broken.

Badly burned by the unexpected deadliness of the white men's fire, the warriors turned and streamed away to the south and were soon lost behind a swirling cloud of dust.

"Crows!" Ready yelled from the hill, feeding shells into his rifle. "And they'll be back, madder'n all hell!"

Suddenly Annie Spencer was at Garrett's side. "I told you to get farther into the arroyo," he snapped, tension riding him.

The woman ignored the rebuke. "Ready says they're Crows," she said. "If they are, they're being led by Weasel and he won't quit until we're all dead."

A small anger flaring in him, Garrett said, "I thought you said he only wanted to kill Charlie Cobb."

Annie's smile was tight. "Grow up, cowboy. We have cattle and horses here, but what Weasel wants most of all is women. He and his young warriors have been out for months without their females. I'd say they figure they'll soon be having themselves a time."

"Best you get the rest of the gals out of sight," Garrett said. "Though if they want women as badly as you say, they won't be shooting in your direction."

"Maybe so, but don't count on it, cowboy," Annie said.

Chapter 10

After the woman stepped away, Luke Garrett glanced out across the flat, where the cloud of dust was slowly drifting back to the ground. Four Indians were sprawled on the grass, but as he watched one of them rose to his hands and knees, his body heaving as he retched black blood. The warrior was a boy, Garrett guessed no more than sixteen. He steadied his rifle and waited, willing the young man to fall to the ground again.

The flat statement of Ready's Henry hammered apart the smoke-streaked silence and the warrior slammed onto his side as the .44.-40 hit hard. The Crow's legs twitched convulsively and Ready put another bullet into him. This time the young warrior lay still, dust sifting over his lifeless body.

Garrett glanced over his shoulder. Jenny and the other women had moved closer to the herd. Durhams were much more placid than longhorns, the oxen even more so, but the shooting had the animals on edge and they were milling around, making no effort to graze—a bad sign. If they decided to run, the women would be right in their path.

Worry nagging at him, Garrett flexed his fingers on the stock of his rifle, his eyes restlessly scanning the open land that stretched away before him. The dust had settled now, but there was no sign of the Indians.

A fly buzzed around Garrett's head and a hot breeze blowing from the south touched his cheeks. He wiped his sweating forehead with the back of his hand. He was still in shock from the suddenness and fury of the attack, his mind empty of thought, concentrating only on the open prairie. In the distance, to the west, wound the thin, worn ribbon of the Whoop-Up Trail, the road to freedom that could take them away from here.

Garrett forced himself to consider the possibility that Weasel had given up the fight, then quickly dismissed the notion as his own wishful thinking.

A slow fifteen minutes passed. The heat grew more intense and Garrett could smell his own rank sweat. Up on the hill Ready was staring into the glare of the sun-scorched prairie. The old puncher looked lean and hard, his hands unmoving on his rifle, untroubled blue eyes shaded by the wide brim of his hat.

Zeb Ready had fought Indians before and he knew what to expect. But for his part, Garrett was at a loss. His frustration growing, he knew he could only wait helplessly for Weasel to make his next move and dictate the course of the battle.

The sullen breeze again wafted against Garrett's face, bringing him no coolness. His mouth was parched, but he resisted the urge to get himself a drink. He had no idea how long Weasel would keep them penned up here, and he calculated they had only enough water for a couple of days, maybe less, because what remained in the barrel would have to be shared with the horses. The arroyo trapped the sun's heat, turning it into a stifling oven, and he was sure that back there close to the cattle and horses, the women must be suffering.

"Luke," Ready called from the hill, "something's stirring out there."

At first Garrett saw only the bodies of the four Crows. Beyond the dead, the prairie showed nothing at all but the same heat waves shimmering across the vast emptiness.

Then he spotted them.

A dozen mounted warriors were riding back and forth, leaning from the backs of their ponies, blazing tree branches in their hands.

They were setting the grass on fire.

"Damn it all, Luke," Ready yelled. "I knowed them Injuns would use the breeze."

The tinder-dry grama grass was going up in flames and a wall of flickering red was racing across the prairie toward the arroyo, pillars of dark blue smoke rising into the sky.

"Zeb!" Garrett yelled. "Where are they? Can you see them?"

"They're coming behind the smoke," Ready answered. "You'll see 'em sooner than you want."

Ready's rifle roared, fired again, but he was shooting blind and Garrett saw no hits.

The fire was closer now, fanning across the grass

in a shallow arc, the smoke rising higher and thicker.

Garrett caught a fleeting glimpse of a galloping Indian waving a burning branch above his head. He fired at the man but did not see the effect of his shot as the Indian disappeared into the smoke.

Suddenly Annie Spencer was at his side, her mouth a tight line as she fought to conceal the fear that was so readily apparent in her eyes. The center of the fire was only a couple of hundred yards away and moving fast. But the outer rims of the arc were much closer, reaching out like arms to clasp the arroyo in a fiery embrace.

"Give me your Colt, Garrett," Annie demanded.

The young rancher hesitated for a moment, then without a word, he drew his gun and handed it to the woman. He had read all he wanted to know in Annie's eyes. He had realized almost from the first that she was well used to men and their ways. No doubt they'd come at her wearing different faces, saying different things, and she had prospered from their needs. But this was different. Nothing in Annie Spencer's past could have prepared her for what would happen to her and the others if the Crows took them alive.

Garrett thought of Jenny and understood. "Annie, if it all falls apart, I'll tell you when," he whispered.

The woman nodded, her face set and determined, then she walked quickly away.

A bullet slammed into the wagon, showering splinters into Garrett's cheek, and another thudded into the wall of the arroyo. He raised his rifle and fired rapidly into the smoke, dusting shots along the length of the wall of flame. He heard Ready shooting steadily, but again saw no hits.

The fire was closer now, and behind it the Crows were firing, the bullets flying into the arroyo, buzzing like angry hornets.

Above Garrett, on the hill, Zeb Ready cried out. A bullet had crashed into the chamber of his Henry and ricocheted with lethal venom, plowing into his left shoulder, where sudden blood was splashed red on his buckskin shirt. The old man swayed to his right and his mangled rifle slipped from his fingers.

"Zeb!" Garrett yelled. "Hold on. I'm coming up there."

Ready, his face ashen, straightened and waved Garrett away. "I can make it!" he hollered. "Stay right where you are."

The old man staggered to his feet, drew his Colt and began firing into the rapidly advancing smoke, the gun bucking wildly in his hand.

Garrett realized their time was short. He glanced behind him and saw Annie Spencer staring intently at him, his gun hanging loose at her side. The woman had been grazed by a stray bullet, and a trickle of blood ran down her cheek.

He only had to utter the word and she would begin shooting. At the others. At Jenny.

Garrett's mouth moved as he tried to say what needed to be said, but only a despairing croak escaped his lips.

Men pray for miracles, but they cannot be summoned. They come at their own pace, at the unlikeliest moment, and usually to those who expect them least. And just as he was about to lose all hope, Luke Garrett got his miracle.

As it will do from time to time on the plains, the breeze that had driven the fire suddenly died away to nothing, and the flames stalled right where they were, settling down to a smoldering line of charred black across the green of the prairie.

"Fire's going out, Luke!" Ready yelled from the hill, telling him what he already knew.

But behind the dying flames, the Indians sat their horses and waited. They would charge again when the fire settled, and since they were much closer to the arroyo, this time there would be no stopping them.

But Garrett was determined not to allow them that opportunity.

"Annie!" Garrett yelled. "Come over here and bring the rest with you!"

The woman did as she was told, yelling to the other women to join her. Aware that time was rapidly running out on him, Garrett simply said, "Help me move the wagon out of the way."

The women surrounded the wagon and bent to the task. At first it refused to move, but as Garrett urged and cursed them to a greater effort, the wheels creaked and began to turn, slowly in the beginning, then faster. When the wagon was clear of the canyon mouth, Garrett took his Colt from Annie, swung open the loading gate and fed a round from his cartridge belt into the empty cylinder under the hammer.

He reholstered the gun, ran into the arroyo where the black was standing, and swung into the saddle. After a single fearful glance at the dying prairie fire, he shook out his rope and rode among the shorthorns, hazing them in the direction of the canyon mouth.

"Zeb!" he called out. "Are you all right?"

The old puncher was feeding shells from his belt into his Colt. "I'm still alive, Luke. If that's what you mean."

"Then cover me!" Garrett yelled.

Ready hollered a question, but Garrett ignored it. He shucked his Colt and fired a shot into the air. The startled Durhams broke into a trot, then a run as they tumbled out of the arroyo mouth and headed into the still smoking prairie.

Garrett strung out the shorthorns and fired again. Normally the cattle would have swung away from the smoke and the last of the flickering flames, but the arcs of the fire smoldering on each side of the herd had them trapped. Thoroughly panicked, they made the choice to charge straight ahead.

Without slowing their pace, the cows ran through the curtain of smoke and into the ranks of the waiting Crows, Garrett galloping hard behind them.

He heard Ready's Colt firing from the hill, and ahead of him a warrior's pony went down, the rider hitting the ground hard. And suddenly Garrett was among the Indians as they fought to control their milling, bucking ponies.

A painted face swam into Garrett's view as the man swung a stone war club at his head. He ducked and triggered a shot into the Crow's chest, but didn't see the man go down as he galloped past him into the clear.

The cattle were scattering across the prairie and the Crows had now recovered from their surprise. Garrett reined in the black as a dozen warriors surrounded him on all sides, their rifles trained on him. He still had his Colt, but the few shots that were left were useless against so many.

Garrett knew it was all up with him, and he made the decision to go down fighting. The last thing he wanted was to be taken alive.

He noticed a tall warrior on a paint pony who was wearing a bonnet of eagle feathers and a war shirt of brain tanned hide, decorated with scalp locks and ermine tails. This had to be Weasel.

Garrett set spurs to the black and charged at the man, triggering his Colt. From somewhere behind him a rifle fired and a bullet burned across the side of his left temple. Stunned, his head reeling, he saw Weasel as an indistinct, shifting shape straight ahead of him. He fired again and again, shooting the gun dry. But the Crow still sat his horse, his Winchester held in an upraised fist. Snarling his anger, Garrett galloped up to the man and cut at him with the barrel of his Colt. The big Indian grinned and easily evaded the blow. His arm came down fast and the butt of his rifle crashed into the top of Garrett's head.

Garrett saw the grass rush up to meet him, spinning at a tremendous speed, and then he slammed headlong onto the ground and every scrap of breath was forced out of him.

Unbidden, a thought flashed into his mind. He'd made a real bad mistake—he was still alive.

*   *   *

Luke Garrett lay stunned, gasping for air, his face buried in the grass. From somewhere he heard the soft footfalls of a horse, then something sharp prodded his back.

"You, get up." A man's voice, harsh and guttural.

Garrett finally caught a breath. He rolled on his back, his hand reaching for his gun. The Colt was gone. It must have fallen when he hit the ground. Now he remembered—it was empty, useless.

The hammered iron point of the lance dug into Garrett's throat, just above the collarbone. He looked up and saw the black silhouette of a mounted Indian against the glare of the sun, a halo of red and yellow flashing around him as his pony moved.

"Up," the man said. The lance dug deeper, its sharp point drawing a trickle of blood.

Garrett struggled to his feet and stood there swaying. The lance was still at his throat.

A rawhide loop was thrown from behind him and when it settled across his upper arms it was jerked tight, almost pulling him off his feet. Garrett again looked at the man on the horse. It was Weasel, his black eyes hard and merciless and full of hate.

Where were Zeb and the others? Where was Jenny?

Garrett turned his head and glanced over his shoulder. He saw no sign of Zeb or any of the women. The arroyo was seemingly empty of life.

Suddenly Weasel swung the lance away from Garrett's throat. He brandished it high above his head, then thrust the iron tip again and again in the direction of the arroyo, yelling something Garrett did not understand.

The twenty or so braves clustered around Weasel yipped their excitement and began to check their weapons.

Garrett glanced behind him to the canyon once more. So Zeb and the women were still alive—Jenny was still alive. Beyond the point where the cattle and horses had been gathered, the arroyo narrowed, its sides becoming much steeper. Canny old Zeb had probably withdrawn to the narrowest spot, where the Indians would have to come at him two or three abreast and he could hold them off with his Colt—at least for a while.

Garrett tested the rawhide rope around his arms, but it was drawn tight and he could not move. He was helpless, and there was nothing he could do to help Zeb. A sense of failure tugging at him, he watched the Crows working themselves up for their charge into the arroyo and he thought about Jenny. Would she be taken alive? Would he live long enough to see what happened to her?

That would be the worst torture of all, more than he could bear. Like Jacob McGee, he would die screaming.

As his head cleared and his breathing eased, Garrett steeled himself. He would run at Weasel and try to knock the Indian off his horse. If he got the chief on the ground he'd try to kill him with the only weapon he had—his teeth. He would die in the attempt, he knew, but better that than watch Jenny stripped naked, then get passed from man to man before they tired of her and killed her.

Garrett felt a slackening of the rawhide rope as the Crow who held the end bent to load his rifle. It had to be now.

He leaned forward, ready to make his run—but stopped dead in his tracks when Weasel's head exploded.

Chapter 11

The large-caliber bullet hit Weasel in the middle of his forehead, just under the blue tradecloth rim of his war bonnet. A crimson halo of blood and brain erupted around the man's head as he fell backward off his pony.

Another Indian went down, and a third crashed to the grass under his wildly kicking horse.

The Crows milled about in confusion as yet another fusillade of shots ripped into them, spreading death.

Garrett felt the rope around him slacken and he dived for the ground. Hooves pounded to his right. He turned his head and saw a line of a dozen horsemen coming on fast, rifles bucking at their shoulders.

Hit hard, their war chief dead, the Crows broke and ran, galloping to the south, leaving six of their number dead or dying behind them.

The horsemen, bearded, wild-looking men in stained buckskins, circled around the fallen Indians, pumping bullets into the quivering bodies until all movement ceased. A few threw shots after the fleeing Crows as others swung off their horses, drew knives and began the grisly task of scalping the dead.

Garrett looked around him, squinting through a shifting veil of thick yellow dust at the bloodstained hands of his grinning rescuers, who were busily tearing away dripping scalp locks.

"This one's worth ten dollars at Benton," one man yelled, holding the scalp high for the rest to see. "Look at them braids, boys. Hell, I've barked squaws that didn't have braids like this'n."

Men laughed and one, a huge, red-bearded man with a savage knife scar down his right cheek, said, "But he don't have teats, Benny. What you gonna do for that new tobacco pouch you wanted?"

The man with the scalp yanked down the Crow's loincloth, his knife poised. "Guess," he said.

The red-bearded man roared and slapped his thigh. "Benny, you're true-blue. I always knowed you was true-blue." He noticed Garrett on the ground and kneed his horse close to him. "Now what in the hell are you?" he asked, his pale eyes amused.

The young rancher scrambled to his feet, found his hat and settled it on his head. "Name's Luke Garrett," he said, wiping his hands on his chaps. He glanced quickly toward the arroyo, saw no sign of life, then added, "I was trailing a herd north when I was took by the Crows."

"That your wagon over there?" the man asked.

The amusement in his eyes had been replaced with a shrewd, calculating look and Garrett realized he was not dealing with a fool.

"Uh-huh. My cook and hired hand lit a shuck soon as they saw the Indians." Garrett managed a smile. "I don't know your name, mister, but I want to thank you for saving my life."

"Think nothing of it, boy. Name's Kane, Thetas Kane."

The mention of the name felt like a knife sliding into Garrett's belly. This was the man Annie feared more than Indians, more than outlaws, more than anything.

He managed to keep his voice neutral. "I'm beholden to you, Mr. Kane. If you're ever in the Judith Basin country look me up and I'll show you a time. But right now I guess I'll fork my bronc standing over there and head out after the herd. No point in keeping you here any longer. I'm sure an important man like you has urgent business elsewhere."

Kane grinned, showing remarkably white teeth, the canines long and prominent, like wolf fangs. "I can see in your eyes that you're keeping something back from me, boy. I reckon you got something hid in that canyon you don't want me to see. You got a woman back there? Your wife maybe?"

"Nah, no woman," Garrett said easily. "I trailed up from the basin with a cranky ol' cuss of a cook and a wore-out puncher."

Kane shook his head. "You're lying to me. I can smell a woman." He turned to the others. "Hey, boys, any of you getting the scent of a female some-wheres?"

A man with rodent eyes and a matted black beard down to his belt buckle lifted his nose in the air and sniffed. "Sure do, Thetas. Smell her right enough, like she was standing here beside me."

Kane nodded. "Thought so. Go take a look-see in that arroyo and bring her out here, Lenny."

"I wouldn't do that if I was you, Lenny," Garrett said. "There's a mean old man back there and he's good with a gun."

Lenny looked at Kane, uncertainty in his glance. "Go see," Kane said. He nodded toward another bearded rider. "Take Cates with you."

"I'll go," Garrett said quickly. "You're right. There is a woman there." He tried a desperate gamble, hoping it would work. "I'll bring her out. See, the old man is my hired hand and he won't shoot at me."

Kane looked down at Garrett, his blue eyes suddenly hard. "I'm starting to take a real dislike to you, boy. You told me your hired hand had skedaddled. I got the feeling you've been stretching the blanket since we first got to talking, and my feelings are never wrong." He turned to Lenny. "Go, bring that sage hen out here. Hog-tie her if you need to."

Anger flared in Garrett. "Look, Kane, I thanked you for saving my life. Now ride on out of here."

"Tell you something, boy, a man without a gun can't afford to get mad," Kane said. "Now you shut your trap or I'll drop you right where you stand."

Helplessly, Garrett watched Lenny and the man

named Cates ride into the arroyo. A couple of slow minutes dragged past, Kane and the others saying nothing, their eyes fixed on the canyon.

A shot echoed from deep between the hills, followed by two or three more in rapid succession. Then silence.

"Garrett, I guess my boys met up with that hired man of yours," Kane said, grinning. "See, Lenny and Cates are pretty good with guns their ownselves."

But as time dragged by, the two men did not reappear. Then a horse walked slowly out of the arroyo, its reins trailing. It was Lenny's horse.

"Damn it, Garrett," Kane yelled. He swung out of the saddle and grabbed the young rancher by the front of his shirt. Kane pulled Garrett close to him, his eyes blazing. "Who's back there?"

"Like I told you before, Kane, a mean old man who's real handy with the iron." Garrett allowed a smile to touch his lips. "Zeb Ready's holed up tight as Dick's hatband and he's got plenty of water and ammunition. If you and your boys want to get at him, it will have to be one at a time, and you'll leave dead on the ground."

Kane backhanded Garrett viciously across the face, and the young rancher tasted blood salty in his mouth from a split lip.

"Ride on, Kane," he said, knowing it would bring another blow. "There's nothing for you here but death."

But Kane did not hit him again. He pushed Garrett away and turned to one of his men who was standing close. "You, bring Deke over here."

The man stepped over to a rider on a big American stud and slapped him on the thigh. Without a word he pointed to Kane, and the rider nodded and kneed the horse forward.

Unlike Kane and the others, all bearded, shaggy-haired men in buckskins, the brown hair of the man called Deke was clipped short, his sweeping dragoon mustache trimmed. He wore a black frock coat, a low-crowned, flat-brimmed hat of the same color, a shirt that was almost white, and a string tie. It was the classic uniform of the frontier gambler/gunfighter, and one he must have carefully chosen to set himself apart from lesser men.

But what Garrett noticed most of all were the .44 Smith & Wesson Russians in crossed belts around Deke's hips and, strangely out of place, the old powder horn that hung on a rawhide string from his left shoulder.

Kane remounted his horse and Deke moved closer beside him, their stirrups almost touching. Now Garrett saw the purpose of the powder horn. The gunman stuck the narrow end of the horn into his left ear and leaned attentively from the saddle. Kane put his mouth to the bell of the horn and yelled, "Canyon! Old man! Kill him!"

Deke nodded, his cold gray eyes expressionless, and swung his horse away, moving toward the mouth of the arroyo, checking the loads in his guns as he rode.

Kane looked down at Garrett and grinned. "That's what years of practicing with six-guns will do to a man. But deaf as a cow skull or no, Deke Pickett is one of the best with the revolver there is." He shrugged. "Well, now I study on it some, maybe Temple Yates down Fort Benton way is faster, I don't know. I'd sure like to see them two go at it, though. Damn close run thing." Kane's grin widened. " 'Course, I'm faster than either of them, and they know it."

"Why are you telling me this, Kane?" Garrett asked, a slow anger burning in him. "You maybe trying to impress me?"

"Nah," Kane said, his good humor vanishing as his eyes turned suddenly icy. "I'm not trying to impress you, on account of how pretty damn soon now you're going to discover just how fast I am."

It was not an empty threat and Garrett knew it. He had no gun, his Colt lost somewhere in the grass, and no way of defending himself—unless, somehow, he could get to a gun. He realized his chances were slim to none, and slim was already saddling up to leave town. It was not a thought calculated to bring comfort to a man.

A few minutes passed, the smell of blood and the smoke of the prairie fire hanging heavy and thick in the still air. Then Deke Pickett rode out of the canyon.

The man waved an arm and hollered something, the words so distorted by his deafness that Garrett could not make them out. But the meaning of the waving arm was clear.

Kane turned to a man with long yellow hair tumbling over his shoulders, pointing at Garrett. "Throw a rope on the puncher and bring him," he said. "And one of you others catch up that black of his."

A loop snaked through the air and settled around Garrett's neck. He was almost jerked off his feet as he was hauled behind the towhead's horse, the rope biting deep as the loop tightened.

He stumbled along behind Kane and the others as they headed for the mouth of the arroyo, his mouth dry and his heart hammering.

There had been no shooting after Pickett entered the canyon. Was Zeb dead? And what would happen to Jenny after she fell into Kane's hands?

As he was hauled across the scorched, still smoldering grass, these were questions Garrett couldn't bear to think about. Yet he knew he would have his answers all too soon.

Chapter 12

Thetas Kane led his riders into the canyon, following Deke Pickett. Garrett was dragged across the trampled grass where his Durhams had grazed, then, as the surrounding hills crowded closer, around a narrow bend made even more cramped by stands of mesquite and cactus.

Beyond the turn, the arroyo opened up again and began to gradually grade upward, and it was there that the bodies of Kane's men lay sprawled and undignified in death, like broken puppets thrown away by a bored child.

The slope continued for a hundred yards, rising to a height of about twenty feet until it met the saddleback formed by the meeting of the hills.

Annie Spencer and three of the other women stood at the top of the slope. Beside them kneeled Jenny, Zeb Ready's head in her lap.

Kane spared hardly a glance for his fallen men, his eyes on the women. "Get down here," he yelled. Immediately Annie and the others started down the rise, but Jenny stayed where she was. "You too, blondie," he hollered. "Leave him. He's already a dead man."

Tenderly Jenny laid Ready's head on the grass. Then she rose and joined the others. Her eyes touched Garrett's, and he saw in them a knot of feelings, fear uppermost but also pity, and what could have been hurt for something she'd found that was soon to be lost.

Garrett looked beyond Jenny to where Ready lay unmoving in the grass. He began to remove the loop from around his neck, but the towhead jerked it tight. "You just stay right there, cowboy," he said. "You ain't goin' nowhere."

Kane sat his horse, looking down at Annie. "Been a long time," he said, a humorless smile touching his lips. "Four years since you walked out on me in Cheyenne."

"That was your own doing, Thetas," the woman answered. "I couldn't take the beatings anymore. And the killings."

Kane nodded, lifting his voice so the others could hear. "The years haven't been kind to you, Annie. You've lost your looks, gone all dried out and scrawny like a wore-out old whore."

The woman's expression did not change, but Garrett saw sudden, raw wounds in her eyes. "I was twenty-one when I met you, Thetas, and I was pretty then," she said. "What I am today, you made me."

"I guess you heard I planned to gun you on sight first time I saw you again," Kane said. "See, I was real mad because you left me." His voice rose again as he looked around at his grinning men. "Now I'm glad as all hell you did."

A roar of laughter went up from the surrounding riders, and when it had died away to a few lingering cackles, Kane said, "Where's Charlie Cobb, Annie? And what are you and the cowboy doing on the Whoop-Up Trail with them others?"

Desperately trying to save Jenny and hoping that Kane might possibly fear Cobb, Garrett intervened. "Kane," he called out, loosening the rope around his throat, "these women are Charlie Cobb's property. They're all virgin brides I'm escorting to Fort Whoop-Up to meet their husbands-to-be."

Another bellow of laughter sounded through the arroyo, Kane laughing loudest of all. Finally he wiped tears from his eyes with the back of his hand and hollered to his men, "Boys, these whores stopped being virgins the first time they couldn't outrun their brothers, Annie included."

After the resulting merriment ended, Kane looked down at Annie. "What's good ol' Charlie got planned at the fort, Annie? There's got to be money in this bride business to interest a goldbrick artist like him."

"You go to hell," the woman said, her eyes blazing.

"Please, Annie, after you," Kane said. He drew his Colt and thumbed back the hammer, the triple click loud in the waiting silence.

"Kane, wait!" Garrett yelled. "I'll tell you."

The man turned and his cold eyes met Garrett's.

"You string another whizzer at me, boy, and I'll gun both you and Annie."

"What I'm about to tell you is the truth," Garrett said. "Cobb told me to collect two thousand dollars from each of the miners for their brides. I'm to take the money back to him at Fort Benton and he said he'd give me five hundred for my trouble."

Kane sat his saddle, his brow wrinkled, thinking it through. Finally he eased the hammer back on his gun and shoved it into the holster. "Catalog brides, huh? Sounds like something Charlie would think up, all right."

Kane swung his horse around, facing his men. "Boys, at two dollars a pelt we could kill wolves all this summer and the next and never come close to clearing ten thousand. I say we take these women up the trail to Fort Whoop-Up and collect the money from the miners ourselves."

"Thetas, what about them?" a man with hot eyes asked, waving a hand toward the women. "Don't we get a taste?"

"You will, but only after we get our ten thousand. I don't want these women all marked up an' bit when they meet the miners. Hell, we'll just take 'em back again and you can share them among you. There's plenty of honey for all."

"Who gets Annie?" the man asked, his tongue touching his top lip. He was young, with a hard mouth, and there were several notches cut on the walnut handle of his gun.

"You want her, Jim, she's yours." Kane smiled. "You like 'em tough and scrawny, huh?"

Amid laughter, the man called Jim said, "Man needs a belly warmer on a cold night. Maybe she's all wore out, but, hell, she'll do."

"Then it's settled," Kane said. "We escort the, uh, virgin brides"—he waited until the laughter he knew would come faded away—"to the fort and collect the money."

"And then we take them back, right, Thetas?" a man called out.

"Yeah, then we take 'em back and have ourselves a little fun while we do some wolf hunting and whatever else comes our way," Kane said.

As a cheer went up from his riders, he grinned and waved an acknowledging hand. "Now let's grab some grub before we move out, boys. Killing redskins gives a man an appetite."

As the wolfers dismounted and began to picket their horses, the man who had been holding Garrett let go of the rope. "You stay close, cowboy," he said. "I see you wandering too far and I'll put a bullet into you."

Garrett took the loop from around his neck and walked toward Ready. Jenny stepped in his way, her face pale. "Luke, I'm scared. These aren't men. They're . . . they're wild animals."

Aware that several wolfers had stopped what they were doing and were looking at him with hard, calculating eyes, Garrett kept his distance from the girl. "Jenny, I promise you, I'll get you out of this," he whispered.

The girl's face revealed her confusion and fear. "But how? There are so many of them."

Garrett had no answer. "Somehow," he said,

managing a tight smile as he brushed past her and walked to Ready. He kneeled beside the old puncher and put a hand on his chest.

"Yeah, I'm still alive, Luke." Ready opened his eyes and gave the younger man a weak grin. "But I'm mighty close to taking the big jump. One of them hoss thieves got a bullet into me." The grin grew wider. "Cleaned his plow for him though, didn't I?"

Garrett nodded. "You sure did, Zeb. You done real good."

"Listen, Luke, all my talkin' is just about done. But I need to tell you something, a thing I never worked up the nerve to tell you afore. Luke, you were my boss, but to me you were a sight more than that, like a son."

Garrett opened his mouth to speak, but Ready held up a hand. "I've done said my piece and you don't have to say anything your ownself. Sometimes silence can be a speech." The old man reached inside his shirt and produced a small buckskin bag. He smiled and said, "I been holding out on you, Luke. I've set money aside every month since I rode for ol' Charlie Goodnight." He shoved the bag into Garrett's shirt pocket. "There's three double eagles in there. Figured we'd have it to fall back on if we ever come on hard times. Use it for that artesian well you've always wanted."

Ready's breaths were coming fast and shallow and the blue death shadows were gathering under his eyes and in the hollows of his cheeks. From somewhere Garrett heard the little brunette let out a shrill, outraged shriek, followed by Kane's lion roar of a laugh and the bellows of his highly amused men. But he ignored the uproar around him, all his attention on the dying Ready.

He patted his shirt pocket and smiled. "This is more than enough for the well, Zeb." Ready had seen death in many forms and knew his time was short. There was no point in pretending otherwise. "I'll put a brass plate on it somewheres with writing on it that says, 'The Zeb Ready Memorial Well.' "

The old man smiled. "Hell, Luke, that's better than a mountain called for me."

Ready was fading fast, his voice barely a whisper, and Garrett leaned closer. "Luke, when we was riding the high country an' camped near the aspens, do you mind that song we used to sing? It was always my favorite."

Garrett nodded, his eyes stinging. "Sure I do, Zeb. Let me see, how does it go now . . . ?"

In a voice so soft it was barely a whisper, he began:

As I was a-walking one morning for pleasure,
I spied a cowpuncher a-ridin' along.
His hat was throwed back and his spurs were
  a-jinglin',
And as he approached me he was singing this
  song.

Ready smiled, his eyes alight, and he joined in the chorus in a weak, unsteady voice:

Whoopee ti-yi-yo, git along little doggies,
It's your misfortune, and none of my own.

Garrett saw the old puncher's eyes flutter, then close, the smile on his lips frozen forever. Zeb Ready had saddled up and was following a dim, narrow trail toward greener pastures. Garrett finished the song alone.

Whoopee ti-yo, git along little doggies,
You know that Wyoming will be your new home.

Garrett laid the tips of his fingers on the dead man's forehead. "Ride easy, pardner," he whispered. Then he rose to his feet, the sense of loss in him a dull, cold ache that he knew would never leave him.

Kane was stepping into the leather and a couple of his men who were already mounted were herding the horses of Garrett's remuda toward the mouth of the arroyo, Jenny and the other women falling in behind them. The young rancher stepped quickly to his black, caught up the reins and had his foot in the stirrup when the towhead's icy voice stopped him.

"Leave that pony alone, cowboy," the man said, taking a step toward him, his hand on his gun. "You ain't goin' with us."

"Going or not, I need a horse," Garrett said, a feeling nagging him that something real bad was about to happen.

The towhead turned and looked up at Kane, who was sitting his saddle watching, casually picking his teeth with a scrap of mesquite twig. "What do I do with the cowboy, Thetas?" he asked.

Kane smiled, spat the twig from his mouth and

drew at the same time. His gun roared and Garrett felt a red-hot sledgehammer crash into his chest. Suddenly he was falling . . . plunging headlong into a yawning abyss of scarlet-streaked darkness.

Chapter 13

Awareness slowly returned to Luke Garrett, stark and merciless. The agony in his chest was a fire that threatened to consume him, made worse by sharp lances of pain that spiked along his ribs on the left side.

He opened his eyes to darkness. The sky above the walls of the arroyo shimmered with stars, as though the hand of God had scattered diamonds across a backdrop of black velvet. A longhorn moon was riding high, surrounded by a halo of silver and pale pink, and the breeze that touched Garrett's face smelled of dust and heat. Nowhere was there a sound or a movement.

For a few minutes Garrett lay still, fearing to sit up and look at the bullet wound in his chest. Out here, miles from any possible medical help, he knew he was done for and his time would be short.

Slow and careful as a naked man climbing a barbed-wire fence, Garrett raised his head. He looked down at his shirt and saw a brown stain of dried blood, about dead center in the pocket of his shirt.

He tried to move and was surprised that he had the strength to sit up, though his head swam and his forehead beaded with sweat from the effort. With unsteady hands, he began to unbutton his shirt.

The hushed rustle of lightly stepping feet padding through sun-dried grass carried like a thin whisper across the quiet of the night.

Garrett froze, his hands on the front of his shirt. The footfalls were coming from his right and he turned his head and looked into the darkness. He saw nothing but night shadows, here and there the silver sheen of the moonlight gleaming on the high slopes of the arroyo.

Had the Crows come back?

Garrett tensed. He was all shot to pieces and his strength was running out fast. But he was determined to sell what remained of his life dearly. He had no gun, but he reached into his pants, found his pocketknife and opened the blade. It was a puny weapon and any fighting he did with it would have to be up close and personal, but it was all he had and he was determined to make the most of it.

The stealthy padding of feet stopped suddenly and the silence again fell around Garrett. "Who's there?" he yelled, his voice sounding hollow as a drum.

The quiet taunted him, the darkness crowding closer, blacker.

A soft stirring in the grass . . . and Garrett knew his time of waiting would soon be over.

He gripped the knife, holding it out in front of him at waist level and braced himself for what was to come. "I'm ready for you, Injun," he called into the night, loss of blood and his own dry fear making him reckless.

But the shadow that emerged from the gloom and took form was not an Indian—it was a timber wolf. The animal's amber eyes glowed in the darkness as it stepped to within five yards of Garrett and stopped, giving him a slow, searching look, its nose lifted to the smell of blood.

Garrett's breath caught in his throat. He had seen wolves before when he'd ridden the high country, but then only at a distance as they moved like gray ghosts through the aspens.

But this big lobo was like no other wolf he'd ever seen.

The animal was much larger than the average male, standing nearly three feet at the shoulder, and Garrett guessed its weight at a hundred and fifty pounds. For long moments the wolf studied him, then it stepped closer, placing each huge paw on the grass with infinite care, its head carried low, though its eyes, reflecting the moonlight, never left Garrett's face.

"Damn you, I'm ready," the young rancher whispered, all his uncertainty and fear leaving him. He gripped the knife harder and shifted his body so he was facing the wolf.

It was then he saw the white scar across the big lobo's face, a deep furrow angling from its muzzle to under its left ear. Only a bullet could have caused a mark like that. At one time in its life, this wolf had been real lucky. An inch farther to the right and it would have been a goner.

The animal came closer, so close its nose was just inches from Garrett's face, its breath hot on his cheek, the intelligent amber eyes calculating and wary. Garrett made no move to use his knife. So far the wolf had shown no aggression. It was curious, as though looking for something.

For long, tense moments, man and animal remained like statues, neither moving, the night closing in around them. Finally the wolf turned and trotted away, soon swallowed by the darkness.

Garrett waited, still grasping his knife in a sweaty palm. A minute ticked past, then another.

From high atop the arroyo, an echoing wolf howl haunted the hushed night, a savage song that spoke of grief and loss and emptiness. Garrett listened, strangely moved, until the song died away and was lost among the hills.

He looked down at his partly unbuttoned shirt. Had the giant wolf joined him in the darkness to tell him it would sing his death song? Garrett had no answer. He undid the rest of his buttons, opened his shirt and saw the wound on his chest.

When he pulled the shirt away, the wound reopened and bled. Garrett's fingertips probed around the bullet hole and touched metal, causing him so much pain in his ribs that he gritted his teeth and a low groan escaped him.

Had his ribs stopped the bullet?

Garrett probed his wound again, his breathing short and fast, hissing between his clenched teeth. He touched something round and hard. The rim of the bullet? Forcing himself to stay conscious, Garrett pinched the rim between his thumb and forefinger and pulled. Pain hammered at him, but the slug refused to budge. Exhausted, he quit for the moment and wiped bloody fingers on his chaps.

The moon was dropping lower in the sky, horning aside a few fleeting clouds, and the breeze touched Garrett's fevered face, bringing him a welcome coolness. The wolf was gone, but the coyotes were yipping out in the darkness and closer something small and stealthy rustled through the grass.

It was time to try again.

This time the bullet moved a little. Again Garrett wiped bloody, slippery fingers on his chaps and grabbed the protruding rim. He pulled the object free—and found himself looking at a bent twenty-dollar gold piece, one of the double eagles Zeb had given him.

Garrett picked up his shirt and took the bloody buckskin bag from the pocket. He tipped the remaining coins into his hand. One had been holed dead center by Thetas Kane's bullet, and the other had a half-moon clipped out of the rim. He figured the round must have gone through one coin, clipped a second then hit the third, bending it and forcing it between his ribs.

Zeb had given him the money to have a well dug, but the double eagles had stopped Kane's bullet and saved his life.

Garrett looked into the darkness, toward where Zeb's body lay, and he whispered, "Thanks, old man. Thanks for everything."

As far as he could tell he had no broken ribs,

but the wound in his chest where the coin had penetrated was raw, nasty and painful.

Garrett rose to his feet, swaying a little as his head spun. When the world around him righted itself, he picked up his shirt, followed the moonlight deep into the arroyo and found what he was looking for, a thick stand of prickly pear.

He kicked off several pads, then he carefully used his knife to filet one, digging out the soft, pulpy center. This he pressed against his wound, holding it in place with the palm of his right hand. The pulp would help keep the wound clean and stop any infection from getting started. It was another thing old Zeb had taught him, a remedy the old man had learned from the Comanches.

There were still several hours until daylight, and, a dragging weariness in him, Garrett spread his shirt on the grass and lay down on top of it. He fell asleep holding the cactus poultice against his chest and knew no more until the darkness surrendered to the light of the new day.

Garrett woke to a bright dawn. He sat up, blinking against the light, and looked at his chest. At some point during the night he had moved his hand and the cactus pulp had dropped to the ground. But the wound looked clean and he felt less pain, so long as he didn't try to move.

He got up and put on his shirt, gingerly adjusting his wide suspenders over the wound, then found his hat. His mouth was dry and he had a raging thirst. But the water was gone with Kane and the wagon, and there was none to be had in that parched country unless he walked clear to the Marias. And he'd never make it that far.

Slowly, every step its own moment of agony, Garrett walked from the arroyo and onto the prairie. The Indian dead were gone, spirited away during the hours of darkness, and so were their ponies. Around him lay a vast emptiness, nowhere a sound or a movement.

Brown blood still stained the grass where the Weasel and his Crow warriors had fallen and Garrett began to cast around, searching for the Colt that had dropped from his hand during the fight. To his joy he found the gun after a few minutes of searching. He punched out the spent shells and refilled the cylinders from his cartridge belt, suddenly feeling less naked and vulnerable.

But he knew it was an illusion.

Summing it all up in his own mind, he was alone on the Whoop-Up Trail, where it seemed that every man's hand was turned against him. Zeb was dead, his herd was scattered all over hell and half of Montana, never to be seen again, and he had no horse. He was weak from loss of blood, thirsty and getting thirstier by the minute, and he was miles from water in a harsh, hot and unforgiving wilderness.

"But on the positive side," Garrett whispered aloud, smiling at his own misery. He waited a moment, then added, "Well, there's sure no positive side to this here situation that I can see."

He took off his hat, wiped his sweating brow

with the back of his hand, then beat the hat against his chaps, freeing it of dust, before settling it on his head again.

The corrugated ribbon of the Whoop-Up Trail lay just to the west, and Garrett studied it for a long while, deciding on his next move. He looked to the south, searching the horizon. In the distance a faint veil of dust lifted against the pale blue of the sky. The mysterious rider, whoever he might be, was still there and, at least for now, seemed to be keeping to the main trail.

Garrett wondered who the man might be. Friend or foe? He had no way of knowing, but he guessed that question might be answered one way or the other very soon. Until then there was no point in harrying the subject.

After a few more minutes of thought, Garrett made up his mind. He'd given Charlie Cobb his word that he would take his women along the trail to Fort Whoop-Up, and that's what he would do, no matter the odds facing him. And there was the matter of the Red Angus bull. Garrett needed the animal if he was to improve his herd, and that was no small consideration. And he had yet another personal stake in the matter. Jenny was out there somewhere with Thetas Kane and his wolfers and he had promised the girl he'd save her.

The only question was how.

Every man is afraid of something. What did Kane fear?

Again, it was a question without an answer, but an answer Garrett decided he must seek if he was to have any chance of saving Jenny and the others and getting through this alive.

But before he took to the trail, he had one last duty to perform.

Garrett returned to the arroyo and laid out Zeb Ready as best he could. There was no question of a burial, but he stood beside the old puncher's body and whispered, "Zeb, I'm not a praying man, but I guess you know that if I had the words I'd sure let 'em rip." He got down on one knee and placed his hand on the old man's forehead. "So I reckon I'll just say . . . *adios, viejo amigo.*"

Rising to his feet, Garrett walked out of the arroyo and into the plain. He didn't look back.

Chapter 14

The sun rose in the sky, burning across the silent, empty land and there seemed to be no limit to its heat, lying heavy on Luke Garrett as he walked. Ahead of him the Whoop-Up Trail stretched on forever until it was lost against the horizon, where shimmering waves danced, blurring the line between earth and sky. On either side of the trail rose shallow hills, cut through by narrow arroyos, and out there nothing moved—not a bird, not a lizard. Even the insects had fallen quiet.

Garrett stumbled on, awkward in high-heeled boots that were never built for walking. His tongue stuck to the roof of his mouth and his thirst was a greater pain than the wound in his chest, a searing dryness that threatened to devour him.

After two hours, as the fiery ball of the sun climbed to its highest point, he left the trail and sought shade in one of the arroyos. But there was no shade, not in the arroyo, not anywhere.

Exhausted, Garrett sat down heavily on the canyon's sandy bottom, no more than a dry wash strewn with rocks. He picked up a pebble and put it in his mouth, trying to work up saliva. But after a few unsuccessful minutes he spat the rock out, his mouth as dry as it was before.

The sun seemed to be suspended in the sky, a brassy ball hanging right above him, so close it looked like he could reach out and touch it and let it burn his fingers.

His head hanging, Garrett made himself think, searching for a solution to his present problem. Before anything else, he had to find water—and soon. He calculated he was about ten to fifteen miles south of the bend of the Marias, an impossible distance under a blazing sun. He would never make it—unless he traveled at night when the heat was less intense.

The more Garrett thought about it, the more he decided it was the only way. He would hole up for the rest of the day and set out for the river at dusk.

He unbuttoned his shirt and looked at the wound in his chest. It was red and angry, painful to the touch, but showed no sign of poisoning. At least that was good news.

Garrett buttoned up and rose to his feet. He walked to the mouth of the arroyo and his eyes scanned the trail to the south. He saw no dust. It seemed that the mysterious rider on his back trail had also sought shade away from the heat.

Entering the canyon again, Garrett found thin cover from the sunlight under a mesquite bush. He lay down on his back and tilted his hat over his eyes. All he could do now was try to sleep and wait for darkness.

Despite the raging thirst that ceaselessly tormented him, he drifted off, lulled by the silence and the surrender to sleep of his tired body.

An hour went by and Garrett did not wake as a quick shadow flitted across his legs, thrown by the noiseless passing of a great gray wolf, its head turned to him, the amber eyes watchful and alert.

The day was shading into night when Garrett woke with a start. He'd been dreaming of water, running cool and clear in the stream near his cabin. In the strange mother-of-pearl twilight between sleep and waking he'd thrown himself on his belly, shoved his burning face into the stream and drunk deep. He'd lifted his mouth from the water, his chin dripping—and had looked into the eyes of a great wolf that had been intently watching him.

A wild cry died in Garrett's throat as he sat upright, the dream slowly fading. He shook his head and, as is the way of men who have ridden lonely trails, he said aloud, "Gettin' spooked in your old age, Luke."

His voice was a hard, dry croak, like the rustle of fallen leaves, and his ravenous thirst was still an agony much worse than the throbbing of the wound in his chest.

Unsteadily Garrett climbed to his feet. He waited for a few moments until his world stopped spinning and came to a lurching halt. Then he set his feet in motion toward the mouth of the arroyo.

When he reached the trail, the waxing moon lit the way ahead, angling to the northwest toward the Marias. His boots kicking up little puffs of dust,

Garrett began to walk. He had gone a mile, maybe less, when he began to stumble and stretched his length on the ground.

It would have been so easy to lie right where he was, his face in the dirt, and let the endless sleep take him. In any case, Garrett doubted he could get up again. Better to rest and perhaps gather his strength. A red mesquite bug crawled past his face, making a small sound in the dust, and headed toward the hills where the shrub from which it got its name grew. As Garrett watched, the insect was soon swallowed up by the darkness.

He lay still, thoughts without form or order tumbling around in his mind. Where was he going? After a while he remembered. He was headed north on the Whoop-Up Trail toward the Marias. There was water there, water that would save his life. But he tried to recall something else— something urgent. Now he brought to mind what it was. He was trying to save Jenny, free her from Thetas Kane.

Garrett shook his head, trying to concentrate, attempting to shove his terrible thirst and his weakness away from him.

Jenny needed him. He had to make the effort.

Gathering the last of his strength he pushed hard on his hands and raised his head and chest, his back arching. For a few moments he let his head hang between his arms. Then he rolled onto his side and struggled to a sitting position, breathing hard.

The wolf had been one with the night, but now it emerged from the darkness and trotted toward

Garrett, a sense of purpose apparent in the way the animal carried its head—low, watchful.

Garrett saw the wolf come at him and he drew his Colt. When the big lobo was a few yards away, it stopped, studying the man, its eyes calm, measured and knowing.

Many considered the wolf to be a savage, merciless killer, imprinting the lowest trait of the human personality on a creature they neither knew nor understood. But the Indians, living closer to nature, understood the wolf well. To them the wolf was a sage, a teacher, and they believed only the mountains had lived long enough not to be stirred by its cry in the night.

Garrett thumbed back the hammer of his gun. "You stay away from me," he croaked, his voice tense. "Or I'll drop you right where you stand."

It is the wolf's business to know when a creature is sick and weak, since this makes the chase and the kill all the easier. But the lobo, aware of the human's sorry state, displayed no aggression. It sat down a few yards from Garrett, and when its eyes brushed his, he saw only a fixed interest in their amber depths.

Garrett had the cattleman's inherent antipathy and suspicion of the wolf, and it was in his mind to gun the animal and have it done. But there was something in the huge wolf's demeanor that gave him pause. It did not act like an animal that planned to attack him.

Then what did it want?

The wolf rose to its feet, trotted away for ten

yards, then stopped, looking back at Garrett. Was it trying to lead him someplace?

Figuring he had nothing to lose, he eased down the hammer of the Colt and shoved it into the holster. After a struggle, he climbed to his feet and walked toward the wolf. Wary now, the lobo trotted into the darkness and was standing patiently waiting when Garrett, moving slowly and unsteadily, caught up with it.

The wolf led him into the darkness of the surrounding hills and entered a wide coulee, a few stunted spruce and mesquite growing on both slopes. In the moonlight the wolf's gray coat gleamed white as it moved like a silent spirit through the gloom. Garrett, weak from thirst, tried his best to follow, though his progress was slow, marked by constant falls that scraped skin off his hands and elbows.

But the wolf's patience was limitless. Each time Garrett stumbled and fell, the animal stood still and waited until he got to his feet. Then it again showed the way.

But to what?

There was a growing suspicion in Garrett's mind that the wolf was leading him into a trap. Perhaps the entire pack was lying in wait just ahead to jump on him and tear him apart.

Garrett smiled into the night, his cracked lips hurting. He was dead anyway. The wolves would just make his dying a lot faster, and maybe that was one of nature's small mercies.

The walls of the arroyo narrowed, so close that

the prickly pear on the slopes tore at Garrett's chaps as he lurched past. From somewhere quite close a horned owl questioned the night, but if the rising moon heard, it did not deign to answer.

Deep in the arroyo the wolf stopped, and when Garrett got close it loped up the side of a hill to his left and stopped on the crest, a silhouette against the star-scattered sky.

Garrett looked around him. There was no sound, no movement. Why had the wolf led him here and then moved on? He shifted his feet and felt the ground give way under his boot heels. He pressed the sole of his right boot on the ground, feeling the dirt yield. Garrett got down on one knee and pushed with his hand. It came away black with mud.

Now he knew what the wolf had planned. It had led him to a seep fed by an underground spring deep beneath the hills, perhaps running all the way from the Marias.

Digging his fingers into the damp dirt, Garrett spread mud on his cracked lips. Then he grabbed a handful and shoved it into his mouth, trying to suck out the moisture. It didn't work. He spat out the dirt and kneeled, frantically digging into the soft ground with both hands.

He'd dug to the depth of a foot before he felt water on the backs of his fingers. Steeling himself to wait, he let a slow minute pass, then another, before he tested the hole again. There was an inch or two of water in the bottom. Garrett lay on his belly and shoved his face deep into the hole. The water was muddy and brackish, but to a thirsty man struggling for survival it tasted like nectar.

Garrett drank the hole dry, then waited, his face covered in mud, until it began to fill again. This time he paused longer, until there was six inches of water in the hole, and he drank deeply again.

For the best part of the next hour, Garrett sat by the seep waiting for the hole to fill up, then drinking. Finally the dehydrated tissues of his body were saturated and his cracked lips had already begun to heal.

He stepped away from the seep and sat with his back against the southern slope of the coulee, suddenly wishful for a smoke. His fingers strayed to his shirt pocket, but found only the buckskin bag with the three mutilated double eagles inside. Then he remembered he'd stashed an emergency supply of tobacco, papers and matches in the pocket of his chaps.

Garrett got out his makings, pleasantly surprised that they were still intact, and built himself a smoke. He lit the cigarette and dragged deep, enjoying the harsh bite of the tobacco, and turned his eyes to the opposite hill.

The wolf was gone.

Garrett wondered why the animal had led him to water. Out of the goodness of its heart? That was hardly likely. Then how to explain the big lobo's unnatural behavior?

It was then that Garrett recalled the terrible bullet scar across the animal's face. Had it been a victim of Thetas Kane and his wolfers? It could have been shot and somehow survived. Wolves mate for life—perhaps the lobo had lost its female to Kane's guns or poison traps.

The giant wolf was an intelligent animal. It could have remembered Kane and planned its revenge, or at least instinctively recognized the man as a predator and danger to the pack that had to be removed. It had chosen Garrett as an unlikely ally, temporarily adopting him as a pack member. Garrett had also been shot by Kane and had the scar to prove it. Thus he and the wolf were kindred spirits, united by the renegade's bullets.

The more he thought about it, the more Garrett figured this had to be the case. Somehow the wild, ferocious creature had figured out that Garrett also planned the demise of the human it either hated or greatly feared. By necessity, it had decided they would unite in a common cause—the destruction of Thetas Kane.

It was a stretch and Garrett knew it. Yet the Indians believed the lobo was a highly intelligent animal that left the pack to seek wisdom, returning after many years to share its knowledge.

Garrett harbored no such illusions. The animal had acted out of pure instinct, yet there was no getting around the fact that a mighty smart, and very strange, wolf had saved his life.

Chapter 15

Garrett finished his cigarette, smoked another, then rose to his feet. He felt stronger, and the wound in his chest did not pain him so badly.

He had no way to carry water, so he lay by the seep and drank again. This time there was maybe half a gallon of water in the hole and he finished it all. When the hole began to fill again, he untied the bandana from around his neck, soaked it thoroughly and washed the mud off his face.

Retying the bandana as he walked, Garrett left the canyon and headed back to the trail. There were still several hours of darkness left, and he must use them before the heat of the day forced him into shelter.

As the moon dropped in the sky the way ahead became shadowed. He stumbled often on deep wagon ruts that had baked hard in the sun. He shared the cowboy's aversion to walking, and as he trudged on through the dark tunnel of night, his skintight high-heeled boots punished his feet. But he gave no thought to stopping. Ahead of him on the trail was Jenny Canfield, the girl he intended to marry, and she would be looking for him to save her.

The girl he intended to marry . . .

That thought surprised Garrett. Yet, as he walked through the darkness he recognized the truth of it. When he'd first set eyes on Jenny he'd felt like the man who had discovered fire, delighting in her warmth, blinded by her bright beauty. To live without loving Jenny would be to not live at all, something he dared not even try to imagine.

After this was all over he would turn his back forever on the Whoop-Up Trail and take Jenny as his wife to his ranch in the long shadows of the mountains.

That thought pleased Garrett immensely and he smiled into the gloom. He was still smiling as the long night began to flee the dawn and the awakening birds rustled among the thickets of juniper and mesquite.

Instinctively the young rancher glanced behind him as the darkness faded into a blue-gray half-light. He stopped and turned. Far in the distance he had caught the pinpoint glow of a campfire, and there it was again, dim as a fading star in a lightening sky. As Garrett watched, the fire winked out and disappeared.

There was still someone dogging his back trail, but he decided he would not let it worry him, at least for the time being.

Because right at the moment he had other problems.

Now that the darkness had gone, he saw where the tracks of a wagon and horsemen had left the trail and turned directly east toward the Marias River. If the night had lasted only a few minutes longer he would have walked right past the spot without seeing it.

Garrett stepped to the place and scanned the distance ahead. The wagon had left wheel tracks on the grass as it swung off the Whoop-Up, and at least a dozen horses had followed. He kneeled and studied the bent-over grama. The blades were already straightening, so the wagon had passed over them many hours earlier, possibly even the day before.

Now Garrett remembered the half-empty water barrel. That was not nearly enough water for Kane's men, the five women, the draft oxen and the horses. Undoubtedly the wolfer must have made the decision to head for the Marias to refill the barrel and water the livestock.

Garrett tried to remember what he'd learned about the trail and the river. He had walked a fair piece in the night and he must be near to the spot where the Marias began a gradual bend before crossing the Whoop-Up about twenty miles to the northwest.

Slowed by the oxen, Kane must have decided it was better to head due east for water, even though the detour would take him out of his way. But the river was much closer at this point, just nine or ten miles, and worth the delay, especially with the blistering daytime temperature climbing well above ninety-five degrees, by Garrett's calculation.

But was Kane still there? He could have watered
the stock and then headed back to the Whoop-Up,
possibly angling across the flat to meet up with the
trail again farther north.

Garrett was at a crossroads, but his own need
for water forced his decision for him. With luck, if
he kept to the trail it would be a couple of days
before he reached the Marias. He would be suffering terribly from thirst by then. If he was unlucky,
something as simple as a twisted ankle could mean
death in this wilderness.

His mind made up, he climbed to his feet and
began to follow the wagon tracks.

Just to the south rose a ridge of low hills, their
slopes covered in stands of cactus and mesquite.
Scattered among them were streaks of goldenrod
with its shy yellow flowers. The air smelled of dried
grass and heat, and as he walked Garrett knew the
rising sun would soon make the morning hotter
still.

He followed the lay of the hills toward the river
and after an hour he stopped in the spindly shade
of a solitary juniper growing at the base of a slope
and built a cigarette.

Around him the land lay still and silent, hammered into meek submission by the heat. Even the
vultures seemed content to glide lazily across the
blue face of the sky, riding the high currents where
the air was cool.

Thirst was again nagging at Garrett and his cigarette tasted harsh and dry. He ground out the butt
under his heel and his eyes lifted to a sudden flicker
of movement on the hill behind him.

The wolf was standing there just below the crest, where it would not be skylined, watching him. Garrett waved to the animal and resumed his walk toward the Marias. He glanced back and the wolf was still there, unmoving, its eyes following him.

He trudged across the grass for another thirty minutes. The sun rose, burning hot and merciless, and his thirst again began to plague him. How much longer to the Marias? As far as Garrett was concerned it could not come fast enough.

Ahead of him the land danced in the heat, the horizon shimmering where it rose up to meet the white-hazed arch of the sky. Once he saw a small herd of antelope walking in the direction of the river. He tried to keep the animals in sight, but the moving veil of distance and heat soon swallowed them, for a moment the legs of the pronghorns looking strangely elongated as they melted into the shifting mirage and disappeared.

A few minutes later another figure slowly emerged from the blurred landscape and Garrett stopped and watched as it grew closer. The gaunt, undulating silhouette settled into a defined shape, all sharp corners with no suggestion of softness. Yet it was obviously the form of a woman wearing a black dress—and it could only be the thin, angular Annie Spencer.

Garrett stayed where he was and let Annie come to him. When the woman was a couple of yards away she stopped, her eyebrows arching in surprise. "Hell, cowboy, I thought you were dead."

"Came close," the young rancher acknowledged.

He touched his pocket so Annie could hear the chink of coins. "Kane's bullet hit these. Drove a double eagle between my ribs and made me bite the ground, though."

Garrett's glance brushed the woman from head to toe. She looked tired and she'd aged even more in the past few days. Her hard eyes betrayed what could have been fear, knotted up with anxiety and mistrust. Finally he spoke the question he'd been dreading to ask: "How is Jenny?"

A slight smile tugged at the corners of Annie's mouth. "She's doing all right so far. A couple of the boys have claimed her. But nothing will happen until Thetas gets the money from the miners at the fort. I guess when the time comes her suitors will settle their dispute over Jenny with guns. That's how they usually decide things."

Garrett shook his head. "That's not going to happen. I aim to rescue Jenny and reckon with Kane"—his fingers touched his bloodstained shirt pocket again—"for this and for Zeb."

Annie laughed, a small, humorless sound in the quiet that surrounded them. "Cowboy, Thetas is way more than a match for you, and so are each and every one of the nine or ten he's got with him. Take my advice—head back to your ranch in the mountains and forget you ever heard of Jenny Canfield. If you don't, Thetas will kill you for sure this time."

Garrett let that go. Annie carried a canteen slung from her shoulder and his thirst raged at him. But he did not ask her for a drink. She would have to make the offer.

"What are you doing out here, Annie?" he asked, his voice a dry rasp. "Did you run away?"

The woman nodded. "Something like that. I knew Thetas was going to kill me when all this was over, maybe even before. So I waited until there was no one around and left. That was just before sunup."

"But why would he kill you? Weren't you two close at one time?"

Annie laughed again. "Thetas Kane gets close to no one. He wants me dead because I walked out on him. That hurt his pride. Despite what he said back there at the arroyo, he doesn't forgive and forget." She studied Garrett's face and extended the canteen. "You look all used up and you sound like a croaky old bullfrog. Here, take a drink."

"Obliged," the young rancher said. He tilted the canteen to his swollen lips and took a swallow. He could have drained the canteen dry, but forced himself to stop. He and Annie might need the water, depending how long it took them to reach the Marias.

As though she'd read his mind, the woman said, "Thetas will have noticed I'm gone by this time and he'll be coming after me. About all we can do is hide in the hills and hope he doesn't find us."

Garrett's smile was slight. "How much chance of that?"

"Slim to none. Thetas is a first-rate tracker."

"Then why did you run? You must have known he'd find you."

Annie nodded, her face somber. "Maybe so, but better a chance in hell than no chance at all."

Garrett looked beyond Annie to the horizon. Nothing moved out there but the dancing land. The oppressive heat pounded at him and he felt sweat trickle down the small of his back.

"We have to get out of this sun," he told the woman. "Like you said, move into the hills. I'll do what I can to protect you, Annie."

The woman shook her head, looking down at the toes of her dusty shoes. When she looked at Garrett again, her eyes were amused. "Luke, you're so true-blue I'm surprised nobody stole you when you were just a pup. Listen, Thetas thinks you're dead. It's me he's coming after. There's no point in us both dying. Just head back to the trail and light a shuck for the Judith Basin country where you belong."

"Can't do that, Annie," Garrett said. He took off his hat and wiped the inside band with his fingers before settling it on his head again. "I told Charlie Cobb I'd take you and the rest of the women up the trail to Fort Whoop-Up and that's what I intend to do." He smiled, remembering. "Well, except for Jenny. I plan on making her my wife."

Exasperation showed on Annie's hard face. "You owe Charlie Cobb nothing."

"I owe him my life," Garrett said. "That means something to me. And I also gave him my word that I'd see you and the others safe. When you think about it, Zeb Ready died helping me keep that promise."

Annie glanced anxiously over her shoulder, then looked back to Garrett. "We don't have much time, so here are a few quick home truths. Charlie's plan is that me, Jenny and the other women make the trip to the fort a number of times. He says miners don't stay in one place for long, so he can make a killing by selling the same catalog brides over and over to different men."

"Taking a chance, aren't you? There's always the possibility you'll be recognized."

"There isn't much chance of that. As I already told you, miners are a restless breed. They come in to the fort to blow off steam and then head back to the diggings. Besides, a woman can change her appearance, dye her hair, wear different clothes." She smiled. "You'd be surprised how different I can look when I put my mind to it."

Garrett decided to let that pass without comment. "Sounds like Cobb had a pat hand. Why did he need me?"

"He wanted an escort for the cat wagon and he needed somebody trustworthy to collect the money at Fort Whoop-Up. He took one look at you, figured you for a rube, and decided you'd fit the bill. That's why he saved you from a hanging.

"As soon as the fees are collected, we're to make our excuse to our husbands-to-be that we need to go pretty up, but we'll head right for the livery stable. A friend of Charlie's will supply horses. Then we'll meet you outside the fort and light a shuck back to Fort Benton."

"And what do you get out of all this?" Garrett asked, his mind on Jenny.

Annie looked over her shoulder again, then said, "Charlie will pay us two hundred a trip. Sure, it's a tough way to make money, but it beats working the line. That's where good ol' Charlie boy found us."

Garrett felt like he'd been punched in the gut. "Jenny—Jenny worked the line?"

"Oh, for heaven's sakes, grow up, Garrett," Annie snapped. "Jenny was an orphan who was shoved from one foster home to another. Most of the time she was treated as a slave, but when she was thirteen she ran away from a Kansas sodbuster who wanted to use her as another, younger wife. Pretty soon after, Jenny worked the saloons and dance halls in Dodge, Ellsworth, Wichita and half a dozen other cow towns. She was just another whore on the line in Helena when Charlie found her. He figured she was ideal material for a catalog bride because she still hadn't lost her looks and she was used to miners and their ways. Needless to say, Jenny jumped at the chance."

Garrett no longer felt the hot sun. He was chilled to the bone, remembering the way the sunlight tangled in Jenny's hair, the sweet innocence of her when she showed him her sketches and talked of her dream of becoming an artist. "I—just can't believe that," he said. "It's hard to take."

"Yeah, well, things are tough all over, cowboy," Annie said. "Now let's get into the hills. If Thetas catches us out here in the flat we're as good as dead."

Garrett looked around at the low, cactus-covered rises and narrow arroyos, trying to get his numbed brain to work. It was Annie who led the way. She walked to the base of the nearest hill and began to climb its gradual slope.

Garrett followed and when he caught up with Annie, the woman turned her head and asked, "How much did Charlie say he'd pay you for getting us to the fort?"

"Five hundred," the rancher replied. "But with Zeb dead and my herd lost, I reckon it wasn't worth it."

Annie laughed, this time the harsh, knowing screech of the saloon girl. "Hell, he wouldn't have paid you anyhow. Charlie Cobb is a dark-alley tinhorn who's cut men in half with a shotgun for fifty dollars. He never intended to give you any part of his profits."

Garrett's smile was stiff and grim. "If we get out of this alive—which I'll admit is looking more and more uncertain—I'll get my money."

"Then good luck with that." Annie grinned. "Charlie will kill you for sure. And if he doesn't, Temple Yates, that fast-draw partner of his, will do it for him."

Chapter 16

Garrett and Annie Spencer crested the hill, then dropped down into a narrow arroyo choked by clusters of prickly pear and white flowering tarweed. They made their way across the arroyo floor, then climbed the opposite hill, this one higher than the rest, its rocky, humpbacked summit obscured by a scattering of mesquite and stunted juniper.

The sun was almost at its highest point in the sky and the late morning was already unbearably hot. Flies buzzed around the mesquite bushes and crickets made their small sound in the grass.

Garrett led Annie into the lean shade of the junipers and looked back toward the Marias. There was no sign of Thetas Kane, but from up here he could see the man coming from a distance and that might help. Just how it might help, Garrett had no idea. He had no rifle and would have to fight Kane at six-gun range. Given Kane's speed and skill with the Colt, Garrett would be bucking a stacked deck and the outcome would be an almighty uncertain thing.

Annie was sitting with her back against the twisted

trunk of a juniper, her eyes on Garrett. "See anything?" she asked.

The young rancher shook his head.

"He'll be coming," Annie said. "He's out there somewhere, already planning what he's going to do with me when he catches up to me. Savoring the moment, you might say."

When Garrett looked at the woman, she tried to meet his glance with defiance, but there was something else in their black depths, a raw dread about what could soon happen to her.

"I won't let him touch you," Garrett said, pretending a confidence he didn't feel.

Annie heard how hollow the young man's assurance sounded, as it must even to him. "Thanks, cowboy, but on your best day you couldn't match Thetas with a gun. He's good. Maybe the best there is."

Garrett forced a smile. "Then I'll take my hits and outlast him."

Annie shook her head. "When he shoots, you'll drop." Her eyes met Garrett's. "Bang, bang, end of story."

"You don't believe in reassuring a man, do you?"

"Just stating fact, Garrett. A short while from now, when Thetas gets here, you'll be dead. Your ranch, Jenny Canfield—nothing will matter a hill of beans."

Garrett's eyes wandered to the flat again. Nothing.

He squatted beside Annie and built a smoke. "Can I try one of those?" she asked.

"Sure."

Garrett passed his cigarette to the woman and rolled another. They smoked in silence for a while; then with that sixth sense possessed by the hunted, the young rancher's eyes fixed on the opposite hill. He had seen a blur of movement where there should have been no movement.

Holding himself very still, Garrett tensed. Then his hand dropped to his gun.

"What is it?" Annie whispered.

"Over there, on the slope. Something moving."

A few taut seconds dragged past. Then a gray shape emerged from the shelter of a mesquite bush. The wolf stood watching them, its wild eyes green fire in the sunlight.

Annie leaned forward, her forgotten cigarette smoldering between the fingers of her right hand, curling blue smoke. She was silent for a long while, her eyes on the wolf, then she whispered, "I'd know that big lobo anywhere. It's Mingan."

Garrett turned his head to the woman, surprised. "I've met him before," he said. Then with a hint of sarcasm edging his voice, he added, "But I never knew until right now he had a name."

Annie dragged deeply on her cigarette. "Thetas gave him that name. It's Cheyenne for 'wolf.' Thetas raised him from a pup and kept him as a pet. Then one day in the Big Sheep Mountain country he got bored with him and shot him. I saw it happen. Mingan ran away, but he was trailing blood from his head and I always figured he'd gone off and died somewhere."

Garrett's eyes lifted to the wolf. "Why did Kane shoot him?"

"Like I told you, he got bored having him around. Thetas is like that, he even gets tired of people, sometimes men, but more often women. Man or woman, he takes what they have to give him, then he discards them, just like he'd toss away a half-eaten apple. Thetas had been drinking and he saw Mingan nosing among the supplies and he just drew his gun and shot him. 'I'm tired of that damn wolf skulking around the place,' he said. Then he went back into his tent like nothing had happened."

"I think Mingan hates him," Garrett said.

Annie shrugged. "I don't know if a wolf can hate, but if Mingan does, he's just one of many, myself included. Not that it matters much. None of us give Thetas a sleepless night."

Ten minutes later Thetas Kane rode out of the shimmering heat waves, distorted and grotesquely elongated, so that man and horse appeared to be twenty feet tall.

"He's coming, Annie," Garrett whispered, though there was as yet no need for quiet. He looked over at the woman and saw naked terror writ large on her face, a fear that mirrored his own.

They avoided each other's eyes, the haunting knowledge that death was now very close lying cold and unspoken between them.

Garrett looked around him. They couldn't stay where they were, skylined and obvious at the crest of the hill. To the east the arroyo angled slightly

as it narrowed to a width of about fifteen feet. It
looked to Garrett that the coulee opened up again
beyond that point and gradually faded to flat where
the slopes of the hills ended.

He would make his stand at the narrowest part,
where a few scattered talus rocks and stands of
prickly pear would give him cover. Kane could
come at him from only two directions—along the
arroyo or behind him. Either way, he and Annie
would have the advantage of the sheltering boulders. Of course, Kane might decide to attack over
the top of either of the surrounding hills. But then
he'd be skylined himself where there was little
cover, and he was too smart to make himself such
an obvious target.

As plans went, it wasn't much and Garrett knew
it. But right then he was dog tired. His feet were
sore and it seemed all his bright ideas had long
since skedaddled. Thin or not, it was all he had and
it would have to do.

Garrett quickly told Annie what he had in mind.
Although the woman arched a slender eyebrow in
surprise, she made no objection. Like himself,
Annie Spencer knew time was short and she was
fresh out of options.

Garrett led the way down the slope and into the
boulders, pinkish chunks of sedimentary rock that
had shaken loose from the surrounding hillsides
during some ancient earthquake. Most were small,
but a few stood as high as his waist and would offer
good protection from gunfire.

After he'd gotten Annie settled in a sheltered
spot, Garrett climbed the hill that they had taken

into the arroyo. He crouched low as he neared the top, then crawled on his belly the remaining distance.

Thetas Kane sat his horse, Garrett's black, just a hundred yards away. The big wolfer's eyes were scanning the surrounding hills, and once they briefly touched the place where Garrett was hidden before moving on. Slowly, making as little movement as possible, the young rancher reached down and drew his Colt. Could he make the shot?

Garrett blinked sweat from his eyes and steadied the revolver in both hands, pushing it out in front of him. He eased back the hammer, the triple click sounding like loud drumbeats in the silence. Kane stayed right where he was. He hadn't heard.

It was no small thing to bushwhack a man, even a cold-blooded killer like Thetas Kane. But Garrett knew he had no other recourse. His own life and the lives of five women depended on what he did next.

Sweat stung his eyes as he laid the front sight dead center on Kane's chest. Then he raised the blade a fraction higher to allow for any possible bullet drop. A fly droned around Garrett's head as he took up the tiny amount of slack on the trigger—and fired.

The roar of the gun echoed through the hills, scattering jays from among the juniper on the slopes. For a while it seemed that time stood still as Kane sat immobile on his horse. Then the man drew with flashing speed and hammered shot after shot in Garrett's direction. A bullet whined off a rock close to the young man's head and another clipped a branch off a nearby mesquite. A third kicked up a startled V of dirt in front of Garrett's face as he ducked, driving gravel and sand into his eyes.

Half blinded, Garrett raised his head, thumbing back the hammer of his Colt. But Kane was already galloping away and by the time Garrett rose to his feet, the wolfer was riding around the hill toward the mouth of the arroyo and was soon lost from view.

Cursing under his breath, Garrett slid down the slope toward the rocks on his rump. He hit the flat on his feet and ran into the boulders, where Annie's frightened eyes were asking an urgent question.

"I missed him," Garrett said bitterly. "Missed him clean."

"Where is he?" the woman asked, alarm spiking in her voice.

"If I'm not mistaken, he's going to be right on top of us very soon."

But minutes passed and there was no sign of Kane. Nothing moved, and now that the jays had fallen silent there was no sound but the drowsy drone of the flies.

Where was the man?

Garrett wiped the sweaty palm of his gun hand on his chaps. His mouth was dry—from thirst, he tried to tell himself, not fear. But Thetas Kane was an ominous threat, his menacing shadow falling across the bright window of the day, and he was a man to be very much feared.

Annie whispered, "Are you sure you missed him, Garrett? Maybe he's dead."

The young rancher shook his head. "I didn't get him." Then, anger and disappointment pulling at him, he added, "Hell, I can't even bushwhack a man."

"That's because you're in the wrong business, cowboy," Annie said. "You should be home in the Judith Basin country, trying your best to outthink cows."

Garrett nodded, his smile slight. "Seems like."

"Where is he?" Annie asked again.

Garrett made no answer as his red-rimmed eyes scanned the arroyo. He turned and checked behind him. There was only emptiness.

The sun was directly overhead, a searing ball of fire blasting the sky and arroyo like a blast furnace.

Garrett put his tongue to his dry lips, then wiped sweat from his forehead with the back of his gun hand. A rock, dislodged from higher up the slope to his right, skittered down the steep incline and bounced off a boulder next to where Annie was sitting. The woman let out a little gasp of alarm as Garrett swung his gun on the hill. But he saw nothing. A moment later a squirrel bounced into the open, loosening more rocks and gravel, and dived into a juniper, chattering its irritation.

Shaking his head at his own jumpiness, Garrett again turned his eyes to the arroyo ahead of him.

Hours slid past like snails, slow trails of time that marked the passing of the sullen afternoon.

The light was beginning to fade when Garrett decided to bring matters to a head, the waiting wearing on him. He cupped a hand to his mouth and yelled, "Kane, show yourself and fight like a man, you damned yellow dog!"

The echoing silence mocked him and only the mute hills seemed to be listening.

Garrett stood and held himself still, his gun raised in his hand. Moments slipped by, then he heard a regular, muffled sound—the soft footfalls of a horse walking slowly through the arroyo toward him.

Chapter 17

Luke Garrett tensed as he heard Annie's sharp intake of breath. "He's coming, Garrett," she said.

There was no hope in the woman's voice, no urging of the young man beside her to action. She was merely stating a fact: Thetas Kane was on his way. What she had left unsaid was that Garrett could not stop him.

The horse had still not reached the bend of the arroyo where it would come into view. For a few moments the quiet fall of its hooves stopped, then started again.

Kane was very close now.

Garrett raised his gun, almost to eye level, the hammer back and ready. If he was lucky he would be able to get off one fast shot and it would have to count. If he missed . . . then Kane would bed him down for keeps.

The horse kept coming.

Garrett touched his tongue to his top lip, fear burning like a cold fire in his belly.

His black walked through the curve of the arroyo and into the open.

Garrett raised his gun higher, his finger on the trigger. But he had no target. The horse was riderless.

"Behind you, Garrett. Turn real slow."

It was Kane's voice. Garrett paused for just an instant, considering his options.

"Turn or I'll drop you right there," Kane said. "Thought maybe you'd like to see it coming."

The thought had flashed through Garrett's mind that he could turn fast and fire. But he just as quickly dismissed the notion. Kane would kill him before he even brought his gun to bear.

Garrett turned slowly, holding his Colt in an upraised hand, knowing his time was running out fast.

"Just open your fingers and let the iron drop," Kane said.

Through the gathering gloom he saw Kane's white smile. "I don't know how you survived the last time I gunned you, boy. But this time I mean to make sure."

The muzzle of Kane's gun lifted a fraction, ready for the shot. "Now let go of that gun like I told you."

Deciding to sell his life dearly, Garrett swung down his arm and leveled his Colt, already aware that he was way too slow.

Kane could have gunned him right then but he never got to pull the trigger.

A flash of gray and the big wolf was on top of him, its wide-open mouth clamping over Kane's face, the fangs digging deep. Kane screamed and fell on his back, Mingan tearing at his face.

Kane lifted his hand, trying to get his gun into a firing position. But the wolf jumped off him and bounded away. His face streaming blood, Kane staggered to his feet and triggered shot after shot at the fleeing wolf. But the animal had been quickly swallowed by the darkness and Kane's bullets went wild.

"Kane!" Garrett's voice cut through the ringing silence that followed the staccato racket of the wolfer's shots.

The man turned, his face a grotesque mask of scarlet blood. White bone showed on his cheekbones where the skin had been ripped to shreds.

"Now it's your turn to drop the gun," Garrett said, his voice soft and easy. "Do it now or I'll kill you."

For a few moments Kane thought about it, and Garrett could see the man's mind working. How many shots had he fired?

Garrett gave him the answer. "You shot your gun dry, Kane. Now drop it on account of how I won't tell you again."

"Damn your eyes, Garrett," Kane snarled as he threw his useless Colt on the ground. "You'd better kill me now because I won't rest until I skin you alive."

"Big talk coming from a man who was just half et by a wolf," Garrett said, smiling, feeling the tension of the past hours draining from him. He stepped toward Kane. "Back off."

The man read something in the grim set of the young rancher's mouth and took a couple of steps back. Garrett picked up Kane's gun and shoved it into his waistband. "Come morning we're headed for the Marias," he said. "You're going to tell those boys of yours to let Jenny Canfield and the other women loose."

Kane's face was streaked with thin fingers of blood, his eyes blazing with rage. "Do that and you'll never leave the river alive," he said.

Garrett nodded. "Neither will you," he said. "This much is certain, Kane. One way or the other you'll die with me."

"Thetas!" Annie Spencer ran to the wolfer's side. "You've been sore hurt," she said. "Let me help you."

Kane sat as the woman poured water on her fingers and began to dab the blood off his face, whispering wordless, soothing sounds as a mother would to a sick child.

Garrett shook his head. There was just no accounting for women. She'd been used and abused by Kane and was deathly afraid of him. And she'd said she hated the man. But that had been a lie. She still loved him, an unnatural, perverted kind of love to be sure, but love just the same.

After taking time to reload Kane's Colt, Garrett stepped to his black and untied the rope from the saddle. He walked back to where Annie was still tending to the big wolfer and said, "Annie, step away from him."

"Why?" the woman asked, turning her head to Garrett.

"Because I said so. Now move!"

"Don't hurt him," Annie pleaded as she rose to her feet.

Garrett shook out a loop, then tossed it over Kane's shoulders, cinching it tight when it fell over the man's upper arms. He stepped closer to the wolfer and wound the rope around him several times, before tying it behind him.

Kane made no protest, but his searching eyes were on Garrett the whole time, his face black with a deep hatred.

"Did you have to do that?" Annie asked, her own eyes blazing. "Truss him up like a chicken that way?"

"Yes, I did," the young rancher answered, not an ounce of give in him. He looked down at Kane and smiled. "Thetas, best you get some rest. You've got a long walk ahead of you come morning."

"Listen, Garrett. When I kill you, it will be real slow. You'll die a thousand little deaths before you go screaming into hell. Damn you, boy. I'll skin your sorry hide piece by piece so it takes you a week to die. You'll beg me to put a bullet into you, but I won't because I'll remember this day and all I'll do is giggle and cut some more."

Garrett smiled. "Kane," he said, "you've got a heart as big as a Brazos riverboat, haven't you?"

The twilight shaded into night. Garrett unsaddled the black, then sat close to Kane, not trusting Annie Spencer. The waxing moon rose and the coyotes began to talk among the hills. A breeze stirred, coming off the Bear Paw Mountains to the west, carrying with it the faint scent of pine and sage.

Kane sat in a scowling silence, Annie close beside him. She had washed most of the blood off the man's face, but could do little about the raw lacerations made by Mingan's fangs. The wolf had scarred Kane and he would carry the marks for life. Now man and animal shared a common bond of mutual hate and terrible disfigurement and the bad blood between them would not go away until one or both of them were dead.

Annie moved, getting nearer to the wolfer. "I'd appreciate it if you'd put some space between you and Kane, Annie," Garrett said. "You're making me a mite uneasy."

"I won't untie him, if that's what you're thinking," the woman said.

Garrett nodded. "That's what I was thinking. Now move away from him."

Annie rose to her feet and walked a few steps away from Kane. She sat and rested her thin back against a rock. "This better?" she asked Garrett.

"Sets my mind at rest. For a spell there, you and Kane were getting too all-fired cozy."

"Thetas was hurt and he needed help," Annie said. "I guess old habits die hard."

"Loving a man become a habit with you, Annie?" Garrett asked.

The woman nodded. "A real hard habit to break, seems like."

Garrett's eyes slid to Kane's face, a dour blur in the gloom. "You told me you hated him."

"I do. How can a woman love and hate a man at the same time? You tell me. I only know that's how it is."

"And that's how come I don't want you going near him," Garrett said.

"I won't set him loose, cowboy," Annie said. "There's no going back to how things once were between us."

Kane's laugh was a hard, cold cackle coming out of the darkness. "You're damned right about that, Annie. Oh, maybe in the night I'd reach out for you, to scratch an itch like. But come first light I'd take one look at you and kick you clear out of bed."

The big wolfer tilted back his head and roared, his laughter even more cruel than his words.

Garrett waited until Kane had fallen silent and shook his head. "Miz Spencer, that bad habit you say you got, if'n I was you, I'd break it real fast."

The woman made no answer, but Garrett heard her sob, a small, wrenching sound in the quiet.

Garrett rose to his feet, sat down beside Annie and put his arm around her scrawny waist, pulling her to him. The woman laid her head on his shoulder and they sat like that for a long time, saying nothing, until Annie's sobs died away.

Later, as he lay on his back and looked up at the stars, Garrett asked himself why he had comforted Annie, a woman who meant nothing to him. He had no answer. Maybe it was just that he couldn't bear to see a wounded creature hurting. Or was he just getting soft? He had no answer for that either.

Chapter 18

At first light Luke Garrett shook Annie awake, then kicked Kane in the ribs until the man opened his eyes.

"That's a dozen more cuts, boy," Kane said, his boiling eyes boring into Garrett's. "I won't forget."

Garrett ignored the wolfer and stepped to his saddle. His saddlebags were still in place and he reached inside and found a rope piggin string. He walked over to Kane. "On your feet."

The man rose and Garrett quickly bound his wrists together with the string. He loosed his rope, then dabbed the loop around the wolfer's neck, pulling the rawhide hondo tight so it settled just under Kane's chin.

Garrett smiled. "Try to make a run for it, Thetas, and I'll break your damned neck."

Kane looked terrible. His beard and long hair were crusted with blood and the cuts on his face were open to the bone, his wild eyes shot through with threads of scarlet. Without his guns he seemed smaller, but the man had lost none of his arrogance and he cursed Garrett viciously, his face a snarling mask of anger.

Last night had convinced Garrett that he could trust Annie not to make an attempt to free Kane. He passed her the wolfer's gun. "If he tries any fancy moves, kill him."

The woman nodded. She held the Colt in both hands, her thumb on the hammer. Kane's blood-shot gaze went to Annie, curious and calculating, but he said nothing.

Garrett saddled the black, picked up the end of Kane's rope and swung into the leather. He kicked a stirrup free and told Annie to climb up behind him. The woman gave Garrett back the Colt, stepped into the stirrup and mounted, hitching up her skirt to straddle the horse, showing a deal of still shapely leg.

"All ready?" Garrett asked her, turning his head.

She nodded and the young rancher kneed the black into motion, tugging on the rope, forcing Kane to stumble after him.

After clearing the arroyo, Garrett rounded the hill, then headed east toward the Marias. A scarlet sun hung low in the sky and the morning was still not unbearably hot. Ahead of him the heat waves had yet to begin to shimmer and the land stood out in stark detail. He could see low-lying brush flats that stretched all the way to the horizon until they touched the blue arch of the sky.

For an hour they rode in silence, the only sound the creak of saddle leather, the soft fall on the horse's hooves on the sand and Kane's shuffling steps. Vultures quartered the sky, gliding in elegant circles, and once a gazing antelope lifted its head to watch them as they rode past.

As the sun climbed higher the temperature rose. Garrett passed the canteen to Annie. The woman drank and so did he. Stepping out of the saddle, Garrett lifted the canteen to Kane's lips and the man took a swallow.

"How far to the river, Kane?" he asked.

"An hour," the wolfer answered. "Maybe less." His eyes met Garrett's. "You don't really think you can ride into my camp and get out alive, do you?"

"You're my ace in the hole, Kane," the young rancher said. "Anybody even looks like drawing a gun and I'll scatter your brains."

Kane studied Garrett, reading him. "You mean that, don't you?"

Garrett nodded. "Uh-huh. You can bet the ranch and all the cattle on it."

Thirty minutes later Garrett struck an old buffalo trail that angled slightly to the northwest. He followed the trail, the black's hooves kicking up plumes of dust, and behind him Kane coughed and cursed as he stumbled forward, breathing a dry, noxious mix of powdered dirt and manure.

Annie Spencer, looking over Garrett's shoulder, saw the cottonwoods along the river bottom first. She pointed them out to Garrett and the young rancher's eyes followed her leveled finger. Now he too caught sight of the cottonwoods, rising like puffs of smoke in the distance.

He rode up on the wolfers' camp just as the sun climbed directly overhead.

Garrett reined up the black and jerked the rope,

yanking Kane alongside his left stirrup. "I'm going to ride in slow and peaceful," he told the wolfer. "But if I see any snake eyes, remember what I said—I'll gun you."

"Big talk, boy," Kane said. "We'll find out if you're still talking so big a few minutes from now."

Garrett nodded. "It won't make no never mind to you, Thetas. On account of how you'll already be coyote bait."

A few men were gathering at the edge of the camp, rifles slanted across their chests. They watched Garrett intently as he quickly scanned the lay of the land.

Cottonwoods and some willows lined both banks of the Marias. A low hill rose just to the right of the camp, on its slope several standing stones that may have had a ceremonial Indian origin. The wolfers' horses and the oxen grazed close to the river in the shade of the cottonwoods and only one fire burned, a blackened pot on a wooden tripod hanging over the coals.

The wagon was standing close to the fire, the women gathered around it, Jenny Canfield's bright hair catching the sunlight.

Garrett had seen all he wanted to see. Keeping Kane close, he drew his gun and kneed the horse forward. When he was still thirty yards away he stood in the stirrups and yelled, "Hello the camp!"

A big towhead Garrett recognized as the man who had put a loop around his neck after the fight with Weasel beckoned him forward.

When Garrett rode closer, the towhead's wary eyes slid from the Colt in the rancher's hand to

Kane. "How do you want us to play this, Thetas?" he asked.

"Do nothing right now, you idiot," Kane snapped. "Can't you see he's got a gun pointed right at my head?"

Ten men now stood in a loose line, facing Garrett. Deke Pickett had his powder horn to his ear and the deaf gunman looked confused as he tried to figure out what was happening. His puzzled eyes darted back and forth from Garrett to Kane and his mouth was working.

At that moment Pickett was the most dangerous of all. If he failed to understand the situation he could go to the gun, figuring he would get all the explanations he needed after the smoke cleared.

The other thing that bothered Garrett was the reckless look in the towhead's eyes. The man was holding himself tense, thinking it over. How fast was he on the draw and shoot? Probably lightning fast, Garrett decided, and his worries grew.

He shoved the muzzle of his gun harder against Kane's head. "Thetas, tell your boys to hitch the oxen to the wagon," he said. "The women are leaving."

Kane stiffened as though he'd been struck, but his voice was steady as he said, "Do as he says, boys. Hitch up the wagon." Then, after a moment's hesitation: "It will be all right, he's not going anywhere."

A couple of men left to round up the oxen, both of them looking back at Garrett.

The young rancher watched them go. Jenny's

eyes were on him, and he told himself so far, so good.

But a heartbeat later it took only one questioning word, strangely distorted from the mouth of the poised and ready Deke Pickett, to open the ball. "Thetas?"

Perhaps spurred by Pickett's confused query, the towhead decided to end it right there. Confident of his speed from the holster, he drew. But the man's gun still hadn't cleared leather when a bullet crashed into his chest.

The towhead's eyes widened in surprise. He looked up at Garrett, trying to determine if it was he who'd killed him, then he fell on his back, blood staining his mouth. A flurry of bullets kicked up exclamation points of warning around the feet of Kane's men, and when the roar of the shooting died away, a man's voice called out from the hillside, "Stay right where you are! I'll kill the first man who makes a move for a gun."

Garrett's eyes slanted to the hillside. A rider on a long-legged buckskin emerged from out of the standing stones and made his way down the slope. He held his rifle upright, the butt resting on his right thigh, and even at a distance Garrett saw the white gleam of teeth as the man grinned.

It was Kane who first recognized the rifleman. "It's Temple Yates, damn his eyes."

Deke Pickett had moved up beside Kane, his thumbs tucked in his gun belts. He never took his eyes off Yates.

"Temple Yates," Pickett said. He looked at Kane

for confirmation, his attentive stare on the big wolfer's mouth.

"I know," Kane said, exaggerating the movement of his lips.

Pickett nodded, satisfied. He took a step back, but now his hands were close to the butts of his Smith & Wesson Russians.

Temple Yates rode near to Garrett and reined up, his searching gray eyes missing nothing, lingering for a moment on the Colt pointed at Kane's head.

Yates was a tall, slender man, riding relaxed and easy in the saddle. He was clean-shaven but for a sweeping dragoon mustache. His dusty range clothes were drab and nondescript, only the band on his hat adding a splash of color. It was silver and obviously decorated by the same gunsmith who had engraved his twin Colts.

The gunman nodded at Kane. "Thetas." His eyes shifted to Pickett, narrowing slightly. "See you still got deef Deke with you. Is he hearing any better?"

"Worse, Temp," Kane answered. "Deef as a snubbin' post." He hesitated a split second and added, "Still real fast with the iron, though."

Yates absorbed that, but said nothing.

Kane tried to take a step toward Yates, but Garrett yanked him back. From where he was, the wolfer said evenly, "You killed one of my boys, Temp."

"Uh-huh. He shouldn't have drawed down on Garrett here."

Garrett was surprised. "How come you know my name?"

"Got it from a mutual friend by the name of

Charlie Cobb." The gunman smiled. "See, that's why I'm here—protecting Charlie's interests, you might say."

Realization dawned on the young rancher. "It's been you on my back trail all along."

The gunman nodded. "I wasn't supposed to show myself until you got the ten thousand and were on your way back to Fort Benton." He waved a hand toward Kane's assembled men. "But then this happened and I had to make a play earlier than I planned."

"Temp," Kane said, "you know I'm not a forgetting man. I'll sure remember this." He nodded toward the dead man on the ground. "Brooks Landstrom there was half Swede, half Mexican and all son of a bitch, but I set store by him."

If Yates was moved he didn't let it show. "That's too bad, Thetas. Maybe if I'd known that I would've just nicked him." He smiled. "But probably not." He studied Kane closely. "What the hell happened to your face? A woman do that to you?"

Kane shook his head. "Had a run-in with a wolf."

"Goes with the profession, I guess," Yates said, his passing interest gone.

"Thetas," Pickett said, his eyes on Yates, "what do you want me to do?"

Kane shook his head, and raised his voice to a shout. "Nothing yet, Deke. The puncher here says he'll scatter my brains and he's just dumb enough to do it." His eyes lifted to his other men. "That goes for the rest of you. You'll get your chance later. Until then, let it lay."

"You men, forget the cat wagon. Get those women on horses and bring them up here," Yates said. "Sack us up some grub while you're at it. Oh yeah, and saddle a horse for Thetas."

The wolfers looked to their leader. Pickett had his powder horn to his ear and seemed uncertain and bewildered. "Do as he says, boys," Kane said. "Saddle my dun."

Yates leveled his rifle on Kane. "Garrett, fill as many canteens as you can find and share them out among the women. From now on we travel light and fast."

It was in the young rancher's mind to tell Yates to fill his own canteens. But the man had no doubt saved his life and he told himself he owed him a favor. By the time he had the canteens ready the five women were mounted, bunched up well away from Yates and Kane.

When Garrett handed a canteen to Jenny, the girl looked down at him, her face and hair bright. "I knew I'd see you again, Luke," she said. "I just knew I would."

Garrett nodded, remembering, this lovely girl's past lying like a dark mist between them. "Think nothing of it. Just doing the job Charlie Cobb is paying me to do."

Jenny picked up on Garrett's curt tone and a small hurt showed in her eyes. "Luke, are you feeling all right?" she asked.

"Hell, look around you," Garrett said, waving an arm that took in the tense and angry wolfers, then Yates and Kane. "I'd say right about now I'm feeling just peachy."

The girl opened her mouth to speak again, but Garrett stepped away from her and handed out the remaining canteens.

Annie Spencer took her canteen and looked at Garrett, raising an eyebrow, a slight smile on her lips. "Quite the gentleman, aren't you, cowboy?" she whispered. "Jenny really cares about you. She didn't deserve that."

Garrett tried to think up something clever to say, but the words wouldn't come. In the end he turned away and walked back to his horse, feeling like he'd just shrunk a couple of feet.

"Ready to pull freight?" Yates asked after Garrett was in the saddle.

The rancher nodded and Yates said, "Seen some of your cows back on the trail. A man could round 'em up if he'd a couple of weeks to spare."

"I'll study on it," Garrett said. "Maybe after all this is over."

Yates gave him a strange, guarded look that Garrett couldn't interpret. But a warning bell was suddenly ringing in his head and he didn't like the sound of it.

"Thetas, you're coming with us," Yates said as the wolfer swung into the leather. He smiled. "At least part of the way." The gunman turned and waved an arm toward the women. "You gals move on out."

Yates waited for a few moments until the women were walking their horses toward the trail; then he swung down his Winchester and shot Deke Pickett dead center in the chest.

Pickett stumbled back, his cheeks ashen. He

clawed for his revolvers but Yates shot him again and a sudden red rose blossomed between the gunman's eyes. This time Pickett fell on his face and did not move.

Stunned by what he'd seen, Garrett yelled, "What the hell did you do that for?"

Yates was smiling through a shifting veil of gray gunsmoke. "I never leave a fast gun on my back trail," he said. He motioned to Kane with the muzzle of his rifle. "Now you, Thetas. Move out."

The big wolfer's eyes were murderous, but he didn't say a word as he swung his horse around and rode toward the women, who had all turned in the saddle, watching, their faces white.

It came to Garrett then that he still had a long ways to travel on the Whoop-Up Trail—and riding with Temple Yates he was in the company of a ruthless, cold-blooded killer who was not entirely sane. And that would make him all the more dangerous.

Chapter 19

Garrett took up the rear, keeping Kane in clear sight, as he and the others reached the trail. The heat of the day was intense, the shimmering horizon melting into a colorless sky. Only in the far distance across the brush flats where phantom lakes sparkled in the sunlight did the sweltering land look cool.

Kane in the lead, Yates' rifle pointed at his back, they followed the trail to the northwest in the direction of the Sweet Grass Hills, three grass-covered buttes rising almost seven thousand feet above the flat.

Garrett could see the peaks through the haze, just a few miles south of the Canadian border. But they looked much closer than they were. It was a three- or four-day ride to the Sweet Grass, and he and the others still had the bend of the Marias to cross.

They rode in silence for an hour, and every now and then Garrett caught Jenny looking at him, her eyes pensive, as though trying to understand where she stood with him.

Garrett had thought he loved her. Did he still? Or had Jenny's past destroyed all that?

The West was a hard, unforgiving place where the weak and the timid went quickly back whence they'd come and only the strong remained and endured and shaped the stubborn land to their needs. Jenny had nothing to return to, no family, no friends, and she had survived the only way she could.

Who was he to judge her? Even now he was part of a crooked scheme to defraud five miners out of their hard-earned money, consoling himself with the thought that the end justified the means. But was a Red Angus bull worth a man's honor, the very thing that made him what he was?

Garrett looked at the sunlight tangling itself in Jenny's hair and realized right about now he was not entitled to be her judge, or anybody else's for that matter. An old Bible verse came to him then, something he'd probably heard around the shallow grave of some poor puncher back along a forgotten trail: Judge not, lest you be judged.

He didn't know who first said it, but whoever he was the man had to have been a right savvy hombre.

As he rode, Garrett thought things through again and again, like a dog worrying a bone, and the next time Jenny turned her head and looked at him, he smiled at her. She didn't smile back.

The sun was dropping lower in the sky, a few puffy white clouds showing to the south, when

Temple Yates threw up an arm and said, "Right. This is far enough."

Garrett rode up beside the gunman. "Why are we stopping? We still have a few hours of daylight left."

Yates nodded. "I know that. But this is as far as Thetas goes."

The big wolfer turned in the saddle, a grin on his scarred face. "I'll come after you, Temp. You know that, don't you?"

Yates didn't answer. He made a chopping motion with his rifle barrel. "Climb down, Thetas."

Kane swung out of the saddle, and so did Yates, slapping the horses out of the way as he stepped closer to the wolfer. He glanced up at Annie Spencer. "Annie, come here."

The woman dismounted and walked to Yates' side, her eyes asking a question.

"I been hearing things in Fort Benton, Thetas," the gunman said, ignoring her. "Well, there and other places."

"What have you heard, Temp?" Kane asked. His wary gaze was fixed on Yates' face. He was obviously wondering what the tall gunman was getting at.

"I heard you're spreading it around that one time back in the Mogollon Rim country you put the crawl on me. I didn't like the sound of that, Thetas. It hurt my feelings, like."

Sensing danger, Kane touched his tongue to his torn top lip. "People say things, Temp. Make things up. You know how it is with people."

"I've never been in the rim country," Yates said. "Strange, that."

Kane nodded. "Yeah, very strange."

"Funny thing is, I heard too that you're telling folks you're faster with the iron than me."

For a few moments Kane held himself. Then he said, "Maybe one day real soon we'll have it out, Temp."

Yates smiled. "No time like the present." He pulled a fancy Colt from his left holster, spun it in his hand and held it out butt first to Annie. "Give Thetas that."

The woman looked at the gun like it was a coiled rattler and backed away, color draining from her face.

"Give it to him!" Yates snapped.

"Let it be, Yates," Garrett said. "We'll let the law deal with Kane. He's wanted in Canada for sure."

"You stay out of this, cowboy," the gunman said. "This is between Thetas and me and you're way over your head here." He turned to Annie. "Give Thetas this gun or I'll drill him square right where he stands."

"Hand me the Colt, Annie," Kane said, smiling as his confidence returned. "Temp's right. It's time some outstanding business between him and me was settled."

The woman bit her lip, then stepped next to Kane, offering him the gun. The wolfer's right hand closed on the butt of the Colt, but his left shot out and grabbed Annie. He yanked her around and pulled her against him, using her as a shield as his gun came up.

With a blurred motion too quick for the eye to

follow, Yates drew and his Colt roared. Hit hard, Annie slammed back against Kane, bumping his gun arm. Kane's shot went wild and Yates fired again as Annie dropped at the wolfer's feet. Hit low in the belly, Kane gasped, his mouth sagged open and he staggered backward. Yates shot again, the bullet higher, smashing into Kane's chest. The gun dropped from Kane's hand and he fell to his knees. He was still in that position when Yates shot him again.

Kane screamed in impotent anger, his bloodshot eyes blazing. He pointed at the grinning Yates and mumbled, "You . . . you . . ."

Then the light in his eyes faded and death took him, his lifeless body crashing facedown in the dirt.

Yates lowered his eyes to Annie and the fallen man, his face expressionless, empty of interest. He punched the spent shells out of his Colt, reloaded and slid the gun into the holster. Pushing through the women who were clustered around Annie, he retrieved his other gun and walked to where Garrett was still sitting his horse.

"Now Thetas and Pickett are dead, we've got nothing to fear from the rest of that riffraff," he said.

His eyes angled to Annie Spencer, who was lying motionless on the ground, the blue death shadows already gathering on her face. "But now we have one woman less. Charlie will sure take it hard, losing two thousand dollars on this deal."

A small anger flared in Garrett. "A woman is dying and that's all you can think about, Yates? Charlie Cobb's money?"

The gunman shrugged. "The woman meant nothing to me. Anyhow, it was Thetas killed her. All he had to do was let her step aside." Yates' eyes narrowed as they lifted to Garrett's. "I detect a chiding tone to your voice, boy. You thinking of bracing me?"

Garrett shook his head, anger making him reckless. "No, but you don't scare me none, Yates. I'm not bracing you. I reckon there's already been enough killing today."

Yates looked pensive. "I don't scare you none, huh? Well, that's a very foolish thing to say, Garrett. You should be very afraid of me, you know."

The gunman clapped his hands together and laughed. "But why are we talking this way? We're friends, you and me, since we both work for the same boss."

"Charlie Cobb isn't my boss," Garrett said.

"Well, the same business associate then." Yates turned and glanced at the sobbing women around Annie. "As soon as the woman dies, we'll move on," he said.

"After we bury her," Garrett said.

Yates shook his head. "We don't have time for a burying."

Garrett leaned forward in the saddle, his hands stacked on the horn. "Yates, we'll make time."

A quick, dangerous light flashed in Yates' eyes, but as soon as it appeared it was gone, replaced by a humorless smile. "Well, have it your way, boy. But all we'll be doing is burning daylight."

Garrett dismounted and stepped to where Annie lay. Jenny moved aside, clearing a space for him, and he kneeled close to the woman. Annie's eyes lifted to his. "Hi, cowboy, come to say so long?" she asked.

"How do you feel, Annie?" Garrett asked.

"I need a drink." Annie's head turned. "Jenny, there's a bottle in the sack tied to my saddle."

The girl nodded. "I'll bring it."

Annie's eyes moved to Garrett's face again. "You take care of that girl, cowboy. She'll need you."

Garrett nodded. "I'll do my best."

"Do better than your best. Don't let her end up like me."

Jenny returned with the bottle. She raised it to Annie's lips, but the whiskey poured from the woman's mouth and over her chin. She was dead.

Later, Garrett and the four women laid Annie Spencer to rest in a narrow coulee a ways off the trail. They used what rocks were on hand to cover her, and Lynette, tears staining her dark eyes, sang "Shall We Gather at the River" in a thin, quavering voice.

When it was over, Garrett fell in step beside Jenny, a silence arching over them that he could not find a way to break. Once the girl turned and briefly looked at him, but her eyes were cool and distant and Garrett saw nothing of himself in them.

Yates was standing by the horses when Garrett and the others got back. "You put the old gal away?" he asked, a smile touching his lips.

"She was twenty-six, Yates," Garrett said, anger still riding him.

"Must have had a real hard life," Yates said. He

nodded to Kane's body. "You wasn't planning on burying him, were you?"

Garrett shook his head. "Leave him right where he lies. The coyotes got to eat too."

"Then let's mount up," Yates said. "We got a heap of ground to cover."

At Yates' insistence they camped that night in a rocky arroyo a mile off the main trail. The gunman kept the fire small, barely enough to boil coffee and brown a few slices of salt pork. They ate beans cold from the can and after the meal was over and the coffee drunk, Yates quickly doused the fire.

He took Garrett aside, out of earshot of Jenny and the other women. "We'll take turns on guard at the mouth of the arroyo tonight," he said. "Four hours on, four off, and I'll take the first watch."

"What's eating you, Yates?" Garrett asked. "Kane is dead and so is Deke Pickett. You said the rest of them wouldn't come after us."

Yates nodded, his eyes shadowed pools in the darkness. "They won't, but this is different. I ran into some woman trouble back along the trail."

Garrett felt something akin to fear stab at him. "What kind of woman trouble?"

Yates shrugged. "Happened just after I left Benton. I was riding close to the Teton and saw a paint pony grazing among the cottonwoods. I rode over to take a look, and there was the prettiest little Indian gal you ever did see swimming naked as a jaybird in the river." Yates' grin was white in the gloom. "Well, I hunkered down among the willows, and when she came out of the water I jumped her."

"You did what?" Garrett asked, alarm edging his voice.

"Jumped her. Hell, man, you would have done the same. Anyhow, swimming all nekkid like that, she was begging for it. So, after I was done with her, I slapped her around a little, then told her to scat. Thing is, she went to her clothes and came at me with a knife. Regular wildcat she was, cussing and yelling like a heathen."

"What happened then?" Garrett asked, talking around the lump in his throat.

"I shot her." Yates shrugged. "It didn't bother me none, nor should it you. She was of no account, just an Indian squaw."

Garrett opened his mouth, trying to find the words, but the enormity of what Yates had just said left him stunned.

The gunman was talking again. "Trouble was, then another Indian showed up. Must have heard my gun. Maybe it was her husband—I don't know—but I took a shot at him. Hit him all right, but he turned and galloped away, to spread the word no doubt."

"What kind of Indians were they?" Garrett asked.

"The red kind," Yates snapped. "How the hell should I know?"

Garrett's mouth set in a grim, tight line. "Yates, we're parting ways right here. I'm cutting you loose."

The gunman's grin grew wider as he shook his head. "Not going to happen, cowboy. I told Charlie I'd see his women safe to Fort Whoop-Up and that's what I intend to do."

"He hired me to escort the women, Yates."

"Yeah, and me to oversee the whole shebang. Charlie's not a trusting man."

Yates' hands were on his hips, close to his guns, and now when he lifted his head his eyes were as gray and hard as steel. "Listen, Garrett, we're in this together. You cut out by yourself and the Indians will come after you too because by now they know we're in cahoots."

Yates managed a cold smile. "When this is over and Charlie has his money, you can come talk to me again, you being such an Injun lover an' all. But when the time comes, you watch your mouth, boy. I don't take kindly to harsh words spoke at me."

Anger flared in Garrett and he threw caution to the wind. "Here are some harsh words, Yates. You're a sorry piece of white trash. Now if you want to shuck those Colts, have at it."

"I've killed men for less than that," the gunman said, his voice low and even. "But if them Indians come at us, I'll need your gun." He stepped closer to Garrett until their faces were just inches apart. "But I don't take an insult lightly and I don't forget, cowboy. From this moment on, consider yourself a walking dead man."

Garrett opened his mouth to speak, but Yates brushed past him and faded into the night toward the entrance of the arroyo.

For long moments, Garrett stood where he was, his mind at work. His chances of getting the promised five hundred dollars out of Charlie Cobb were slim, and getting slimmer all the time. In any case, he did not relish the thought of cheating the miners. All things considered, maybe now was the time to cut his losses and head back to his ranch.

And, to his own surprise, he badly wanted Jenny Canfield to go with him.

Chapter 20

The four women were huddled together in the dark, Annie's death hanging heavy on them. They had been in earnest, whispered conversation, but when they lifted their heads to look at Garrett, they fell suddenly silent. He could read nothing in their expressions, their guarded eyes looking like they'd been painted on the white faces of porcelain dolls.

Garrett sought Jenny in the gloom. She sat with her legs drawn up, her chin on her knees, the moonlight touching her hair.

"Jenny," he said, his voice sounding too loud in the quiet, "can I talk to you?"

The girl studied him for a few moments, as though she was making up her mind about something. Then she rose to her feet, picked up her sketching pad and said, "Sure."

Garrett put his arm around Jenny's slender waist and led her toward a bend of the arroyo angled by deep blue shadow. The sky was aflame with stars, the moon riding high, and out in the badlands the ragged coyotes were yipping.

Taking time to build a smoke, Garrett lit the cigarette and inhaled deep before he said, "I want to ask you a question, Jenny. And I can't give you much time to study on the answer."

"I'm intrigued already." The girl smiled. "Ask away."

"Remember I told you about my ranch, about the mountains and the mornings so quiet and peaceful a man can hear his own heartbeat?"

Jenny nodded. "I remember. It all sounded so wonderful."

"Will you leave this place and come with me, Jenny? Head for the mountains tonight and never look back?"

The girl made no answer. She opened her sketchbook and found the page she was seeking. Tilting the page so it caught the moonlight, she said, "Look."

Garrett glanced down at the book—and saw himself. Jenny had drawn a wonderful likeness, only he looked grumpy and out of sorts, his mouth under his mustache drawn back in a tight, solemn line, his forehead wrinkled in a frown. The image was so funny he laughed with genuine humor. It was the first time he'd been able to laugh out loud since Zeb Ready had died and it felt good. "Do I really look that crabby?" he asked finally.

"Most of the time," Jenny said. "Well, recently at least."

"Does that mean you don't want to share a ranch

with a testy old grouch?" Garrett said. He had asked the question lightly yet feared the answer.

"Luke, you don't know anything about me," the girl said.

"I do. I know all about you. Annie told me."

"And it didn't trouble you?"

Garrett hesitated. "At first it did. Afterward I thought it through and decided I had some fast growing up to do."

"Then you know why I never want to go back to that kind of life," Jenny said. "I don't want to end up a diseased line-shack whore, using morphine to ease the pain of waking up in the morning and still being alive. A few more trips for Charlie Cobb and I can support myself for a while in Boston or New York, hopefully long enough for my pictures to sell." The girl's eyes were damp with tears. "Luke, I can't be a rancher's wife. Don't you see that?"

"I love you, Jenny. Does that make a difference?"

"Love has nothing to do with it, Luke. I want to be like Sarah Peale, find fame and fortune back east as a woman artist. That's my dream and maybe it will never become reality, but I have to try."

Garrett shook his head. "I've no idea who Sarah Peale is, but this much I do know—it's all going bad. Annie Spencer is dead and I think we may be heading into more Indian trouble. It's time to call off the whole deal."

"I can't do it, Luke. Charlie Cobb's money is the only chance I've got. Maybe it's not much of a chance, but it's all I have and I can't pass on it."

Jenny stretched out a hand, her fingertips lightly touching Garrett's chest. "Luke, if it's any consolation, I could love you. I could love you very much. Who knows? Someday I might come looking for you, ride up to your ranch house in a fine carriage drawn by four high-stepping horses and ask for my man."

Garrett nodded, the hurt in him deep. "I'll be there, Jenny."

The girl smiled. "You'll have to tell me how to find you."

"Just look for the mountains and follow the silence."

It was shortly before midnight when Garrett relieved Yates at the mouth of the arroyo. The gunman, his expression surly, said nothing, stepping around the young rancher before walking into the darkness.

Garrett's eyes searched the night. The moonlight touched the brush flats with silver and a million stars cascaded down the high arch of the sky toward the dark veil of the horizon. The coyotes were talking still, sleepless with hunger. He knew now he couldn't leave.

Jenny had refused to become his wife, but he would not turn his back on her, not now, not ever. He was losing her because she was intent on reaching out a hand to clutch at the very stars that were hanging above him. But maybe when she discovered just how distant and unobtainable they were, and how cold, she would change her mind and return to him.

It was indeed a slender straw of hope, but he held on to it like a drowning man, all the time knowing how slight were his chances.

In the meantime he would not leave her to the mercies of a man like Temple Yates. The gunman was pure poison, spawned from hell, made even more malignant by a violent past. He was a rattler coiled and ready to strike, his venom lethal.

Garrett was not a fast gun and he knew if it came to a showdown he wouldn't stand a chance against the sudden lightning strike that was Temple Yates. The thought brought him no comfort, only worry about tomorrow and the days after that.

Yates relieved Garrett once more, a couple of hours before dawn. When the young rancher walked into the arroyo, Lynette had just stepped beside the other women, smiling as she buttoned up her dress. The brunette's eyes angled to Garrett, defiant and challenging, but he said nothing. What the girl did with a man like Yates was her own concern.

Garrett found a spot that was relatively free of rocks and lay on his back, his hat tipped over his eyes. To his surprise, Jenny left the others and lay beside him.

"Sweet dreams, Luke," she said.

He didn't answer. He didn't know what to say.

They took to the trail again just after sunup. The Sweet Grass Hills stood out in stark relief against a lemon sky streaked with bands of red and jade, the peaks looking very close but in reality still many miles distant.

Garrett took the point, ahead of the four women, and Yates dallied at the rear, his head constantly turning to check his back trail and the surrounding coulees. The man seemed to be on edge, as though he heard a rustle in every bush.

Smiling, Garrett was pleased. Let Yates sweat. If they ran into Indian trouble the fault would be all his.

But they saw no sign of Indians that day or the next when they crossed the loop of the low, sluggish Marias without difficulty and refilled their canteens with more silt than water.

Another uneventful day came and went after Garrett led them across Willow Creek, and they rode into pleasant, rolling country with plenty of buffalo sign but no trace of Indian presence.

Yates relaxed as he put more distance between himself and the Teton, though he and Garrett avoided speaking to each other whenever possible. The gunman preferred to spend his nights away from the others, fading into the whispering darkness with his arm around Lynette.

But on the morning of the fourth day, hell came to the Whoop-Up.

Chapter 21

Luke Garrett rode past the West Butte of the Sweet Grass Hills, just a few miles south of the Canadian border. The sky was a washed-out blue, shading to a pale pink at the horizon, where a last, laggard star stubbornly gleamed bright.

Around Garrett lay hilly grazing country, the slopes of the cone-shaped butte covered in buffalo grass and, except for a raw outcropping of rock to the east, scattered stands of juniper and mesquite.

Early in the morning the air was relatively cool and smelled sweet with pine and the newly blossoming sagebrush buttercup. The air was so clear Garrett could turn his head in any direction and see forever.

Jenny rode beside him, looking bright and clean as a new penny, the trail not seeming to take any toll on her. She sat astride her horse, her oval knees bare, and it was in Garrett's mind that he had never in his life seen any woman so pretty and so alive.

As they rode, he pointed out to the girl the

things he knew, a cougar track on the soft ground alongside the trail, stands of prickly pear where the pack rat made its home and hoarded its treasure, a collection of shiny pebbles and bits of metal, a dusty depression in the grass where buffalo had wallowed.

"Indians like fresh buffalo, but if there's plenty of meat in camp, they prefer to hang their ribs and steaks until they start to decay, and then they'll devour them and lick their fingers when they're done," Garrett told her. "I've seen the Blackfoot wait on riverbanks during the spring breakup and haul in rotting, bloated carcasses floating downstream. They eat those right away, and enjoy them just fine, even if their bellies are full of fresh buffalo."

The girl was interested in anything and everything, her pencil dashing across the sketch pad as she rode, stopping only now and then to ask a question. A pleasant hour passed as they cleared the horizon to the east and the sun began its climb into the sky. Once a small buffalo herd walked out of an arroyo and headed north, toward the Milk River, the big, mature bulls out in front, on the prod and spoiling for a fight.

Garrett was telling Jenny about the problem of getting cattle out of slot canyons at roundup time, when an alarmed shout from Yates interrupted him.

"Garrett! Behind you!"

The young rancher turned in the saddle and saw a thick dust cloud rising to the south. As his eyes grew accustomed to the distance, he made out the naked forms of mounted Indians coming at a fast gallop, their faces painted for war.

"Jenny!" Garrett yelled. "The rest of you women, light a shuck out of here!"

Seeing what was coming behind them, the women needed no further urging. They kicked their horses into a run as Garrett faded back alongside Yates.

"This will be a running fight," the gunman said. "Shuck your rifle and maybe we can hold them off."

Garrett slid his Winchester from the scabbard under his knee and levered a round into the chamber. Beside him Yates did the same. They swung their horses around and galloped after the fleeing women.

Yates was turning in the saddle, firing steadily, but Garrett saw no hits. A warrior in a feathered war bonnet decorated with weasel tails was out in front, a rifle to his shoulder. Garrett drew a bead on the man and fired. The Indian's pony went down, hitting the ground headfirst, and the warrior sailed over its neck. He was quickly swallowed by the swirling dust cloud kicked up by the horses of the other warriors.

A bullet split the air above Garrett's head and he urged his black into a faster gallop. Beside him Yates looked grim, dust already settling into the seams of his face.

"They're Bloods, Yates!" Garrett yelled. "And they'll keep coming."

Ahead of him he saw Jenny glance over her shoulder to look at him, her eyes wide. The land ahead of the women promised nothing, just shallow, rolling country stretching all the way to the border. There was no place to stop and make a stand, not a scrap of cover. Yates had been correct—this would be a running battle.

A bullet smashed into the pommel of Garrett's saddle, ricocheting away with a venomous whine, and an arrow whipped past his head. He turned in the saddle, threw his rifle to his shoulder, fired and fired again. Another Indian pony staggered and went down, crashing head over heels into the dirt.

"Hold your fire, Garrett!" Yates yelled. "Put some distance between us and them. Then stop when I do."

Garrett nodded and set spurs to his black. Gradually he and Yates, riding bigger, stronger horses, opened up the stretch between themselves and the Bloods. Bullets were still cutting the air around them, and now and again an arrow zipped past in a vicious blur of movement.

Yates slid his rifle into the scabbard and spurred his mount, the brim of his hat flattened against the crown. He turned and checked the location of the Bloods, then yelled, "Draw rein!"

Garrett yanked the black to a skidding halt. The animal's rump slammed into the ground, kicking up a cloud of yellow dust. Yates swung his horse around and drew his guns with flashing speed. He hammered shot after shot into the Indians, so fast the roar of his Colts sounded like a drumroll.

"Pour it into them, Garrett!" he yelled.

Garrett threw his rifle to his shoulder and worked

the lever as fast as he could, hardly taking time to aim. A couple of Bloods had dropped to Yates' fire, and his deadly bullets had taken the steam out of their charge. The Indians split, widening out on each side of the trail. Wary of the gunman's accurate Colts, they were now shooting at a distance.

"They're trying to cut the trail ahead of us, Yates," Garrett hollered. "Let's get out of here."

Yates holstered his guns, swung his horse around and charged after Garrett. Too late. A dozen or so Bloods were blocking the way ahead, others streaming after the women.

The Bloods may have expected the two white men to stop, perhaps turning and going the other way. But Garrett and Yates charged into them, their rifles flaring. The tactic surprised the Indians and they quickly tried to swing away from the deadly fire, their ponies crow-hopping in their haste to beat a retreat.

A big warrior, his entire face painted black, was right ahead of Garrett's rifle, not ten yards away. Garrett fired into the man's chest and saw him tumble off his pony. Yates was firing deliberately, trying for kills. One Blood went down, then a second.

A bullet tugged at Garrett's sleeve, staining his shirt red, and then he was through them. Yates was right behind him, no longer firing.

The Indians had recovered from their initial surprise and were yipping their anger as they charged after the two white men. Holding his rifle in his left hand, Garrett drew his Colt, swung around in the saddle and emptied the revolver into the oncoming warriors. He scored no hits that he could tell and he hadn't even slowed the Indians' pace.

Looping the reins around his chewed-up pommel, Garrett quickly reloaded his Colt. Ahead of him a large party of Bloods were closing the distance between themselves and the fleeing women.

He saw Jenny's horse suddenly stumble and go down, throwing the girl clear.

Garrett swung toward Jenny, who was on her feet but looked dazed and bewildered. An Indian rode at her, a lance upraised in his right hand. Garrett got off a fast snap shot and the warrior reeled, a scarlet stain splashing his muscular brown back. The Blood continued to gallop toward Jenny, but when he was still several yards away, he slid sideways from his pony and hit the ground hard, dust kicking up around him.

The dead Indian's horse tossed its head and turned broadside to Garrett as he rode closer to Jenny. His big black, outweighing the paint by two hundred pounds, T-boned the animal at a fast gallop and sent it flying. The pony staggered to its right and crashed onto its side, its legs flailing. Garrett swung past the downed paint and leaned from the saddle, his left arm extended as he rode closer to Jenny.

From somewhere he heard Yates yell, "Damn it, leave her!"

Garrett ignored the man. Without slowing his pace he scooped up the girl and lifted her onto the front of his saddle. Jenny said nothing, her face white with shock, and he felt her body tremble violently against him.

The black loved to run and despite its added burden it plunged ahead, its neck straight out, the bit in its teeth. Behind him Garrett heard Yates' rifle slam, then slam again. Two Indians chasing after the other women tumbled off their ponies. Lynette was bent over the neck of her horse. Garrett saw an arrow buried deep in her back, six inches of shaft and the turkey flight feathers sticking out just under her left shoulder blade.

It was a terrible wound—a wound no one could survive.

A killing anger in him, Garrett drew his Colt and fired at the Bloods riding ahead of him. Yates' rifle was hammering and their combined fire took its toll on the Indians. A warrior threw up his arms and tumbled from his mount, and another swung off the trail and pulled up his pony, his head hanging.

The Indians were looking behind them now, and began to ride wide of the trail, some looping back toward the main body of the warriors. The Bloods had a dozen men dead or dying on the ground and were losing their will to fight.

A few long-range rifle shots chased Garrett and Yates as they closed with the women, but there was no pursuit. The Bloods were milling back along the trail, and spirited arguments seemed to be breaking out between the young warriors and older, wiser heads, who did not deem this a good day to die.

Finally the Bloods dismounted and began to gather up their dead. They would fight no more that day.

Garrett slowed the black to a trot and tightened his arm around Jenny's waist. "Are you feeling all right?" he asked.

The girl nodded, clinging to him. "I'll be fine." She looked over at Lynette, who was lying over her horse's neck. "What's the matter with Lyn—" Then Jenny saw the arrow embedded in the girl's back and let out a small, horrified shriek.

Lynette Briggs, an eighteen-year-old small-farm girl from Ohio who dreamed of marrying rich and returning home a fine lady, died just as the day shaded into night, and the coyotes sang her requiem.

A pall of grief hung over the surviving women. Jenny did her best to console them, one a pale, insipid blonde named Abbie Lane who had just turned nineteen, the other Paloma Sanchez, a pretty, dark-eyed girl with Mescalero blood in her. She was twenty-eight, older than the others, and she had an easy, knowing way around men.

The fight with the Indians and Lynette's death had left Garrett feeling drained. He sat near the women with a cup of untasted coffee cradled in his hands, watching the small flames dance in the buffalo-chip fire.

But there was no grief in Temple Yates. He was spitting mad, the death of a girl he'd recently held in his arms apparently a matter of supreme indifference to him.

He stood over Garrett, his thumbs tucked into his crossed gun belts. "Listen, cowboy," he said, "we're down to just three head o' females and

Charlie's business deal is going downhill faster than a six-legged jackrabbit."

Garrett lifted hostile eyes to the gunman. "What do you want from me, Yates?"

"Just this—you got to get more money out of those miners. Raise the ante. Tell them Charlie was double or nothing." He jerked a thumb toward the three women. "When those rock rats see what Charlie's offering, they'll gladly pay more for their belly warmers. Hell, they got pokes full of gold and nothing else to spend it on except whiskey."

"Tell them yourself," Garrett said.

Yates shook his head. "Can't do that, cowboy. I don't know if Charlie told you or not, but me and him ain't exactly welcome at Fort Whoop-Up. Charlie had a little misunderstanding with the redcoat police over selling whiskey to the Indians. And me, I got into a shooting scrape with a couple of miners, and if the Mounties catch me, they'll hang me for sure."

"Handle your own dirty work, Yates," Garrett said. "I want nothing more to do with you or Charlie Cobb. I'm taking Jenny to the fort because that's what she wants, and then I'm done with it."

"You're forgetting something, Garrett. There's five hundred in the deal for you."

"I'm forgetting nothing. But I think my chances of collecting that money from Charlie are pretty slim."

Yates held himself for a few moments. Then he said, "All right, let's try another tack. You up the stakes on the miners and maybe I'll forget about killing you, cowboy. I can't say fairer than that."

"Yates," Garrett said, his voice slow and deliberate, his hand close to his gun, "you go to hell."

The gunman thought about it, thinking so hard Garrett could see his mind working. The young rancher tensed, getting ready for the draw. But the moment passed, as Yates finally let it go.

"Garrett, the only reason I'm keeping you alive is because the damned Indians might not be finished with us. Well, that and the hope you might still change your mind about squeezing more money out of the miners. Maybe you just want to be coaxed, like."

Laying his coffee cup aside, Garrett rose to his feet and stood close to Yates, his hand on his gun butt, a wild recklessness spiking in him. "I'm not changing my mind about anything. Now get the hell away from me, Yates."

The gunman shrugged. "Your funeral, cowboy." He smiled. "And I really do mean that. It will be very soon, you know."

Garrett sat by the fire again. He glanced over at Yates, who had taken Paloma aside and was engaging her in earnest conversation. Garrett knew the gunman had been telling the truth when he said he was keeping him alive only because of the Bloods. But after the women were delivered to Fort Whoop-Up, his usefulness to Yates would be over. And then what? To Garrett the answer was obvious. Yates would call him out and kill him.

It was as simple and direct as that, and as chilling.

Jenny had been sitting with Abbie Lane. Now she got to her feet and came to sit beside Garrett.

"Luke, you were right," she said. "I'll never do this again. All the killing and dying, it just isn't worth it."

Hope flared in Garrett. "Then you'll leave with me tonight?"

The girl shook her head. "We're so close, I want to finish what I started. Two hundred dollars won't be much, but I can make it last."

Garrett opened his mouth to speak, but Jenny held up a hand. "No, please don't, Luke. We've already said all that needs to be said on the subject." She rose to her feet. "You saved my life today. That's something I will never forget."

"I plan to see you safe back to Fort Benton." Garrett smiled. "And I aim to convince you that a woman can be a rancher's wife *and* a famous artist."

Rising to her feet, Jenny said, "Just . . . just you take care of yourself, Luke." She stepped out of the circle of the firelight, took her place again beside Abbie and left Garrett puzzled.

Why had she told him to take care of himself? It was almost like Jenny thought she might never see him again. Was that because of Yates—or something else?

Garrett had no answers, only a sense of deep foreboding about a future he could not see or even guess at, a future that might offer him nothing but an unmarked grave in lonely country.

No matter. All he could do now was play the hand he'd been dealt and hope the cards fell his way.

Chapter 22

The Sweet Grass Hills fell behind Luke Garrett as he and the others cleared the Canadian border and rode into the badlands of southern Alberta. The Milk River lay ten miles to the north, and they swung toward Verdigris Coulee where they planned to cross, riding through dry, barren country of eroded sandstone, weathered into craggy arches and cone-shaped boulders that the first trappers who visited the region named hoodoos.

Clumps of sagebrush and juniper clung to the eroded walls of the surrounding coulees, home to rock wrens and prairie rattlesnakes. Evening primroses with large pink petals grew along the clay bottoms and the vivid yellow flowers of buffalo bean struggled to survive amid tumbled heaps of shale talus.

A meadowlark sang its flutelike song as Garrett rode past and a white-tailed jackrabbit burst from under the black's hooves and bounded away, bouncing over the grass like a rubber ball.

The Blackfoot considered the badlands sacred,

and Garrett rode high in the saddle, ready for trouble.

It was not long in coming.

The sun had climbed directly overhead when the Milk River came in sight, high cottonwoods lining its bank. Beyond the river a ridge rose three hundred and fifty feet above the flat, cut through by wide channels formed in ancient times by water running off melting glaciers. One of those channels was Verdigris Coulee. Garrett planned to cross the river at a point opposite the coulee, then loop to the east across the rich grasslands of the ridge all the way to Fort Whoop-Up.

Jenny was riding beside him, Abbie Lane behind her, then, a ways to the rear, Yates and Paloma Sanchez. The day was scorching hot and every step taken by the horses lifted stifling yellow dust. Sweat trickled down Garrett's back and he squinted burning eyes against the glare, looking longingly at the blue ribbon of the river as it drew closer.

Jenny was sketching the trees along the riverbank, humming tunelessly to herself, and Garrett followed her gaze to the cottonwoods, amazed at how well she had captured every branch and leaf. Suddenly a small flock of grasshopper sparrows burst out of the underbrush at the base of the trees, scattering dead leaves and a few drifting feathers.

"Pull up, Jenny," Garrett said as he yanked his Winchester from the scabbard.

"What is it?" the girl asked, confusion in her eyes.

Her answer came a split second later as puffs of gray smoke appeared from among the cottonwoods, followed by the staccato roar of rifles.

Garrett's black staggered and went down. The young rancher hit the ground hard, rolled clear of the horse's flailing hooves and came up on one knee, his Colt already in his hand.

Behind him he heard Yates yell, followed by the crash of the gunman's rifle.

"Jenny, get away from here!" Garrett yelled. He didn't wait to see what the girl did next. He hammered shot after shot into the trees, then rose to his feet and backed off, reloading his Colt as he went.

Suddenly Yates was beside him, working his Winchester. "Who the hell is it?" he yelled.

Garrett shook his head. "I don't know."

A bullet cut the air next to Garrett's left ear and another kicked up dust at his feet, but he held his fire. The range was too long for revolver work. What he needed was his rifle.

He made a dash toward his dead horse, but bullets were thudding around him and one put a neat hole in the crown of his hat.

"Forget it!" Yates yelled. "They'll be coming after us!"

The gunman swung his horse around and galloped after Jenny and the other women.

Garrett gave a momentary glance at his rifle in the scabbard, but decided the risk was too great. Whoever the bushwhackers among the trees were, they now had the advantage. Bullets were splitting the air perilously close to him.

He turned and ran after Yates, and saw Jenny riding toward him.

Waving his outstretched arms in her direction, he called out, "Get back!"

The girl ignored him. Her horse was running flat out in a fast gallop, a shredding ribbon of dust streaming away from its hammering hooves. Jenny wrenched her mount to a skidding stop, white arcs showing in the animal's eyes as its head came up, fighting the bit.

"Behind me!" Jenny yelled.

Bullets were kicking up dirt in vicious spurts around them as Garrett holstered his Colt and leaped onto the horse. Jenny kicked her mount into a gallop and they hightailed it across the flat, searching shots buzzing after them like angry hornets.

Yates had swung off the trail and was forted up on the steep bank of a dry wash that angled toward the river. His rifle was out in front of him, his eyes squinting into the distance. Jenny hit the wash at a run. Her frightened mount balked at the bank and reared, kicking up a shower of sand and gravel. Garrett slid off the animal's haunches and landed on his feet. He reached, grabbed the reins and man-handled the horse down the slope of the wash, then helped Jenny dismount.

"Who the hell are they?" Yates yelled. "Are they Indians?"

"Don't know," Garrett said, taking a place alongside the gunman. "But I get the feeling we'll find out real soon."

Eight mounted men emerged from among the cottonwoods a few minutes later. To a man they were shaggy, bearded and unkempt, dressed in greasy buckskins, but the sunlight winked on rifle barrels that were clean and oiled.

"Yates," Garrett said, without turning, "remember those wolfers you said wouldn't come after us? Well, they're coming after us."

The gunman nodded and spat, a note of grudging admiration in his voice. "Them ol' boys don't buffalo worth a damn, do they?"

Yates turned his head and looked down the wash at the women. "When the shooting starts, you three hold on to the horses real good. We may have to come a-runnin'."

The wolfers rode forward, then stopped just outside of rifle range. A man on a tall roan left the rest and walked the horse closer to the wash. When he was about thirty yards away he stood in the stirrups and yelled, "Temp, I'm comin' in under a flag o' truce."

"I don't see no damn flag," Yates called back.

The wolfer sat back on the saddle. "Hell, then just imagine I got one." He rode closer, stopped and this time in a normal voice said, "Name's Bill Tetley an' I got a proposition for you boys, and it's fair and square as ever was."

"Let's hear it," Yates said.

"Us 'uns ain't borrowing trouble, Temp," the wolfer said. "And we got nothing agin' you fellers, even though you gunned Thetas an' them." He shrugged. "Hell, let bygones be bygones—that's what I always say."

"I said to speak your piece, Tetley," Yates snapped. "We got faith in rifles here and we aren't sitting on our gun hands."

The wolfer nodded. "So be it. What we want is the women, just like Thetas promised us. That's saying it plain and straight-out an' no mistake."

"And if we give you the women, what then?" Yates asked.

"Why then you ride away from here free as birds." The man smiled, showing a few rotten teeth. "Hell, me and the boys, we'll be too busy to notice, like."

"Tetley, the price for the women is twelve thousand dollars," Yates said. "You got that much?"

The wolfer shook his head. "Sure don't. We don't have a tail feather 'atween us an' I guess that's a shame for you."

"It doesn't matter much anyhow," Garrett said. "We aren't selling. The women stay with us."

"Is that the cowboy?" the wolfer asked.

"Yeah, it is."

"You should have stayed on the ranch, boy. A sight safer that way." The wolfer leaned forward in the saddle. "One more time, Temp. Give us the women and you can ride clear."

"No deal," Yates said, "unless you can pay for them."

The wolfer shook his head. "Well, I'm right sorry to hear that. Now I guess we'll just have to kill you boys an' grab them little sage hens our ownselves."

Yates nodded. "I guess that's about the size of it, except you won't be around to see it happen."

Shock and fear showed on the wolfer's face. "Now lookee here, Temple, I got me a flag o'—"

The man never completed the sentence because Yates rapidly worked his rifle and put two bullets into his chest.

Yates watched the wolfer slide off the side of his horse; then he turned to Garrett and grinned through a gray drift of gunsmoke. "I'd say that feller had nothing under his hat but hair. Ah well, one down, only seven to go."

"Uh-huh, and now the fat's really in the fire," Garrett said. "Here they come and they're burning the breeze."

The remaining seven riders had shaken out into a loose line and were riding hard for the wash. Here and there a rifle flared, and bullets kicked up plumes of sand around Garrett and Yates.

The gunman was firing steadily and already he'd emptied a saddle. But the range was as yet too far for a six-gun and Garrett held his fire.

One of the wolfers split from the others and looped to the west, then rode straight for the wash, his rifle banging.

"On your left, Garrett!" Yates yelled.

"I see him."

Garrett fired at the man, missed and fired again. The wolfer, a huge redhead with a thick beard down to his waist, kept coming. He jumped his horse into the wash and charged at Garrett, his rifle to his shoulder. The wolfer fired and missed, but his horse slammed into Garrett and the young rancher crashed against the sandy wall of the wash, spun and fell on his back.

The man drew rein on his mount and swung the animal in Garrett's direction. He threw his rifle to his shoulder again just as Garrett fired from the ground, aiming his Colt at arm's length. But it was another wolfer who took Garrett's bullet. A rider had just charged past Yates and jumped his horse into the sandy floor of the wash, whooping like an

Indian. Hit hard, the man threw up his arms and plunged out of the saddle, hitting the ground with a tremendous thud. Garrett had no time to see if the wolfer was alive or dead. The big redhead was now clear for a shot, and he and Garrett fired at the same time.

The wolfer's bullet grazed Garrett's cheek, drawing blood, but the man was hit square in the middle of his chest. He gasped and reeled in the saddle, cursing. But he recovered quickly and kicked his horse into a run, charging toward Garrett, holding his rifle in front of him like a pistol. The young rancher grasped his Colt in two hands, raised the gun to eye level and fired.

Hit again, this time the wolfer left the saddle and fell across Yates' legs. The gunman swore and kicked the body away from him. Then he rose to his feet and emptied his rifle in the direction of the river. Garrett thumbed fresh cartridges into his Colt and scrambled up the bank of the wash.

Two dead men lay sprawled on the ground a few yards in front of Yates' position, their horses grazing with their reins trailing. The other wolfers, one hurt and slumped over the saddle horn, were riding fast toward the river.

Yates slid down the incline of the wash and ran to his horse. He swung into the saddle and his mount was already at a gallop when he hit the slope and charged after the fleeing wolfers.

Garrett looked around him. Both of the men he'd shot were dead, and only a smoke-streaked stillness remained. Jenny and the other two women were unhurt, but they were staring at him with wide, frightened eyes. He knew how he must look to them, a wild thing covered in sweat, blood and dust, thin red trails from his cut cheek trickling down his unshaven chin.

Garrett ignored the women and took off his hat. He used the back of his gun hand, still clutching his smoking Colt, to wipe sweat from his forehead, then settled the hat on his head again.

He walked to the prancing horse of one of the dead wolfers, a leggy, mouse-colored grulla, caught up the reins and whispered calming words into its ear. The animal, liking the sound of the man's voice, settled down and Garrett stepped into the saddle.

The grulla bore a Running W on its left shoulder, the brand of Captain Richard King's enormous Santa Gertrudis ranch down Texas way, and Garrett made a mental note never to ride the animal south of the Brazos or he'd risk getting hung for a horse thief.

There was no sign of Yates or the wolfers when Garrett rode out of the dry wash and back to where his dead black lay in a spreading pool of blood. He stripped his saddle and switched it to the grulla. He was about to put his foot in the stirrups when he heard a flurry of gunfire in the distance. Then came a few moments of silence followed by several more bangs. Judging by the sharp sound of the shots, they were made by a six-gun.

Garrett swung into the leather, his eyes scanning the riverbank, now shimmering in the ferocious afternoon heat. He waited, his rifle across the saddle horn, ready for whatever might come next. This much he knew: this was bad luck country, and the sooner he was back in the Judith Basin the better. Despite everything, could he convince Jenny to give up her dream and leave with him? That was unlikely, but as of now she was still with him, and sometimes the future can be purchased by the present. At least a man could only hope that was the case.

A figure rode slowly through the mirage near the river, his shape broken up and distorted by the shimmer. But as he emerged he gradually took on the solid form of Temple Yates.

The gunman reined up close to Garrett. He was smiling. "Killed 'em all," he said. "The last one died hard. I had three bullets into him before he dropped."

Yates' pale eyes searched Garrett's face. "You did all right back there, cowboy. If them two had gotten behind me I'd have been done for." The gunman's smile widened into a grin. "Damn it all, Garrett, I like you. I think for sure I'm going to gun you in the end, but hell, I like you."

"I wish folks wouldn't get to liking me so much," Garrett said. "Maybe then they wouldn't be so all-fired set on killing me."

Chapter 23

The summer drought had lowered the level of the Milk River, and when Garrett led the others into the crossing point opposite Verdigris Coulee, the water was only knee-high to their horses and almost without current.

Keeping the big bend of the Belly River to their west, they rode across featureless low-lying grass and brush country, and on the morning of the third day, just as their meager rations were exhausted, Fort Whoop-Up came into sight in the distance.

Yates trotted his horse alongside Garrett and said, "This is as far as I go." He reached behind him and took field glasses from his saddlebags. "Take a good look at the fort yonder. I want you to know the layout before you and the women ride in there."

As Yates narrated a sketchy history of the outpost, Garrett put the glasses to his eyes and scanned the place. It was solidly built of logs in the form of a hollow square, with ramparts and loopholes for defensive gunfire and bastions at opposite corners. A heavily fortified gate hung open, perhaps to catch any passing breeze. Nearby, the flag of the United States hung limply on a pole, informing the traveler that though the fort might be in Canada it was considered by its founder, the notorious whiskey trader John J. Healy, to be American territory.

Garrett adjusted the focus of the glasses and looked closer. A small cannon was mounted on one of the bastions and the other housed an alarm bell, a mountain howitzer and an artesian well. Through the yawning gate, Garrett noticed that all the doors and windows of the compound's buildings opened onto the central square, another defensive measure.

The post seemed crowded with men, but of their type and nature, at that distance Garrett could not guess.

"Seen enough?" Yates asked.

Garrett nodded and handed back the glasses. Yates shoved them into his saddlebags, then swung down from his horse. "Get down, cowboy," he said.

Stepping from the leather, Garrett purposefully walked closer to Yates until only a few feet separated them. The gunman knew the reason, and his eyes showed guarded amusement. "Not a trusting man, are you, cowboy?" he said.

Garrett held himself ready. "Man says he plans on killing me, my trust spreads thin. You're faster than me, Yates, but up close and personal like this I reckon I'll still have time to get my work in."

For a few moments, Yates' face was expressionless. Then he broke into a wide grin. "Damn it, boy, but you're true-blue. Hell, I'm not going to gun you. As that feller said back at the Milk, let bygones be bygones."

"Yeah," Garrett said, "and look what happened to him."

Yates laughed, showing teeth as long and yellow as piano keys. "Nah, no guns. You and me are going to reach an understanding, right here, right now." He waved an arm. "Look around you, Garrett. What do you see?"

Without taking his eyes off Yates, Garrett answered, "I know what I see—miles of grass and over there a solitary white spruce."

"Right, and that's where I'll be this evening. When you and the women skedaddle from the fort, meet me here."

"Yates," Garrett said, "I told you I won't be a party to fleecing those miners."

"Nor will you be," Yates said, smiling and spreading his hands wide. "We'll leave that to the little gals."

Before Garrett could answer, Yates turned to the women, who were still sitting their horses, listening to the men talk. "You ladies step down and get over here," he said. "We got plans to make."

The women did as they were told and Jenny's eyes sought Garrett's. Gone was the horror he'd seen after the fight at the dry wash, replaced by a softness and warmth he'd never seen before, a look that should have reassured him, but didn't, and he couldn't tell why.

Like a schoolteacher lecturing his students, Yates said, "You remember the names of your husbands-to-be? Jenny?"

"Hiram Van Sickle," the girl answered.

Yates' eyes shifted to the next woman. "Abbie?"

"Bob Rucker."

The gunman nodded. "Paloma?"

"I know his name," the woman snapped, her face flushing. "We're not children here."

"Say it anyhow," Yates said. His voice was suddenly low and flat, the threat obvious.

"Ezra Hacker," Paloma said, reading the gunman and not liking what she was seeing. "How could I forget a name like that?"

"All right, you know the deal," Yates said, ignoring the woman. "You make real nice to those miners. Get yourselves baths, splash on the perfume, and then unbutton some. Show them what will be on the menu for their wedding night. Hell, tell them if you have to, but get them to up the ante to four thousand each. Even at that, it's cutting Charlie Cobb's profit mighty thin."

Yates turned to Garrett. "Don't worry, cowboy. You'll get your five hundred."

"I told you, Yates," Garrett said. "I want no part of this. All I want is to see Jenny safe back to Fort Benton." His eyes angled to the girl. "Or my ranch if she'll change her mind about things."

To his surprise, Jenny smiled at him and said, "That might happen, Luke. A woman changes her mind all the time."

"Do you mean that, Jenny?" Garrett asked, sudden hope rising in him.

Yates interrupted. "You two can talk pretties and make calf eyes at each other later. Right now we have more business to discuss." He stepped closer to the women. Jenny looked as pretty and fresh as ever, and any man would think Paloma close to being beautiful. By contrast, Abbie looked plain and mousy, her fair skin peeling off her nose from the sun.

"Listen up," Yates said. "You get the money from the miners, then make some excuse to leave for a few minutes. Then you head for the livery stable, where Garrett will be waiting." He turned. "Cowboy, we don't need anyone else to supply horses and that cuts down on expenses. You saddle the mounts the women are riding right now and then escort the gals back here. After that, we all light a shuck for Benton."

"Suppose the miners don't pay us up front?" It was Abbie, looking uncomfortable, who asked the question. "And maybe they shut the gates at night."

"The gates won't be shut. It gets as hot as hell inside that stockade and they keep the gates open unless hostile Indians are in the area. As for the money, you tell them miners that Garrett is Charlie Cobb's specially appointed representative and he's demanding immediate payment." Yates' lips thinned. "Do anything you have to, but get that money. Hell, you're all whores, give 'em a taste if need be. Whet their appetites, like." He paused for effect, then his lips pulled back from his teeth in a wolf grimace. "Just get the four thousand from each of them."

Garrett stiffened, anger spiking at him, but he caught Jenny's warning glance and held his tongue. If he braced Yates now it would lead to gunplay and Jenny could get hurt. He couldn't risk it, especially now that the girl seemed willing to go to the ranch with him.

He would also probably die, and that would ruin everything. Garrett smiled at the thought, at the terrible finality of a killing and how a man didn't have to seek death—it had a way of finding him.

"Right." Yates was speaking again. "Mount up and get this thing done."

Garrett stepped into the saddle and glanced at Yates. The man stood straddle-legged, his thumbs in his crossed gun belts, his cold eyes missing nothing. He looked hard and mean and ready for anything, more than able to handle any trouble that might come his way.

Yates, Garrett decided, was a bad enemy, and he didn't think for one moment that the gunman would let him live after he got Charlie Cobb's money. He was not a man to forgive and forget, nor one to trim his boss's profit margin.

Garrett led the women toward Fort Whoop-Up, crossing open ground that allowed the fort's defenders an excellent field of fire against marauding Indians.

The Canadian Mounties were doing their best to stamp out the illegal whiskey trade, but they were spread thin and men like Johnny Healy still prospered. When the redcoat police were near, Healy traded guns, cooking pots, axes, ammunition, sugar, flour, tea, salt, knives, tobacco, cloth and blankets to the Indians for buffalo robes, rather than the intoxicating firewater that would surely land him behind bars.

Once a visiting Mountie moved on, the going rate was two cups of whiskey for a robe, and for a fine pony the Indians expected four gallons of Healy's rotgut, raw alcohol diluted with water and spiked with red pepper.

The whiskey trade was devastating the local Indian population, a fact well known to the Blackfoot and the Bloods. Both of those proud tribes hated whiskey traders and had often attacked the fort, but had never succeeded in breaching its sturdy defenses.

But now Luke Garrett rode unchallenged through the gates, the women with him an open passport to anywhere, their presence already attracting a curious throng. The press of men around the horses forced the four riders to a stop, and Garrett sat his saddle and looked around him.

There seemed to be several hundred men in the compound, mostly bearded miners in plaid wool shirts and heavy boots, all of them carrying revolvers and huge bowie knives on their belts. Here and there aloof buffalo hunters in elegant buckskins, beaded and chewed to the softness of fine suede by Indian women, watched the proceedings, Sharps rifles cradled in their arms. The skinners, lesser mortals, were undistinguishable from the miners except for their bloodstained clothing and pervading stink. Mingled with the rest were the usual flotsam and jetsam of the frontier, gamblers with white faces and thin fingers, shaggy wolfers as wild as the

animals they hunted, thugs and gunmen of all
stripes, and ragged drifters with hollow eyes who
lived as best they could, trapped at the fort by the
lure of forty-rod whiskey or the lack of funds for
a miner's outfit or a good horse. Foulmouthed
freighters jostled missionaries in black broadcloth
who preached the Christian God to the Indians,
and a few of those blanket-wrapped natives stood
at the edge of the crowd, watching what was going
on with empty faces that revealed only defeat.

Garrett saw several whores in the sea of people
around him. They were unattractive women who
looked as worn and used up as old saddles and they
studied Jenny, Abbie and Paloma with calculating,
hostile eyes.

A big miner wearing a battered plug hat and
a belligerent expression lurched from the crowd.
Garrett glanced at him and their eyes met. The
man had been drinking and he was either on the
prod or ready for a woman, and the latter proved
to be the case.

"You, little lady," the man said, ignoring Garrett
as he pointed a finger at Paloma. "How much fer
a poke?"

"She's not for sale," Garrett said, the sharp lash
of his voice quieting the crowd who'd been lustily
cheering the miner's question.

"You keep out of this, mister," the big man said.
"This is between me and the young lady."

"I told you, she's not for sale," Garrett said.
Then, to placate the man, he added, "She's promised to another."

For a few moments the miner stood in silence, slowly shaking his head as he looked down at the toes of his boots. When his eyes lifted to Garrett again, they were hot with anger. "Right. Mister, I told you to keep out of this. Now I'm gonna clean your plow for you."

The big miner roared and his huge, hairy arms shot upward to pull Garrett from the saddle. But quickly the young rancher drew back out of range as he shucked his gun. In a single fast movement he sideswiped away the reaching arms with his left hand, then leaned forward and lifted the plug hat off the miner's close-cropped head. The barrel of the Colt chopped downward and slammed onto the man's skull with the sound of an ax hitting a log. His eyes rolling in his head, the miner staggered back a step, groaned deep in his throat, then dropped like a felled ox.

Up until that moment the crowd around Garrett had been good-natured, keen for any diversion, but now an angry growl went up and a few guns were drawn. A man's voice, loud and clearly used to command, stopped the uproar. "What's going on here?"

Garrett had his gun held high and ready as the mob parted to allow a small, stocky man in an ill-fitting frock coat to stomp his way forward, his face flushed. The man looked tough but wore a starched collar, and to Garrett, that meant he'd have to prove himself. The newcomer glanced down at the fallen miner, then his icy blue eyes lifted to Garrett. "Did you do this?"

Garrett nodded. "That man mistook my female companions for ladies of easy virtue. I corrected his mistake."

"Did you now?" the small man said. His eyes swept the three women. "I'd say it's a natural enough error to make in a place like this." He looked up at Garrett again. "My name is John J. Healy and I own this fort. What are you and your . . . ah . . . female companions doing here?"

Before Garrett could answer, Healy held up a warning hand. "Before you say a word, let me tell you that disorderly conduct means immediate expulsion from Fort Whoop-Up. Do I make myself clear?"

"Clear as ever was," Garrett said. Then, deciding that the times called for a speech, he rose in the stirrups and his voice lifted to the crowd. "The young ladies you see before you are catalog brides, pledged to three lucky men at this post. They have traveled all the way from Fort Benton and suffered through Indian attacks, drought and hunger, so eager were they to get here and meet their future husbands. Surely they should have expected to be treated with respect, not manhandled. These are innocent brides, not fancy women."

"Hear, hear!" somebody yelled. Garrett couldn't see the man but he silently thanked him.

Healy held up a hand to quiet the chattering crowd and spoke directly to Jenny. "Who are these three lucky men, young lady?"

In a breathless, little girl voice that sounded wonderfully virtuous, Jenny answered, "Oh, kind sir, my name is Jenny and I am pledged to wed Hiram

Van Sickle, Esquire." She waved a hand toward the others. "Abbie has plighted her troth to Mr. Bob Rucker and Paloma to Mr. Ezra Hacker." She dabbed a tear from her eye with a tiny handkerchief. "There were two more of us, but, alas, they fell to Indians and bandits."

"Shame!" a man yelled, and others took up the same chorus.

Looking up at Garrett, Healy asked, "Who is the marriage broker? You?"

Garrett shook his head. "No, I was hired as an escort. The man who arranged it all goes by the name of Charlie Cobb."

Jenny slanted a warning glance to Garrett and said sweetly, "Mr. Cobb is such a kind man."

"I've heard Charlie Cobb called a lot of things," Healy said, "but kind wasn't one of them."

A roar of laughter went up from the crowd, but again Healy held up a hand and silence followed. "Be that as it may, the three gentlemen of whom you speak, Miss Jenny, are enjoying a refreshment at my bar this very moment. All three have struck it rich at the diggings, and I know for a fact that from time to time they . . . ah . . . pine for female companionship. It comes as no surprise they have chosen you lovely ladies to be their wives."

Healy waved an arm toward one of the log buildings facing the square. "Boys, here's a lark! Let's carry the brides to their prospective grooms. And the first drink is on me!"

Amid rousing cheers, Garrett watched helplessly as Jenny and the other women were pulled off their horses, lifted onto the broad shoulders of miners and carried away in the direction of Healy's tavern amid roaring laughter and coarse comments.

Within a few moments, Garrett was left alone, the dust cloud kicked up by the miners' boots already settling. The big man he'd buffaloed rose groggily to his feet, looked after at the departing crowd, then searched around for his plug hat. Garrett forgotten, he waved the hat in the air and yelled, "Hey, wait for me!" Then he went pounding after the rest.

Garrett gathered up the reins of the horses and his eyes scanned the compound, trying to locate the livery stable.

A buffalo hunter in buckskins with foot-long fringes and elaborate, geometric Blackfoot beadwork paused to look at him, taking in his wide hat, spurred boots and shotgun chaps. "Fair piece of your home range, ain't you, cowboy?" the man said.

"Some," Garrett acknowledged.

The hunter nodded toward a barn and pole corral at the southeast corner of the fort. "You can put up your horses there. Cost you two bits a day, an' that includes hay. Oats are fifty cents extry."

Garrett touched a finger to the brim of his hat. "Obliged."

He kicked the grulla into motion, but the hunter's voice stopped him. "Heard you mention Charlie Cobb," he said. "Last I remember—it was a few years back, mind—he was run out of Cheyenne for goldbricking the rubes." The man shook his head. "Times change, and now ol' Charlie's in the catalog bride business. Well, I'll be damned."

Garrett nodded, prepared to be sociable. "Like you say, times change."

The hunter lifted cool eyes to Garrett. "Times change, but Charlie doesn't. You step careful around him, cowboy. He's gunned his share and not a one of them took a bullet in the front."

"Obliged again," Garrett said. "That's something to remember."

He rode past the hunter and made his way toward the barn. When he glanced back, he saw the man standing in the middle of the square, watching him.

Chapter 24

An old-timer who had tried his hand at the diggings but had never hit paydirt ran the livery stable. He called himself Ethan, a watchful, silent man who didn't offer conversation but readily answered questions.

After he unsaddled the horses and forked them hay and a bait of oats, Garrett wondered where he could get a bath, a new shirt and a meal.

"A shirt and a meal can both be had at Healy's store across the square," the old man said. "As for a bath, young feller, I just filled the horse trough with water. You can strip an' wash the trail dust off'n yourself in there." He grinned. "An' that's the only bath you'll get at Fort Whoop-Up and the territory around for maybe a hunnerd miles."

A dip in the trough was better than no bath at all. The trough was around the side of the barn, a zinc tub fortunately out of sight of most people who might be passing by. Garrett stripped, pleased to see that the wound on his chest was almost healed, and lowered himself into water fresh from the well and still icy cold.

He washed as best he could without soap, then used the scrap of rag Ethan had tossed to him to get at least partially dry. He settled his hat on his head, then dressed quickly.

"Hope the horses don't mind me using their drinking place as a bathtub," he told the oldster, pulling on his boots.

The man shrugged. "Horses don't mind. Around these parts they've drunk worse."

A few minutes later Garrett crossed the dusty square. The sun was dropping lower and the sky was pale red, a few streaks of purple cloud showing to the west. He estimated it would be dark in a couple of hours when he would need to have the horses saddled and ready. There was still time to buy a shirt to replace the bloodstained and ragged one he wore and get a meal.

Loud voices and laughter came from Healy's bar, a log cabin situated between a blacksmith's shop on one side and a row of bunkhouses on the other. Not wanting to be seen by those inside, Garrett walked wide of the bar and found the store, drawn by a painted wooden sign that hung outside and proclaimed:

JOHN J. HEALY
SUPPLIES, CLOTHING
& SUNDRIES
Mining tools a specialty—sold at cost

Garrett stepped inside, into a low, gloomy cabin with shelves on either side. The place smelled of just about everything under the sun, the rich tang of plug tobacco, the leather of belts and boots, fresh-ground coffee, dried and pickled fish, and the musty odor of bolts of colorful cotton fabric, woven in the mills of northern England. A burlap bag of green coffee stood by the door and near it a barrel of sorghum, leaking black drops onto the floor. Bright candy canes stood on end in jars along a stretch of the counter to Garrett's left, next to rounds of yellow cheese, some of them cut into thick, V-shaped slices. A barrel of crackers, the lid off, shouldered against a hogshead of sugar, and on its other side a barrel of pungent sauerkraut was surrounded by open boxes of gingersnap cookies.

Slabs of smoked bacon on iron hooks hung from the ceiling, and beneath them were piles of hickory shirting in stripes and plaids and more bolts of cloth, this time calico and gingham. A hand-drawn sign directed female attention to a stack of canvas skirts, split for riding, an eastern fashion that was now becoming all the rage farther west. On the shelf to Garrett's right were rows of shoes, mule-eared boots, coffeepots, bags of gunpowder, canned goods of all kinds and boxes of rifle and pistol ammunition. And stacked high were piles of banjos, the miner's handy short-handed shovel.

Garrett stood still for a few moments, enjoying the coolness of the store and its wonderful variety of smells.

"Can I help you?" A man stepped through a curtain at the back of the cabin, rubbing his hands on a stained white apron. He was small and bald, with apple cheeks framed by huge, bushy sideburns.

"I need a shirt," Garrett said, "and some supplies."

"You've come to the right place," the man said, his smile slight and professional. "My name is Bill Bates. What can I do you for?"

"I need a shirt," Garrett said again.

"You surely do." Bates grimaced. He cast an eye over Garrett, gauging his size, then stepped behind a counter and after a short search came back with a blue shirt. "Just like the one you're wearing," the man said, "except it smells better."

Garrett held up the shirt, sniffed the cloth, then nodded and said, "Mind if I change into it here?"

"Please, by all means."

Garrett slipped his suspenders over his shoulders, stripped off his old shirt and buttoned up the new one. "Fits real good," he said, pulling up the suspenders again before putting the bag with the double eagles in the pocket.

Bates smiled. "It's perfect." He made a face and picked up Garrett's discarded shirt between the thumb and forefinger of his right hand. "I'll just get rid of this," he said. The man disappeared behind the curtain and returned a couple of moments later. "The shirt will be two dollars. Anything else?"

"You know, I don't always wear a shirt until it falls apart," Garrett said, figuring that a small defense of his personal cleanliness was necessary.

The storekeeper pursed his lips. "No, no, I'm sure you don't. Now will there be anything else?"

With an eye to his return trip along the trail with Jenny, Garrett had Bates sack up a slab of bacon, another of salt pork, and some coffee, sugar and flour. "Throw in a small coffeepot, tobacco and rolling papers and a half dozen of those peppermint candy canes," he said, thinking they might be something Jenny would enjoy.

Garrett reached into his shirt pocket where he'd stowed Zeb's three double eagles and rang the holed coin onto the counter. Zeb had given him the money to dig an artesian well, but Garrett imagined he'd understand his present necessity.

"Oh, deary dear," Bates said, holding up the coin, his eye to the bullet hole in its center. "This has certainly been in the wars."

"Target practice," Garrett said.

"A silver dollar would have been cheaper," the storekeeper said, his small mouth tightening in disapproval. He stepped to the end of the counter and came back with a small gold scale. "Young man, this twenty-dollar coin should weigh 33.4360 grams." He dropped the double eagle onto one of the pans and placed a small brass disk on the other. "Ah, just as I thought. The bullet has removed ten grams of gold." He lifted bleak eyes to Garrett. "I can only allow you fifteen dollars on this coin, and at that I'm being more than generous."

Realizing that arguing would be useless, Garrett nodded. He picked up the sack and his change and turned to step out of the store, but Bates' voice stopped him.

"Are you going to the wedding eve celebration down at Mr. Healy's bar?" he asked. "I understand some rich miners are planning quite a shindig down there tonight." Bates shrugged. "Something to do with beautiful mail-order brides, I'm told."

"Thinking about it," Garrett said, not wishing to be drawn into a conversation.

He stepped through the door and out into the waning afternoon before the storekeeper could say more.

A cabin in the row of bunkhouses had been set aside as a restaurant. When Garrett stepped inside, he was the only customer. He took a seat on a bench at a rough wooden table and a taciturn waiter who had the look of a range cook about him took his order for the only plate on the menu—buffalo steak, potatoes and wild onions.

The food was reasonably good and the coffee strong, but it cost Garrett all his change from the double eagle he'd used at the store. He took that hard, knowing from experience that money was tough to come by and even tougher to keep.

When he stepped outside, the day was shading into evening and a single sentinel star glittered in the lemon sky to the north. Garrett noted with relief that the post gates were open, and no one seemed to be standing guard. It looked like the entire male population of the fort was at Johnny Healy's bar, drinking whiskey that was no doubt only marginally better than the pop skull he peddled to the Indians.

As he crossed the square in the direction of the stable, Garrett thought he heard Paloma's laugh ring high and false above the bellow of men's voices. Like Jenny and Abbie, the woman would be holding herself, drinking little, knowing she had to wheedle Charlie Cobb's money from her unsuspecting suitor and then leave Fort Whoop-Up in a mighty big hurry.

As he reached the stable, Garrett had made up his mind. He could not let Cobb cash in on his elaborate confidence trick. To allow him to do so would mean that the man would profit by the deaths of Zeb Ready, Annie Spencer and so many others.

He was going to return the money, then get Jenny and the other women out of the post real fast before things turned ugly. Healy, for all of his whiskey trading, seemed like a square dealer, at least toward the miners whose business he valued. Garrett decided that if he handed the money to him, it would get to the right parties and no questions asked since the man wouldn't want a riot on his hands. At least he hoped that would be the case. But first he would give each of the women the two hundred dollars Cobb had promised her. Under the circumstances, after all they'd suffered on the trail, it was the least he could do.

There was only one problem—he'd have to tell Temple Yates that he'd returned Charlie's illgotten gains, a mighty uncertain thing given the man's temperament and skill with a gun.

But to Garrett that was just another river to cross, albeit a dangerous one, and he'd take the hurdle when the time came.

To the young rancher's relief, the man called Ethan was not at the stable. No doubt he was celebrating with the others at the bar. Quickly Garrett saddled and bridled the horses, taking some time with the grulla after it acted up some, refusing to take the bit. Then he found an empty stall and settled down to wait.

Now it all depended on Jenny and the other women getting there without being seen. On his own way out of the fort, Garrett would give Healy the money and be well on his way back along the trail before any hue and cry began.

His plan was thin and he knew it. It would take only one suspicious groom to go looking for his bride to upset the whole applecart. The trick was to get the women out of the fort as quickly and silently as possible.

As Zeb had once told him, "Luke, if you're ever fixin' to pull freight in a hurry, do it kind of casual—like you wasn't even noticin' it your ownself."

Now he was going to take that advice.

Garrett leaned his back against the stall partition, tipped his hat over his eyes and within a few minutes was dozing.

He woke with a start as footsteps sounded hollow on the wood floor of the stable. A lantern was bobbing toward him, a halo of orange light in the gloom, but the person holding it was lost in darkness.

Garrett drew his gun, thumbed back the hammer and said, "Stop right there or I'll drill you dead center."

"Luke, don't shoot. It's me." Jenny's voice.

The girl lowered the lamp and stepped into the stall. She was wearing one of the canvas riding skirts Garrett had seen in the general store, a man's shirt and a new hat and boots. She held the lantern in one hand, a bottle of whiskey and two glasses in the other.

"Are you ready to leave?" Garrett asked. "Your horse is saddled."

"Soon," Jenny answered. "When the others get here."

Alarm flared in Garrett. "Where are they?"

"The last I saw them they were at the store, buying outfits like mine." Jenny smiled, but it was a forced grimace, devoid of humor. "Our husbands-to-be insisted we get outfitted for a trip to their diggings." She waved a vague hand. "Somewhere in the badlands north of here. They plan on selling their claims, then heading for honeymoon bliss in Denver or Cheyenne or who knows where."

Jenny set the bottle and glasses on the floor. "I think every man in the post is over at the store watching Abbie and Paloma get changed. That's why I was able to sneak away and join you, Luke."

"Did you get the four thousand?" Garrett asked.

Jenny's laugh was a faint rustle of sound in the silence. "Four thousand? Hiram bets that much on the turn of a card. I told him I had to pay you the matchmaker's fee and he just grinned and dug into his pocket and stuffed a bunch of notes into my hand." The girl reached into the pocket of her skirt and pulled out a wad of bills. "I counted it. There's just over five thousand dollars here. I'm sure Abbie and Paloma will get as much."

"It's got to go back, Jenny," Garrett said. "Every penny of it, less the two hundred Charlie Cobb promised you. I plan on giving the money to Healy and then lighting a shuck."

To his surprise the girl nodded. "I understand how you feel, Luke. No matter how you cut it, taking this money is stealing. Those three men are all hot and impatient for their wedding night and they plan on tying the knot just as soon as a preacher can get to the post. Healy is planning a big celebration, going to kill the fatted calf, he says. Only the brides won't be here."

"Jenny, I don't want you to ever do this again," Garrett said. "Your involvement with Charlie Cobb is over."

"I won't," the girl said. "I've learned my lesson."

Garrett leaned over and kissed Jenny's full lips, a lingering kiss it seemed she never wanted to end. But at last their lips parted and the girl said, "Let's drink on our agreement."

She filled both glasses and passed one to Garrett. "To us," she said.

"And our future together," he added.

Jenny nodded. "Yes, Luke, to our future."

He was not much of a drinking man, but Garrett drained the glass of raw whiskey, its fire immediately helping to unknot the tension in him.

"Good?" the girl asked.

Garrett nodded, feeling suddenly relaxed. "Real good. In fact I didn't think Healy sold whiskey that . . . that . . ."

He couldn't think of the words, and it looked like Jenny was moving away from him, as though she was slowly backing down a dark tunnel. "Don't go, Jenny," he said, hearing his words slur. "There's time . . . all the time in the world . . . time . . ."

"I'm so sorry, Luke," the girl whispered, tears

staining her cheeks. "Sometimes we have to sacrifice even the people we love to put form and substance to our dreams."

Jenny's face was a pale blur in the darkness, and Garrett shook his reeling head, trying to focus. He reached out a hand to the girl, but his arm was impossibly heavy and he let it drop.

"You'll be fine, Luke, just fine. I know you will." Jenny rose. "One day I'll come looking for you. I promise, Luke, I promise."

Paloma and Abbie, both dressed like Jenny, stepped beside her. "Is he out yet?"

Jenny shook her head. "Not yet."

"But Annie told us those knockout drops never failed," Abbie said, her voice spiked with alarm. "What's taking so long?"

Garrett tried to raise his head, to look up at the woman, but it rolled on his shoulders and his chin dropped to his chest. He tried to rise, but fell back against the stall with a crash and his legs slid from under him.

"He's gone," Paloma said, her voice sounding like it came from a long distance away. "Now we've got to get out of here. They'll come looking for us."

"No," Garrett whispered. But the women did not hear him. He tried to rise again but slowly collapsed on his side. He groaned and let the darkness take him.

Chapter 25

Luke Garrett returned to consciousness with a pounding headache and a mouth so dry it felt like it was full of dust. He opened his eyes and saw Ethan's hairy face hovering over him.

"Thought for a spell you were dead, young feller," the man said. "And you soon will be if'n you don't fork your bronc an' ride."

"Jenny?" Garrett whispered.

"Gone," the old man answered, "with the other two. They sure played hob and now there's all kinds of hell to pay." Ethan cackled. "Them three miners know they've been took and they're mad enough to bite the sights off'n a six-gun."

Helping Garrett to his feet, Ethan led the young rancher to his horse. "I've tied your sack of supplies to the saddle horn. Now climb up on that grulla and get out of here before one of them drunks thinks to shut the gate."

"I'm obliged to you," Garrett said, swinging heavily into the saddle.

"I didn't aim to take sides in this," the old man

said. "I'm not what you might call a doin' man, more of a watcher. But I'll see no man lynched. Saw it one time afore and the sight of that ranny choking and kicking at the end of a rope has never left me."

"I planned on giving the money back," Garrett said, looking down at Ethan from the saddle. "I want you to know that. Tell the others that too when they've calmed down enough." He shook his head. "Jenny . . . Jenny put something in my drink."

"All that don't make no never mind now, son. Them miners are drunk and they're riled. You led those three thieving women here and if they catch you they won't ask no questions. They'll just string you up, probably right here in this barn."

"Ethan, I'm beholden to you," Garrett said.

As the old man waved a dismissive hand, Garrett kicked the grulla into motion and left the barn at a gallop. He swung toward the gate, hearing the drunken shouts of angry men around him.

"There's one of them!" somebody yelled. "Stop him!"

The gate was twenty yards away. Guns banged and a bullet tugged at Garrett's sleeve. Another cut the air by his left ear—and ahead of him a couple of men were running to close the gate!

Raking the grulla with his spurs, Garrett charged. One of the men had closed his side of the gate, but the other half was still a third of the way open. Luck was with Garrett. Instead of closing the gate fully, the man to his right left off pushing and went for his gun instead.

As Garrett reached the opening, the miner fired. But whiskey and the crowding darkness did nothing for his aim and the bullet went wide. Just to keep the man honest, Garrett drew and slammed a couple of shots into the dirt at his feet. The miner jumped back a step, cursing, then tripped and fell on his rump—and Garrett was through the opening and flapping his chaps for the trail.

Behind him there were more angry shouts and guns fired. A few bullets came close, zinging viciously past his head. But the night quickly swallowed him and the shooting came to a ragged halt.

The grulla's pounding hooves beat like a muffled kettledrum on the hard-packed dirt of the trail as Garrett headed south in the direction of Verdigris Coulee. The moon was rising alone in a purple sky, and every bush and clump of bunchgrass was touched by silvery light.

Garrett scanned the land ahead of him, looking for the white spruce where Temple Yates said he'd be waiting. Aware of the shots he'd fired at the fort, he reined in the grulla and reloaded his gun, filling all six cylinders. He might well be grateful for that extra round when he met up with Yates.

The coyotes were calling around him as Garrett rode up on the spruce at a walk, the tree's spreading branches black against the brightness of the night sky. Where was Yates?

Swinging out of the saddle, Garrett let the grulla's reins trail as he stepped to the spruce and looked around into the darkness, his gun in his hand. "Yates," he whispered, "are you here?"

The answering silence mocked him. The coyotes had fallen into quiet, but now, as Garrett scouted the area, they began to talk again.

Suddenly the grulla lifted its head, its ears pricked forward, listening to the night.

"Easy, boy," Garrett whispered. He stepped to the horse and gathered up the reins. "Yates, is that you? Show yourself, damn it."

The grulla snorted and pranced backward, up on its toes, white arcs of alarm showing in its eyes. Uneasily Garrett looked around him, trying to penetrate the threatening shadows that angled across the moonlit prairie.

A stealthy rustle near the base of the spruce.

Garrett's Colt came up, hammer back and ready. "Step out where I can see you," he said. "I got me a finger lookin' for a trigger here."

A few moments slipped past as Garrett stood alone in his small world of silence and darkness. Then the night parted and a huge gray shape emerged by the base of the spruce. The wolf Mingan stopped and watched him, its eyes burning with a golden fire.

Now that the predator was closer, the grulla whinnied in fear and reared on its hind legs, ready for fight or flight. Garrett fought the horse, holding tight to the reins as it plunged and bucked, attempting to turn and run. Finally the grulla calmed down enough that Garrett could throw a glance over his shoulder at the spruce. The wolf was gone and only the darkness remained where it was.

Garrett stepped into the saddle and swung the horse away from the tree. In the distance, heading toward him through the gloom, bobbing torches glowed like scarlet stars and men's angry voices were raised, yelling back and forth to each other.

The miners were coming after him and they'd be carrying hemp.

Time was running out on Luke Garrett, but he forced himself to fight down his clamoring panic and think.

Jenny and the other women had obviously decided to keep all the miners' money for themselves—but in doing that had they made a fatal mistake? Yates could have taken advantage of the darkness to move closer to the fort and he could have seen them leave. He might even now be chasing them. If that was the case, Jenny was in mortal danger.

But what direction had the women taken?

To the west lay Blackfoot country and the formidable barrier of the Rocky Mountains. It was unlikely they'd headed in that direction. If they'd ridden east they could swing south into the Sweet Grass Hills country and link up with the Whoop-Up Trail. Fort Benton would present a problem because Charlie Cobb was there. But it was unlikely he'd try to harm three young women with the vigilante committee watching his every move. Jenny and the others would be free to thumb their noses at Cobb and board an eastbound steamboat at the levee. And nobody would know that better than Temple Yates.

The risks were great, but the stakes were high because each of the women was gambling on her future, especially Jenny, with her dreams of being an artist.

Yates must know he could not let the women reach Fort Benton alive. He had to overtake them, kill them and take the money. It was a simple, effective solution to the problem and it was the gunman's way.

The burning torches were closer now, and the miners had spread out to cover more ground. Garrett moved the grulla to the east, swinging away from Verdigris Coulee back in the direction of the fort. He held the grulla to a walk, worried that the noise of its hooves on the bone-dry ground could betray him.

Garrett rode steadily for ten minutes, crossing a shallow creek lined with cottonwoods and drooping willows before the land ahead of him leveled out, flat and featureless. The torches of the miners' posse were now just pinpoints of light as they fell behind him. The riders were headed for the Whoop-Up Trail, guessing that a man on the run would flee in that direction.

The moon was dropping lower in the sky, the shadows deepening, as the flat land gave way to gently rolling hills, raw outcroppings of rock visible on their grassy slopes.

Around Garrett the land was quiet and nothing moved, the only sound the creak of his saddle and the soft footfalls of the grulla. But he was uneasy, with the feeling a man gets when he's being watched by unseen eyes.

Was Yates out there somewhere, stalking him?

Riding high in the saddle, every nerve in his body alert, Garrett rode down the steep slope of a coulee, crossed its sandy bottom and drew rein before allowing his horse to scramble up the opposite side. He sat his saddle and listened.

He heard only the silence. Even the coyotes had ceased their yammering. Then, very close, rose the howl of a hunting wolf, the sound that makes a man sit bolt upright in his blankets in the dead of night and search the darkness with wary eyes.

Garrett listened and wondered, the grulla shifting uneasily under him. Mingan was staying close. But why? He owed the big wolf his life, but in turn, the animal was beholden to him for nothing.

Shaking his head in bafflement, Garrett urged the grulla up the slope of the coulee, its hooves slipping on loose rock until they topped the rise and regained the flat.

It had been the wolf that had been watching him, but for what reason Garrett could not even guess.

After another hour of riding, he decided the night would yield him nothing. And there was always the chance he could stumble into Yates' gun in the darkness. He fetched up to a dry wash that carried floodwater from the Milk River during the spring melt and made a dry camp. At first light he would saddle up again and resume his search for Jenny.

If Temple Yates didn't find her first.

Chapter 26

Just as the gray dawn light was shading into the pale blue of morning, Garrett found the body of Abbie Lane.

The girl's life had been hard, her death no easier.

She was naked, lying on her back, her body scratched and bruised by Temple Yates, the result of his frenzy to tear off her clothes. Her left eye was swollen almost shut—by a backhand slap, Garrett guessed—and her shoulders were bitten, arcs of the man's teeth still livid red on her white skin.

Abbie had not been shot. She'd been strangled, her windpipe crushed by a man with much sinewy strength in his hands.

Near the body lay the purse the girl always carried, a treasured possession that she pulled closed with a pink ribbon drawstring. The bag's contents had been strewn over the grass, but if Abbie had been carrying money, it was now gone.

Garrett picked up a cheap silver-plated locket and opened it. Inside was a hand-colored photograph of a man and woman, their cheeks unnaturally rosy. The man was solemn and bearded, a farmer probably, and the worn-looking woman could only have been his wife.

Abbie's parents? Garrett guessed they had to be. As to whether or not they were still alive, he did not know. He closed the locket and slipped it into the pocket of his chaps. Maybe one day, if he could track them down, he would return it.

There was no doubt in his mind that it was Yates who had raped and killed the girl. Her pony was grazing nearby, and when the animal moved it favored its left foreleg. Abbie's horse had pulled up lame. As far as Garrett knew, neither Jenny nor Paloma was armed. It looked like Abbie had dropped behind and Yates had caught up to her. The other women, hearing the girl's screams, had panicked and fled.

Now Jenny and Paloma were out there, running scared, with Yates close on their trail. Garrett knew he had to ride, and ride fast, but he could not bring himself to leave Abbie the way she was.

Awkward and fumbling with women's fixings, he managed to dress her as best he could, not wishing others who might pass this way to see her nakedness as he had done. Then he took off his hat and bowed his head. But having none of the words, he stood in silence for a while, remembering what little he could of her, the skin that always peeled on her nose, her freckles, the sound of her voice and her laughter.

When it was over, Garrett settled his hat on his head, knowing what he'd done for Abbie Lane was little enough.

The saddle on the girl's pony had shifted and was hanging under the animal's belly. He removed the saddle, threw it aside, and remounted the grulla. There was no fear in Luke Garrett now, only a hot, killing rage.

He raised his face to the blue sky and roared his hurt into the quiet of the morning.

He was telling the world how badly he wanted to smash and destroy Temple Yates.

Garrett rode east until noon. The tracks left by the women and Yates still scarred the grass and were easy to follow. Some twenty miles north of the Milk River, the tracks swung south, toward the upper reaches of Elkhorn Coulee.

This was game country, and Garrett startled a large herd of antelope watering at a narrow stream that seemed to have its origin a ways farther west in the Cypress Hills. Coveys of up to fifty quail ran from his horse, fluttering into the air for only short distances before landing again in a flurry of wings. Once he saw a ragged and skinny coyote skulking around a stand of prickly pear, ready to pick off an unsuspecting mouse.

But he saw no sign of Yates.

Jenny and Paloma would keep on riding for as long as they could stay in the saddle. But eventually they'd have to stop to rest their horses. Yates was heavier and his mount would tire faster, and he was enough of a frontiersman to know that he couldn't push his horse indefinitely. The animal would need to be unsaddled and given time to graze.

For his part, Garrett walked more than he rode,

leading the grulla across gently rolling country thick with grama, coarser buffalo grass growing on the top of the rises. The day was hot, the sun merciless, and there was no breeze. The buzzards were riding high currents, looking like black flies against the pale blue window of the sky, and thin brushstrokes of white cloud showed to the south.

The land was dry, and with a pang of unease, Garrett realized he and his mount were raising dust, visible for a long distance.

Temple Yates might already know that he was being followed.

Sliding his Winchester from the scabbard, Garrett balanced the rifle across his saddle horn, his eyes restlessly scanning the distance ahead of him where the heat waves were already dancing.

By the time the still far off peaks of the Sweet Grass Hills came in sight, the day was beginning to shade into night. An arroyo offered Garrett shelter, and after drawing rein and studying the place, he rode into the narrow flat between its eroded slopes. The grulla was tiring and once it stumbled as a rock rolled under its hoof on the sandy bottom. After half a mile, Garrett rode up on a green oasis of cottonwood, willow and a few mesquites, tall grass growing among the roots of the trees. Through the branches he caught a glimpse of water. The grulla saw it too and quickened its pace, tugging at the bit. But Garrett reined in the horse and levered a round into the chamber of the rifle. He waited, listening. A night bird called from one of the cottonwoods and he heard the chirping of an insect in the grass.

Warily, he rode between the trees and came up on a small, shallow pool, the grass around it dark green. There was no sign of life. This was a remote and isolated place that Garrett had stumbled on by accident, and if humans had ever visited here it had been a very long time ago.

A weariness in him, he stepped from the leather and stretched the aches out of his tired body. He dropped the reins and let the grulla drink, then unsaddled the horse and led him to the grass around the pool.

There was dry wood aplenty around the bases of the trees and Garrett built a small fire. He filled his new coffeepot with water, threw in a handful of Arbuckle and set the pot on the coals to boil. He found a niche in the slope of the arroyo that protected him on two sides, sat and built a cigarette.

Relaxed by the smell of boiling coffee and tobacco and the small sound of the grazing horse, Garrett's thoughts returned to Jenny.

It would be easy to ride away from her, abandon her to her fate. He loved her, but it seemed that she did not love him enough in return. She'd made that clear when she'd drugged him and then left him alone at the fort. But Garrett's love for the girl was unconditional, his whole world reduced to a single person.

He thought about how much he loved her, an emotion he'd never in his life felt before. He figured there is love like a lamp that goes out when the oil is gone, or love like a high meadow stream that dries up when the spring rains end. But there is also a love that goes on forever, a spring gushing out of the heart of a mountain that keeps flowing endlessly and is inexhaustible.

That was what his love for Jenny was like and why, after all that had happened, he still had a willingness to forgive and forget. He did not question how he felt. He just knew it existed. That it was.

One day, in a future he could not yet see or dare to imagine, they would be together. In the meantime, his love could only help him grow and become stronger.

Garrett smiled and shook his head. He was getting sentimental in his old age, mooning about a girl he might never have, like one of those pale poets with lank hair and a quill pen that writes his verse about lost love, then curls up and dies.

He could die, and very soon. But it would not be from love—it would be from a .45 bullet fired by Temple Yates.

After all his brooding about love, the down-to-earth practicality of that thought made Garrett laugh out loud, so loud that the grulla lifted its head and stared at him.

Still smiling, he rose and poured himself coffee as the darkness of the night crowded around him and the sleepless coyotes began to talk.

Garrett was in the saddle again at first light. He left the arroyo, then spent fifteen minutes cutting for sign before he found his first track. He rode southeast toward the Sweet Grass Hills, sitting high in the saddle, alert for any sign of trouble.

Around him the bad luck country rolled away forever, featureless except where shadows gathered in the arroyos and scattered stands of juniper and mesquite showed up a darker green than the surrounding grass.

The sun was just beginning its climb when Garrett saw buzzards sliding across the sky in the distance. This time they were much lower, gradually losing height as their endless circles narrowed.

Buzzards are regarded as caretakers of the dead, but on occasion they will attack and tear apart a living animal if it is wounded or sick and unable to fight back. They will also readily shed their fear of humans and rip at a weak and dying man, first going for the eyes and kidneys. And they'll do the same to a woman.

Fear spiking at him, Garrett pulled his Winchester and eased back the hammer. He rested the butt of the rifle on his right thigh and swung in closer, his intent gaze constantly scanning the silent land around him.

Now the buzzards were almost directly overhead, unhurried, knowing that no matter what, their time would come.

Garrett saw the dead horse first. He stood in the stirrups and studied the ground around the animal, flat grassland with clumps of prickly pear and a few yellow cactus. He walked the grulla closer, the horse acting up as it sensed death, and caught the smell of blood. The carcass still wore its saddle.

Paloma Sanchez was lying facedown and still. She was partially hidden by the long grass, but there was no mistaking the midnight black of her long hair. A round-shouldered buzzard crouched several feet away from her. The bird flapped into the air when Garrett stepped from the saddle and walked to the girl's body. He got down on one knee and read what had happened.

A bullet had crashed into Paloma's back, neatly placed between her shoulder blades, where it had broken her spine. Garrett rolled the girl over. Her eyes were shut and her beautiful face was tranquil, as though she was asleep. Paloma had been dead when she hit the ground and probably never knew what hit her.

Piecing it together, Garrett figured that Yates had killed the girl's horse but Paloma had been thrown clear. When she'd gotten up and started to run, he'd put a bullet in her back.

Garrett's eyes lifted to the sea of grass rolling all the way to the horizon. Now only Jenny remained, and Yates must be close on her trail.

There had been saddlebags behind Paloma's saddle, but these had been rifled and then thrown on the ground. Like Abbie's, the money Paloma had been carrying was gone.

Taking off his hat, Garrett wiped sweat from his forehead with the back of his hand. He could do nothing for Paloma now. His concern must be for the living.

He settled his hat back on his head and stepped into the saddle.

Somewhere out in that wilderness of grass, cactus and sun Jenny was alone and no doubt terrified of the cold, relentless killer on her trail.

Garrett knew she needed him, more now than ever before.

He lifted the grulla into a distance-eating lope. Time was not on his side.

Chapter 27

The morning was far advanced, but the sky was still streaked with red, band after band stretching clear to the horizon. There was blood on the sky, a bad omen, and Garrett's lean, unshaven cheeks were touched by scarlet light.

Ahead of him lay the Milk River, and already the West Butte of the Sweet Grass Hills stood out stark and clear in the distance. Garrett slowed the grulla to a walk for a mile or so, then again spurred the horse into a lope.

The flat statement of a rifle shot hammered apart the silence of the morning. A moment's pause, then a pair of shots, very close together, came from the south.

Garrett drew rein on the grulla and stood in the stirrups, looking ahead of him. But the raw land offered nothing but distance and emptiness. Fear spiking at him, he spurred the grulla into a fast gallop, going he knew not where. Sound travels far across the flatlands, and all he could do was head in the direction of the gunfire.

And hope he could save Jenny in time—if she wasn't already dead.

Garrett rode across level ground, his horse stretching its neck, eager to run. He estimated that the gunshots had originated due south of him, in the direction of the Milk, but the featureless land ahead showed no sign of horses and riders.

He was about ten miles east of the Whoop-Up Trail, the only freight route into western Canada. As a result, the badlands he was crossing were not much traveled except by Indians. But Garrett rode past two mounded graves, one with its rough wooden cross askew but still intact, probably the last resting place of a couple of miners who had died here on their way to the gold rivers of Alberta.

To Garrett it was yet another bad omen in a hostile land that seemed full of them.

After several miles, the level ground began to gradually slope away from him, giving way to sandier country covered with less grass but more cactus, scattered mesquite and blackthorn bush. Over the course of the next two miles the land dropped in elevation about a hundred feet toward the U-shaped bend of a tree-lined creek running off the Marias.

When he was a couple of hundred yards from the creek, Garrett drew rein, reluctant to ride up on any place without first trying to determine what lay before him.

He slid his Winchester from the scabbard, his eyes carefully scanning the trees. There was no sound and nothing moved. Was Jenny down there somewhere? And was she alive or dead?

Garrett swung out of the saddle and stepped to

a jumble of rock spiked through by thickets of prickly pear. He got down on one knee, the rifle up and ready.

A bullet whined off a rock near his left leg and another kicked up a sudden fountain of sand a few yards in front of him. Garrett saw smoke drift among the trees, but he held his fire, afraid of hitting Jenny if she was down there.

"Garrett! Can you hear me?" Temple Yates' voice.

"I can hear you, Yates."

There was a moment's pause, then, "I got the girl here with me. Come any closer and I'll scatter her brains. You know me, Garrett. I'll do as I say."

"Jenny!" Garrett called. "Are you all right?"

A minute slid past with agonizing slowness, then Jenny answered, "I'm all right, Luke. He . . . he killed Abbie and Paloma."

"And I'll kill this one too, Garrett, less'n you back off from here."

"Yates, harm Jenny and I'll hunt you down," Garrett yelled. "Damn you, I'll kill you any way I can."

"Big talk coming from a man hiding behind a rock," Yates hollered. "Now listen here to me, Garrett. I could have nailed you, but I just fired a couple of warning shots. See, I mean you no harm."

"You're a liar, Yates. You did your best to bush-whack me. Trouble is, you may be fast with the Colt, but you're no great shakes with a long gun."

"Garrett, we can talk this thing through. I'll give you the five hundred and you and Jenny can ride away from here."

"Is that your deal, Yates?"

"Sure it is. But like I said, first we talk. Just lay down your rifle and step to the creek. Hell, you can even keep your belt gun. I can't make it any fairer than that."

"No deal, Yates," Garrett yelled, knowing the man was trying to draw him into a close-range revolver fight that he'd be bound to lose. "Just let Jenny go and you can light a shuck, free and clear."

"Too thin, Garrett, too thin, so it ain't going to happen that way. Listen up. Me and the gal are riding out. If I see dust on my back trail between here and Benton, I'll scatter her brains. If I even spot your shadow in the distance, I'll kill her and her dying won't be easy. Do you understand me?"

A terrible sense of defeat tugging at him, Garrett fought down his urge to charge the trees and take his hits, just so long as he got Yates in his sights. But he knew he'd be dead before he even covered half the distance, and Jenny would be in even worse trouble than before.

"Did you hear what I said, Garrett?" Yates yelled.

"I heard you, Yates. I won't come after you."

"One false step, just one little mistake on your part and she dies. Hell, if you even blow her a kiss I'll gun her. Remember that."

"Damn you, Yates, I'll remember."

"Just see you do."

A couple minutes later Garrett watched Yates and Jenny leave the shelter of the trees lining the creek. He had his rifle cocked and ready, but Yates made sure he kept Jenny between himself and the slope. Garrett could not get a clear shot at the gunman without running the risk of hitting the girl.

Miserably he saw them ride south, then swing west toward the Whoop-Up. He watched until they were out of sight; then he mounted the grulla.

The situation was brutally apparent to Garrett. If he tried to rescue Jenny between where he was and Benton, Yates would shoot her without hesitation. There was a good chance he'd kill her anyway before riding into the settlement. As it stood at the moment, Jenny was a burden to Yates, but she was also insurance that he'd reach Benton without having to fight every step of the way.

But once the Missouri came in sight and he no longer needed the girl, he'd get rid of her.

Garrett knew he could not let that happen. There had to be a way. All he had to do was find it.

Garrett rode to the creek, where the sandy soil gave way to good grass and a slight breeze talked among the trees. He unsaddled the grulla, propped his back against the trunk of a cottonwood and tipped his hat over his eyes. He slept soundly until the light of day began to die around him and the sky shaded from blue to pale violet and the first stars appeared.

Rising to his feet, Garrett collected wood from among the tree roots and built a fire. He filled the coffeepot and, as the water heated, cut thick slices of bacon and skewered them on a stick to broil.

After he'd eaten, he threw the last of the coffee

on the fire, then saddled the grulla. He stepped into
the leather and swung toward the trail, the darkness throwing a dusky cloak over the land.

Garrett welcomed the night. Any dust thrown up
by his horse would be lost in the gloom, unseen by
Temple Yates. From now on he would sleep by day
and ride under the canopy of the stars, and bide
his time.

He rode up on the Whoop-Up Trail and followed
it south and at some point in the darkest part of
the night he crossed the Milk. He paused on a wide
bar to smoke a cigarette as the moonlight cast
horse and rider in silver and spread their thin shadows on the sand.

Just before dawn, Garrett rode into Montana and
passed the Sweet Grass Hills. By first light he was
already asleep in a coulee just south of West Butte
and the long day came and went before he woke
and again took to the trail.

Under a wide moon, he splashed through Willow
Creek and as he regained the opposite bank a shad-
owy shape emerged from the long grass under the
cottonwoods and walked with him, adjusting its
pace to that of the horse.

The grulla didn't like it much and began to act
up, but Mingan kept his distance, never coming any
closer than twenty yards to Garrett.

"Wish I knew what you wanted with me, wolf,"
Garrett said aloud, a habit of men who ride lost
trails. He smiled. "Less'n you're planning on
eating me."

If the wolf heard and understood, it made no
sign, slipping like a gray ghost from patches of

moonlight to shadow, its burning eyes never leaving the trail ahead.

Ten miles north of the big bend of the Marias, Garrett spotted the winking crimson light of a campfire. He drew rein and calculated the distance. A mile, no more than that.

Mingan sat, waiting, and when Garrett kicked the grulla into motion, the wolf followed.

Garrett rode at a walk for half a mile, then stopped to listen. Ahead of him the campfire still burned, but there was no sound. The air was close and stifling, smelling of grass and the hot earth. Heat lightning flashed gold in the sky to the west as Garrett swung out of the saddle and slid his Winchester from the scabbard.

On cat feet he crouched low and began his walk toward the fire. He left the trail and crossed a patch of open ground, stepping around outcroppings of prickly pear. Garrett's eyes narrowed as he stood and scanned the distance in front of him. The campfire still glowed, but as yet he could not make out the lay of the land around it. He rubbed a sweaty palm on his chaps and touched his tongue to dry lips.

Was Yates even now watching him, sighting his rifle?

A booted and spurred horseman, Garrett knew he wasn't cut out to sneak across open country, but he saw no alternative. This might be his only chance to catch Yates unaware and get close enough to where the Winchester could nullify the gunman's deadly speed and accuracy with the Colt.

He stared gloomily into the darkness, at the flut-

tering light of the fire, and forced himself to
move again.

A hundred yards farther on, Garrett made out
one wall of a shallow coulee, the other side eroded
to a low hump rising a couple of feet above the
flat. The fire burned in the shadow of the higher
wall, casting a dancing circle of scarlet and yellow
on the grass.

Getting down on one knee, he studied the space
around the fire. There was no coffeepot on the
flames, no blankets spread, no picketed horses. The
camp was deserted.

Garrett rose to his feet. Holding the Winchester
high across his chest he stepped into the firelight,
the only sounds the snap of burning wood and the
chime of his spurs.

He saw the note pinned under a rock almost
immediately.

> GARRETT, YOU ARE TOO CLOSE.
> IF YOU WANT TO SEE THE GIRL
> ALIVE AGAIN BACK OFF.

Garrett read the note, then scanned it one more
time, as though hoping the words would suddenly
change before his eyes. But Yates' warning was
clear. He knew he was being crowded and if Garrett didn't put some distance between them Jenny
would pay the price.

A feeling of hopelessness tugging at him, Garrett
tossed the note into the fire, where it burned, curling like a black rose.

He could only hope Temple Yates would keep

Jenny alive until they reached Fort Benton. There she'd be safe, at least for a while.

But if that happened, the solving of one problem would create another. Some overdue vigilante justice by way of a hangman's noose was waiting for Garrett at the settlement. It would take only one idle porch percher to recognize him and his chances of rescuing Jenny and getting out in one piece could stack up to be mighty slim.

The young rancher glanced at the sky. There was blood on the moon. It was another bad omen in a bad-luck land.

Chapter 28

Luke Garrett rode into Fort Benton sitting slumped in the saddle, his hat pulled low over his face. The grulla was beat from the trail. Puffs of dust lifted from its plodding hooves and its head hung, the tired horse taking no interest in what was going on around it.

The streets of the settlement were crowded with freight wagons urged on by mule skinners and bearded, profane bullwhackers, their long whips snapping like Chinese firecrackers. Horsemen and people on foot scurried this way and that, their preoccupied eyes fixed on the way ahead of them, intent on their destinations, looking neither to the left nor the right.

Men of uncertain character and doubtful means of support were a common sight in the town, and no one slanted a second glance to the tall, unshaven rider who swung out of the saddle at the nearest saloon and pushed his way through the batwing doors.

Garrett's eyes searched the room as he walked

inside. A man with thin sandy hair, dressed in a collarless shirt and brocaded vest, stood behind the bar. A couple of men, teamsters by the look of them, sat at a table nursing warm beer that was growing warmer by the minute in the afternoon heat.

The bartender wiped a rag across the rough pine bar in front of Garrett and asked, "What will it be?"

"Rye and some information," Garrett answered.

"Rye I got. Information"—the man's black eyes measured the rough-looking stranger—"well, that all depends on what a man wants to know." He took a bottle and shot glass from behind the bar and poured the whiskey. "If it's about women now, I can—"

"I'm looking for a man," Garrett said. He tossed off the rye, then extended the glass for another. "Last I heard, he was calling himself Charlie Cobb."

A guarded look crept across the bartender's face. "Here, are you the law?"

Garrett shook his head and pretended a cheerfulness he did not feel. "Nah. Ol' Charlie and me, we go way back."

One of the men at the table had been studying Garrett closely, his eyes moving upward from the young rancher's big-roweled spurs to the top of his battered hat. "Mister, you got a way about you that looks familiar. Don't I know you from somewhere?" he asked.

"Ever been to the Pumpkin Creek country, southeast of here?"

The mule skinner shook his head. "No, I haven't."

"Then you don't know me from somewhere."

"Hell, I could have sworn—"

Garrett didn't want the man to push it any further. Maybe the teamster was just trying to be friendly, but he might be a vigilante. He turned his head toward the man, his eyes suddenly cold, and said, "You don't know me."

There was something in Garrett's look that the man didn't like and he let it go. "My mistake, stranger. No offense."

"None taken," Garrett said. He turned to the bartender again. "We were talking about Charlie Cobb."

The bartender and the man at the table had just recognized a quality in Luke Garrett of which he himself was completely unaware. There had always been iron in him, but all he'd endured on the Whoop-Up Trail had tempered that metal into hard, unbending steel.

In just a couple months he'd grown much older. His face had become taut and brown from the sun and there wasn't an ounce of him that was not muscle and bone. He looked tough, capable, and ready for anything and there was a recklessness about him that showed in the way he held his angular body and wore his holstered Colt like it was a part of him. He had acquired the kind of challenging, steady gaze that makes lesser men look away, and now the bartender found it difficult to meet his eyes.

"Mister, there's no telling where Charlie goes by day." The bartender topped off Garrett's glass. "No charge," he said. He leaned closer. "But he's here most nights." The man turned and waved a hand to a corner table. "Sits right over there. Plays poker sometimes. Other times he doesn't."

Garrett finished his drink and nodded. "I'm obliged." He fished in his shirt pocket for one of his two remaining double eagles and laid the coin on the counter. "Take my drinks out of that."

"Too early in the day to make that much change," the bartender said. He pushed the dented coin toward Garrett. "Pay me when you meet up with Charlie tonight."

Picking up the double eagle, Garrett nodded his thanks and turned to leave, but the man's voice stopped him. "Young feller, I don't know you and you don't know me, so I'm saying this for your own good. If you've got a beef with Charlie, step careful. Temple Yates got into town a couple of nights ago and he'll be with him. I don't know if you've heard o' Yates, but he's poison mean and lightning fast with the iron."

At the mention of Yates, Garrett turned so fast that the bartender's eyes widened in alarm. "Did Yates have a girl with him? Blond, real pretty"— he stretched out a hand, palm down—"about this tall?"

The bartender nodded. "Now you mention it, Charlie Cobb and Yates had a girl like that with them last night. I hear Charlie plans to have her to work the line down by the levee. Looked like a real nice girl, though kind of pale and frightened maybe, like she'd just got in from the sticks." He shrugged. "Takes all kinds, I suppose."

So Jenny was still alive. Relief flooded through Garrett. It seemed that Yates had decided it was better to make money out of the girl than kill her. And Charlie Cobb had agreed.

From all he'd heard, the whores along the levee catered mostly to the steamboat roustabouts—and were considered only a tiny cut above the lowly soldiers' women who plied their trade in the cow towns.

It was a harsh fate for any woman, a high percentage of the levee whores dying within three years of disease, morphine or drunken violence.

Garrett knew he would not let that happen to Jenny.

One way or another, it was all going to end—tonight.

Garrett stepped out of the saloon and gathered the reins of his tired horse. He looked around him as he crossed the street toward the livery stable, walking past a pile of stinking buffalo robes as tall as a man on horseback. He noticed that the jail had never been rebuilt, now an abandoned, empty shell missing two of its walls and the roof. But the gallows still stood, though the red, white and blue bunting was gone.

The street was still crowded, teams of mules and oxen and iron-rimmed wheels kicking up thick clouds of dust that hung in the air in a swirling fog. The town smelled of heat, raw timber, buffalo offal and the all-pervading stench of manure. Down by the levee a steamboat whistle screeched, holding its shrill note for almost half a minute, then fell silent, leaving Garrett's ears ringing.

A young stable hand showed Garrett to an empty stall. He gave oats and hay to the grulla, then asked if there was a place he could eat. The youngster nodded his head in the direction of a timber building with a canvas roof. "That's as good as any in town and better than most," he said.

Garrett touched his hat to the stable boy and again walked into the street. So far he'd seen no sign of Simon Carter. The vigilante chief might be away from the settlement, which would greatly reduce Garrett's chances of being recognized. He hoped that was the case. From what he'd learned about Carter, he was not a forgetting man.

Stepping well wide of the barbershop where he'd been shaved for his hanging, Garrett walked to the restaurant and stepped inside, a brass bell above the door tinkling. There were no customers at this time of day, the hours between lunch and dinner, and the benches on each side of a long pine table were empty.

A curtain opened at the rear of the cabin and an old woman stepped out, smiling. She was thin as a bird and looked too frail to lift the heavy cast-iron fry pans that were the tools of her trade. "Judging by the way your shadow has holes in it, I'd guess you're ready to eat, young man," she said.

Garrett nodded. "I could use some grub. I'm missing my last six meals," he said.

"Then you've come to the right place." The old lady turned. "Let me get you some coffee."

She returned with a cup and a blackened pot and poured coffee for Garrett. "I have a beefsteak stew, first time in months," she said. "The strangest thing, a buffalo hunter was up on the Teton and came on a shorthorn steer grazing along the bank as nice as you please. He shot it, of course, and packed back the meat. It's good and fresh."

Now Garrett knew the sad fate of at least one of his cows. "Got anything else?" he asked, a slight lump in his throat.

The old woman was surprised. "No beef stew?" She studied Garrett for a few moments, puzzled, then said, "Ah well, everyone to his own taste. Young man, I can burn you a buffalo steak and I've got eggs. Do you like eggs?"

"Sounds good to me." Garrett smiled. "Maybe half a dozen over easy with the steak."

"I think I only have five. Is that enough?"

"That will do just fine."

When the food arrived the old lady sat on the bench opposite and watched him eat, her bright sparrow eyes curious. "You don't look like a buffalo hunter to me," she said. "More like a puncher."

Garrett spoke around a mouthful of steak. "Uh-huh, I'm a cattleman. Just passing through."

The woman nodded. "We had a cattleman here a while back, and that awful Simon Carter was fixing to hang him. But somehow the young man escaped. Blew up Carter's jail doing it, and that made our vigilante chief real mad, I can tell you."

Trying to keep his face expressionless, Garrett said, "Saw what looked like a jail when I rode in. I thought maybe it had burned after being hit by lightning or something."

The old woman shook her head. "No, it was giant powder did that. Or so I was told." She smiled. "Well, anyhow, I'm glad the young man escaped. There's been too much hanging around here recently if you ask me. Maybe that's to do with the fact that Carter is the town undertaker."

She rose and disappeared back into the kitchen. Garrett finished his meal, then built a cigarette. He was drinking the last of his coffee when the woman reappeared, a plate in her hand. "Thought you might like a piece of apple pie. I baked it myself."

She busied herself by removing Garrett's dinner plate and when she came back to the table, she again watched him eat. When he'd finished the pie to the last crumb, she asked, "Feeling better now?"

Garrett smiled and nodded. "Considerable."

He reached into his shirt pocket and extended the bent double eagle to the woman. "Sorry. I've nothing smaller."

"I can make change," the old lady said. She rose and walked to a cash drawer and returned with paper money and some coins. "Fifty cents for the steak and eggs. The coffee and pie are on the house."

Garrett stuffed the change into his pocket and got to his feet. "I'm obliged, ma'am. Now I got to be moving on."

"One thing before you go, young man," the

woman said. "Call it a word of warning if you like. Simon Carter is in town, and he prides himself on how he never forgets a face."

"You know it was me he was fixing to hang, don't you?" Garrett asked.

The old lady nodded. "As soon as you walked in the door. You see, I never forget a face either."

Chapter 29

Luke Garrett walked slowly into the street, then turned right and headed toward the livery stable. He passed the saloon, which showed little signs of life, and threaded his way through a throng of freight wagons, horses and people before reaching the barn.

There was no sign of the stable hand and Garrett stepped to his saddle hanging over the partition of the grulla's stall. He slid the Winchester from the scabbard, wiped off the action with his bandana, then fed extra shells into the chamber.

Satisfied, he retied the bandana around his neck and looked around him. The sun was still high in the sky and beams of light where dust shimmered angled into the barn through chinks in the pine roof. The grulla snorted and pawed the floor of its stall, and over in a corner by the door a restless rat rustled.

Suddenly weary, Garrett found an empty stall and stretched out. He tipped his hat over his face and laid the rifle by his side where it would be handy. He closed his eyes and, lulled by the quiet and drowsy heat, he let sleep take him.

Garrett awoke to the blue haze of twilight. He picked up his rifle and got to his feet. Despite the crowding darkness, everything around him stood out in sharp detail—the straw on the floor, the bulky shapes of the horses in their stalls, the shifting puddle of orange light cast by a lantern on an iron post just beyond the barn door.

He stood there for a few moments, taking everything in, appreciating the sights, the smells and the small noises made by the animals. A man who is about to face death takes stock of such things, knowing that soon, in a single hell-firing moment, they could all be taken away from him forever.

Luke Garrett had known little but hard work in his life, and nothing he owned had come easily. Before he'd taken to the Whoop-Up Trail, he'd been a young man with a ready smile and an easy-going way about him, his only real worry trying to raise the wherewithal to buy a Red Angus bull.

But the trail had changed him and he was not smiling now.

Temple Yates and Charlie Cobb might already be at the saloon across the street—and the time of the reckoning was racing relentlessly toward him.

Garrett settled his hat on his head, racked a round into the chamber of the rifle and stepped to the door of the barn. Across at the saloon the lamps were lit, two windows to the front casting rectangles of yellow light on the dirt of the street.

Lamps were also being lit in most of the surrounding cabins and tents against the crowding darkness, and over by the levee a steamboat was embarking passengers, its tiered decks made dazzlingly brilliant by scores of reflective lanterns.

Walking into the street, Garrett stepped slowly toward the saloon, his spurs ringing. Now, as darkness was falling, there was less traffic. He stopped to let a mule wagon piled high with buffalo bones pass, its driver smoking a reeking pipe that scattered tiny red sparks into the air.

Out among the coulees the coyotes were talking. Then, as he started to walk again, Garrett heard the long, drawn-out howl of a wolf. Mingan was out there someplace, a gray ghost that for reasons he could not fathom refused to leave him.

From the saloon, he heard a piano playing a tune he did not recognize, each note dying a separate little death as it failed to compete with the constant roar of drinking men.

Reaching the batwing doors, Garrett stepped inside, the Winchester ready in his left hand.

The saloon was crowded. Ragged buffalo skinners rubbed shoulders with sleek businessmen in broadcloth and miners wearing plaid shirts and mule-eared boots. Hunters in beaded buckskin talked robe prices with bearded mule skinners, and the few women in the place, their gleaming shoulders bare, were in demand by everybody.

No one noticed Garrett as he stepped inside, a long-geared man with searching green eyes who tried his best to mingle with the crowd and remain unseen.

Because of the press of bodies, he could not see the corner table where the bartender had told him Charlie Cobb held court. Carefully, so as not to offend anyone, he made his way slowly through the crowd, holding the rifle down by his leg.

But a tall, grim-faced man can't go unnoticed forever. Eyes see, minds begin to wonder, and a timid few begin to fear.

Garrett was hardly aware of the crowd parting in front of him, the men not liking what they were reading in the tall man's eyes, the women drawing back, sensing danger.

Temple Yates saw Garrett first.

The gunman was sitting near Cobb, his back to the saloon wall. Jenny, looking pale and tired, sat between them, her eyes downcast on the table in front of her, seeing nothing.

Yates unwound to his feet gracefully, like a poised rattler, a slight smile on his lips. In the sudden hush of the saloon his voice was very loud. "Well, well, if it ain't the cowboy." His lips twisted into a sneer. "Didn't I tell you to stay away from me? Now I'm going to have to kill you."

"Let it go, Temp," Cobb said, his arm waving as though he was brushing away an annoying fly. "He's nothing." The man's eyes sought Garrett's. "What do you want?"

Aware of men moving away from behind him, out of any line of fire, Garrett said, "I want only two things from you, Charlie. I want Jenny and I want the twelve thousand dollars you stole from the miners at Fort Whoop-Up."

"Harsh words, Garrett," Cobb said. "Wounding

words. You surely do disappoint me, boy. Such bald-faced lies, and in front of all these people too. Come, I'll give you twenty dollars. Go get drunk in some other saloon."

Before Cobb could say more, Yates asked, "And me, cowboy. What do you want from me?"

"Only your death, Yates," Garrett said, his voice flat, emotionless. He lifted the muzzle of his rifle higher. "I aim to shoot you down like the wild animal you are. And I'll be doing it for Annie Spencer and Abbie Lane and Paloma Sanchez, the women you murdered."

As talk rippled through the crowd, Yates' face turned ugly. "Now you're beginning to get tiresome, Garrett," he said. "It's time I cut you down to size." And he drew.

Garrett swung up the rifle fast and fired from the hip. His shot and Yates' sounded as one. Something red-hot burned across Garrett's left side, just above the gun belt. But as he levered the Winchester he saw that his own bullet had hit Yates hard. Bright scarlet blood was splashed across the front of the man's shirt. The gunman slammed against the wall, recovered, and swung his Colt on Garrett. The young rancher fired again, this time aiming lower. His bullet hit Yates in the belly and the man screamed his rage, knowing he'd just received a killing wound.

Yates, his face gray, eyes wild, advanced on Garrett, his guns slamming. Behind him Garrett heard a woman scream and people stampeded for the door.

A bullet thudded into Garrett's left thigh and he

dropped to one knee, his rifle roaring. Hit again, Yates staggered a step back, an unbelieving horror on his face. In that instant he knew he'd lost. He'd lost everything, the miners' money, his fearsome reputation as a gunman, Jenny. His life.

"Damn you, Garrett," Yates shrieked. "Damn you to hell."

"You first, Temp," Garrett said. And he fired into Yates again.

The gunman stood on his toes, then fell on his face. He hit the ground hard and rolled on his back, his gun coming up. Garrett stepped to Yates and kicked the Colt out of his hand with a casual boot.

"I let a two-bit cowboy buffalo me," Yates whispered, his stunned eyes seeking Garrett's.

"I know," Garrett said, smiling, no give in him. "And just as things were lookin' up for you, too."

Yates shook his head, still unable to believe the fact of his dying. Then life left him and his eyes were staring into nothing but darkness.

"Luke!"

Jenny leaped up from the table and ran toward Garrett, her face alight with a smile. But she never made it. Cobb drew from a shoulder holster and fired. He was aiming at Garrett, but his bullet hit the girl in the back and she fell at the young rancher's feet.

Cobb was standing with his right leg extended, his Colt high and held out in front of him in the duelist pose. He thumbed back the hammer to fire again, but Garrett slammed a shot into him. Shooting from the hip, he hit Cobb three more times before the man slowly slumped to a sitting position on the floor, trailing a wide red streak down the saloon wall.

Garrett kneeled, laid aside his rifle, and cradled Jenny in his arms, gray powder smoke drifting around him. The girl's face was white with shock and blood stained her pale lips. "You're going to be all right, Jenny," he whispered. "I'll get you to a doctor."

The girl smiled. "I knew you'd come for me, Luke. I just knew you would."

One of the saloon girls leaned over Jenny. "You'll be just fine, honey," she said. She wiped blood from the girl's lips with a tiny lace handkerchief. "Just you lie there real still now."

Men were crowding into the saloon, some looking down at Jenny, others talking among themselves as they examined the bodies of Yates and Cobb.

"One of you get a doctor," Garrett yelled.

From somewhere in the crowd, he heard a man say: "I'll get Doc Shortridge."

"Yeah, if he's sober," another man said.

Garrett gently shifted Jenny's position and looked at the hand that had been on her back. It was covered in blood.

"Where's that damned doctor?" he called out, fear and panic spiking at him.

"I'm here," a man's voice said. "No need to get uppity."

A short gray-haired man in a frayed black coat brushed the saloon girl aside and kneeled beside

Jenny. He unbuttoned her shirt and examined the wound in her back. When he finally looked at Garrett his eyes were bleak. "You the husband?"

Garrett shook his head, searched for the right word, and finally settled for "I'm a friend."

The doctor took off his coat, folded it under Jenny's head, and stood. "Step away," he said. He nodded. "Over there. I've got to talk to you."

With a lingering glance at Jenny lying still and pale on the floor, Garrett drew off a couple of steps and the doctor followed. "Will she be all right, Doc?" he asked.

Shortridge's craggy face was stiff, like it had been chipped from granite. "Son, the bullet is in deep, maybe close to the heart. It would take a better doctor than me to cut it out of there, and even then the prognosis would not be good."

Garrett shook his head, a vague anger rising in him. "What the hell does that mean?"

"It means all you can do now is pray for a miracle."

"I'm not a praying man," Garrett said.

"Then you'd better learn how," Doc Shortridge said. "And fast."

"Take the bullet out of her, Doc," Garrett said. "You can try."

The man nodded. "Sure I can try, but I'd kill her. Right now she's got maybe one chance in a thousand. If I start in to cut that deep, she'll have no chance at all."

Garrett opened his mouth to speak, but he heard a step behind him and something hard pressed into the back of his neck.

"Move a muscle and I'll blow your head clean off your shoulders with this here Greener," a cold voice said.

It was Simon Carter's voice.

Chapter 30

"Turn real slow and let me take a look at you," Carter said.

Garrett did as he was told and turned—and saw recognition dawn in the man's eyes.

"What happened here?" Carter asked. It seemed to be enough for him at the moment that Garrett knew he recognized him. The vigilante's eyes searched the crowd. "You, Simpson," he said, nodding toward a buffalo hunter in fancy buckskins. "What happened?"

The man called Simpson shrugged. "Temple Yates drew down on the cowboy here. But the young feller upped his rifle and cut Temp's suspenders for him."

Carter turned to Garrett, with a look that was part disbelief, part admiration. "You killed Temple Yates?"

"He had it coming," Garrett answered.

"Maybe so," Carter said. He turned back to Simpson. "And over there, who's that?"

The hunter turned his head and motioned to the

corner. "That there is Charlie Cobb. He threw a shot at the cowboy but hit the girl instead. The cowboy bedded him down too. I'd say he don't stack up to being any kind of revolver fighter, but he's right slick and fast with the rifle."

Carter thought all this through for a few moments, then said: "Well, if ever men needed killing it was them two." His glance angled to Garrett. "I guess we owe you a vote of thanks for ridding the territory of that pair."

"Listen," Garrett said, "Cobb has twelve thousand dollars that he stole from three miners up in Fort Whoop-Up. If you send the money to Johnny Healy, he'll see they get it back."

"I know Healy," Carter said. "He's honest enough." He glanced down at Jenny, who was being comforted by several women. "Want to tell me how all this came to be?"

In as few words as possible, Garrett told of Cobb's catalog bride scheme, his trip up the Whoop-Up Trail, and how Yates had murdered three women. He talked about losing his herd and their brushes with Indians and outlaws. He did not mention Cobb blowing apart the jail to get him out, figuring that might be a sore point with the vigilante.

When he was finished speaking, Carter's sad vulture eyes searched Garrett's for a long time. Then he said, "That's a tear squeezer of a story for sure, boy. But you ought to have known that whores don't live in the company of poor men. A man like you who owns nothing but a two-by-twice ranch and a hoss and saddle gets involved with whores, trouble is bound to follow." He motioned to Garrett with his head. "Step outside. We need to talk."

"I can't. Jenny needs me here."

"She's not going anywhere, and this will only take a minute. Step outside, boy, and this time, I ain't asking. I'm telling."

So far Carter had not revealed Garrett's identity, and Garrett decided he could trust him, at least for now. He stepped over to Jenny and kneeled beside her. "How are you feeling?" he asked.

"I'll be just fine, Luke," the girl said, a wan smile on her white face. "I know I'll be fine."

The young rancher nodded. "I'm just stepping outside for a minute and I'll be right back."

He rose and followed Carter out the door of the saloon and into the darkness of the street.

"Garrett," the vigilante said, his shabby frock coat and battered top hat making him look more like a molting crow than ever. "I told you once before I liked you, and I still do. Taking into consideration what happened to your woman and the fact that you got rid of Yates and Cobb for me, I'm letting you go." He smiled. "I don't plan on hanging you no more, at least not today."

Relief flooded through Garrett. "I'm obliged to you, Carter," he said.

"Just one thing, though. I want you out of Benton tonight. I'll get the ferryman to take you across the river."

Garrett shook his head. "I can't do that. Jenny needs rest, and lots of it."

"Then she can stay, but you go," Carter said, a

hard man who saw his duty clear, no give in him. "I'm the law here, Garrett, and I don't want a gun slick like you in my town. Trouble follows you, boy, and I want no part of it."

Garrett's eyes sought Carter's in the darkness, and he saw only the grim determination of an unbending man. Finally he nodded. "Then I'll be on my way, Carter. Make sure you take good care of Jenny until she's fit to travel."

"I'll see she gets the best of care, Garrett. Depend on it." The vigilante glanced around him. "Where's your horse?"

"At the livery. He's a grulla that don't look like much."

"I'll saddle him and then roust the ferryman. See you're ready to leave by the time I get back."

Garrett watched Carter fade into the darkness toward the stable. Then he walked back into the saloon. Men with wary eyes stepped aside to let him pass as he went to Jenny and kneeled beside her.

"Jenny," he said, "the vigilantes won't let me stay. But once you're well again, I'll come back for you."

The girl's breathing was labored, her face very white, dark shadows gathering under her eyes. "I'm—I'm coming with you, Luke. I want to live at your ranch." She managed a slight smile, blood bright on her lips. "A woman should stay close to her man. Once—once she realizes she's loved him all along."

"It's a long trail, Jenny," Garrett said, talking

through a tight throat. "You have to rest, get strong. In no time at all, you'll be well and I'll come for you."

The girl shook her head. "Take me with you, Luke. Tonight." Her eyes grew distant. "Tell me about it again . . . tell me how your ranch is, about the mountains and the quiet."

Garrett tried to talk, failed, then tried again. "Jenny, I built my cabin in the shade of the tall mountains and the air smells of pine and the aspen in the high places. And in the morning . . . in the morning, it's so quiet, the silence lies on the land like a blessing. That's how it is. Most times, maybe all the time."

"Take me there, Luke. I don't want to stay here and watch your back as you leave. Promise me."

Garrett bowed his head, afraid that men might see the redness in his eyes. "I'll take you there."

"Tonight?"

"Tonight."

He took the girl in his arms and carried her through the throng of watching people to the door of the saloon. He turned and backed through the batwings and stood outside, waiting for Carter. He looked at Jenny's face, impossibly white in the moonlight, and he heard the sound of her labored breathing, his hands soaked with her blood.

"Are we going home now, Luke?" the girl asked.

Garrett nodded. "Sure thing. We'll be there by sunup, maybe tomorrow, maybe the day after that. All we have to do is follow the first bright star that points south."

Jenny laid her head on his shoulder. "I'm tired,

Luke, so very tired. But I'm going to stay wide-awake. I want us to follow our star together and go where it leads."

The Blackfoot had been raiding to the west and that morning had surprised three freight wagons on the Mullen Road, killing and scalping seven men.

They were riding through the darkness just north of the Highwood Mountains, heading for their village on the Teton, when they saw a solitary rider sitting a grulla horse heading down the trail toward them.

A man alone was fair game and the fifteen Blackfoot drew rein, letting him come to them, their hands tightening on their weapons.

The rider came on at a walk, moving through dappled shadows cast by the moon shining through cottonwoods lining the nearby creek.

It was only when he got closer that the warriors saw the woman in the rider's arms and the huge gray wolf that trotted at his horse's heels. The woman's head was hanging, her blond hair unbound and swaying with every step of the horse, so long it almost brushed the ground. The rider looked neither to his left nor right, his eyes fixed on the shadowed trail ahead.

The man rode closer, his face showing not a trace of fear, the soft footfalls of his horse now loud enough for the Indians to hear.

The Blackfoot had a superstitious dread of the insane, and who but a crazy man would hold a dead woman in his arms as he rode through the darkest part of the night?

One by one, their black eyes glittering, they drew back, hissing their fear. The man passed through them, the noiseless wolf moving beside him like a gray ghost in the gloom.

The Blackfoot watched the rider until he was swallowed by the night.

And only the silence remained.

SIGNET BOOKS

"A writer in the tradition of Louis L'Amour and
Zane Grey!" —*Huntsville Times*

National Bestselling Author
RALPH COMPTON

**Available wherever books are sold or at
penguin.com**

Joseph A. West

"I look forward to many years of
entertainment from Joseph West."
—Loren D. Estleman

"Western fiction will never be the same."
—Richard S. Wheeler

Donovan's Dove   0-451-21250-9
Zeke Donovan walked away from a poker game with $125, a
gold watch, and a fallen dove named Nancy. Unfortunately,
his opponent was gunfighter Ike Vance—and he doesn't take
kindly to losing.

Shootout at Picture Rock   0-451-21814-0
Returning home to Dodge City after tracking down a band of
killers, Deputy U.S. Marshal John Kilcoyn is greeted by Bat
Masterson with a ransom note demanding $10,000 in
exchange for a local doctor and his daughter. The note is
signed by Jake Pride—an ex-lawman turned thief who
Kilcoyn put in jail. Now, Pride is out of jail, and out for
bloody revenge.